Praise for
Three Days to Darkness

"*Three Days to Darkness* is a fast-paced, vivid read that incorporates all the elements of a superior mystery, thriller, and fantasy. It's certainly not a portrait of a predictable afterlife, a conventional Heaven, or a banal post-life mission. All these facets merge to create a uniquely involving story blending amusing moments with engrossing encounters between disparate forces; each with their own special interests and agen-das. And Darius? He's in it for the ride, and takes readers along with him in an unexpected journey through Heaven, Hell, and beyond."
—*Diane Donovan, Senior e-book Reviewer, Midwest Book Review*

"Enjoyable writing and pace. Hard to put down after the first few pages."
—**Kirkus Discoveries Book Review**

"The plot is straightforward, but like many great books, there's more to it than just a plot. Why are there so many bad things in the world? Can people really be happy? What do we want out of life, and why does it often not make sense? Author Dave Gittlin uses an interesting cast of characters to take an enjoyable stab at answering some tough questions."
—*Joseph Canzano, Author*

"*Three Days to Darkness* is a well-scripted page-turner; one I would like to read again for the thrill of it. Just don't make the mistake of reading it alone at night!"
—*Readers' Favorite*

Three Days to Darkness

DAVID GITTLIN

Entelligent Entertainment, LLC

Three Days to Darkness is a work of fiction. Names, characters,
places, and inci-dents are the product of the author's imagination
or appear in the story ficti-tiously. Any resemblance to actual persons,
living or dead, events or locales is en-tirely coincidental.

Cover design by David Gittlin and Illumination Graphics
Interior design by David Moratto, www.davidmoratto.com

Published in the United States by
Entelligent Entertainment, LLC

ISBN 978-0-9882635-1-2

In Memory of
My Father, B. Morton Gittlin.
He was as much a hero as my main character,
Darius McPherson.

CONTENTS

THE FIRST DAY OF FOREVER

DARIUS MCPHERSON NEVER saw it coming. His thoughts were elsewhere. On the kids. The ones he could save. They weren't kids, really. Some of them were older than him. They were all tough and uneven around the edges, but a few of them were diamonds in the rough. They were the ones he considered his kids. They had real potential. They just needed someone to care about them. They needed a role model and some inspiration. Darius was happy to provide both. Not a bad summer gig for a guy waiting for his first year of law school to begin.

He pressed the bell on the side of the barred wooden door. The royal blue paint under the ugly bars gleamed in the direct sunlight and looked completely out of place in the burned-out industrial neighborhood in midtown Detroit.

He waited patiently to be buzzed into the youth counseling center.

"Be right with you, Darius," his supervisor said through the intercom. He liked Allison Turner. In her late thirties and twice divorced, she had managed to stay kind-hearted despite rough circumstances. She was also extremely capable. Allison had taught him more about inner-city teenagers than he could have learned in a decade on his own.

The door opened and a group of youthful offenders burst into the street. Darius knew several of them. They were attending classes at the center as part of their plea bargains. Darius smiled at them, even though he knew most of them were as dangerous as plastic explosive wired to detonate at the slightest provocation.

"Hey La Vonn" Darius called to the tallest boy in the group. "I hope you learned something today."

"Yeah. How to stay outta' the crowbar hotel," the slender boy replied.

"Do you mean learning how to game the system or how to stay out of jail?"

Darius noticed La Vonn's eyes open wide. He turned around in time to see a gray Lincoln Navigator with shiny, twenty-inch wheels and dark tinted windows round a nearby corner. No rap music blared from inside the car, which made Darius suspicious. He heard the sound of footsteps running away from him. He thought it undignified to run. And why would anyone in the neighborhood want to harm him?

When the windows came down in unison, a cold chill went through his body. Darius saw young men wearing ski masks inside the car. He had no time to react. The first shots hit the cinderblock wall of the youth center. *Not unlike fireworks on the Fourth of July,* Darius remembered thinking before a bullet pierced his chest. At first, he felt like an ice pick had stabbed him in the chest. Then there was a burning sensation. He remembered seeing his body lying on the cracked sidewalk in a pool of blood. The last thoughts that went through his brain were of his parents, his older brother and younger sister, and of course, Rebecca. After that, he sensed his awareness swirling down a dark tunnel opening at the far away end into some kind of scintillating light.

THE BIG EMERGENCY

DARIUS THOUGHT HEAVEN was supposed to be a peaceful place.

It had been anything but that for the last fifteen minutes. Like so much of what had happened to him since his sudden death in a drive-by shooting, Darius had only the most elementary understanding of what was going on around him. New arrivals were normally the beneficiaries of an extensive orientation program, he had heard. That was before "The Big Emergency" erupted.

The crisis broke a few weeks after Darius awoke from a sleep that seemed centuries long. Angels normally paid little attention to time, Darius soon discovered, unless there was an issue of world war proportions brewing. What his superiors referred to as "The Big Emergency," because they didn't have time to think of a better name, appeared to have all of the ear markings of a genuine apocalypse. At least it seemed so from Darius McPherson's inexperienced perspective. Everyone was scurrying around with serious expressions and talking about important priorities. They barely had time to welcome Darius and explain to him where he was and why he was there. It would be nice to know, for example, what he was doing in heaven at such a young age. Was a premature, violent death his reward for trying to prevent inner-city teenagers from spending most of their lives in prison?

Then there was the million-dollar question: If there was a God in heaven, why had He ripped apart an ideal couple like Darius and Rebecca Donahue when their love was in full bloom. Would he go on longing for her through the rest of time? He had about a hundred questions after these two five-hundred-pound blockbusters.

Nothing made sense anymore, including the events unfolding before his eyes.

It was shocking to watch the Directors bicker like children in the midst of an emergency assembly. He expected these famous examples of higher consciousness to be proposing solutions to the problem, rather than shouting at one another rudely.

There was a lull, as the Archangel responded to a question from one of the Director Angels.

"If we allow this new drug to be marketed, the evolution of human consciousness will be thrown completely off track. I must say, I've never seen the Chief this concerned before."

The Archangel, whose square features and intense expression reminded Darius of Burt Lancaster in the role of Elmer Gantry, addressed the Directors from a round podium in front of fifty, grim-faced Director Angels seated at a glass conference table. The table stretched so far away that Darius had trouble seeing the Directors sitting at end of it. The view was some sort of an optical illusion.

One of the first things Darius learned about heaven was that nothing appeared to newcomers as it truly was. The rules allowed new arrivals like Darius to see the shapes of things like a room, or a person's face, as familiar objects imported from their former, mortal lives. Darius came to understand this filtered perception as a kindness, a sort of bridge between two worlds. The great arched meeting hall; the appearance of the eleven other Junior Operatives seated around a mahogany table with Darius; and the fifty Directors bearing an uncanny resemblance to famous people; all would remain, until further notice, figments of Darius' imagination.

It was no surprise to Darius that many of the Directors resembled well-known actors. He was an avid reader and a model student. He spent a healthy portion of his twenty-one years on Earth with his face crammed into adventure novels and school textbooks. Aside from his participation on the Grambling College track team the only relief from the disciplined existence he had led as a mortal was his love of movies, both classic and contemporary. Darius' father liked to catch a movie with him on weekends when he stole a few hours away from his business of building custom furniture for wealthy customers. Darius also missed the closeness and encouragement he shared with his mother, Corrine, and the camaraderie with his older brother, Seth. The ache in his heart was as painful as the hole the bullet tore in his chest when he had lost his life for no good reason.

Something else was bothering him. Where in heck were all of the Senior Operatives? Their table was deserted.

Questions from Junior Operatives were not welcome in general assembly meetings. Otherwise, his hand would have been up and waving long ago. As he pondered the mystery of the missing Senior Operatives, another Director rose to speak. She was a dead ringer for Julianne Moore.

"There seems to be no alternative," Ms. Moore said. "One of us must go."

"I don't agree," the Archangel replied. He regarded the entire director corps with a level, piercing glare. "You've all become a bunch of squealing, spoiled brats. I doubt any of you can still follow orders."

Julianne Moore wore an FBI jacket. She spoke in a commanding voice, like the cop she played in the sequel to "The Silence of the Lambs."

"Please Archangel, not in front of the Junior Operatives."

The Archangel's prickly response surprised Darius right down to his African American bones—or whatever substance his body was actually made of these days.

Another Director, who resembled Denzel Washington, rose to speak. He was dressed in a casual tropical outfit with a brightly patterned shirt, open wide at the neck.

"Who else besides one of us is qualified to go?" the Denzel look-alike said.

"One of the Junior Operatives," the Archangel replied without the slightest hesitation. "They haven't had time to develop your self-important attitudes."

"Have you fallen out of your tree," Denzel responded with every bit of righteous indignation he was used to injecting into his screen characters.

A Director with the features of Jett Li had the audacity to imagine this happening. His thought patterns appeared in full color on the domed ceiling. Darius observed the imaginary Archangel falling from a giant redwood tree and bouncing off the ground like Wiley Coyote falling off a cliff in a Road Runner cartoon. The Archangel sat up and a few walnuts from the tree bounced off his head. The walnuts were a good touch, Darius thought.

Most of the Directors struggled to keep a straight face. Nicolas Cage, or someone who looked just like him, lost it and broke out laughing. That started more Directors laughing as the images faded from the ceiling. Darius and the other Junior Operatives stared straight ahead without a sound.

"Was that really necessary?" the Archangel admonished Nicolas Cage.

Darius raised an arm—a reflex reaction he immediately regretted. One of his seminary teachers, crusty old Brother Lucius, had often scolded him for being impetuous. Inappropriate spontaneous behavior was an unruly habit that clung to Darius like a stubborn crab despite his earnest character improvement efforts.

"We don't have time for questions from Junior Operatives," the Archangel reminded Darius.

"I just wanted to make a suggestion," Darius heard himself say.

The Archangel stared at Darius sternly. He brought his hand up to his chin, as if pondering some ancient Chinese riddle. A terrible thought struck Darius. Perhaps the Archangel was considering demoting him to some menial rank below Junior Operative, if there was such a thing.

The Archangel broke the heavy silence.

"Since we haven't heard anything useful from the Directors, something tells me I'd better listen to your suggestion. Just make it quick."

Darius wished he had not lost control of his reckless right arm and then opened his big mouth.

"I can't imagine we're going to solve anything by yelling at each other," he said reluctantly.

An oppressive silence fell on the room once again. Darius firmly believed he had succeeded in ruining his career as a Junior Operative before it had even begun.

Then Julianne Moore applauded. More Directors applauded, until every Director at the conference table was clapping.

The Archangel did not clap. Instead, he glared at Darius sharply. Darius felt a twinge of pain between his eyes. He removed his rimless glasses and began cleaning them meticulously. The applause subsided. All attention now focused on Darius. His chest tightened. His heart rate took off. It felt like a jet fighter catapulted from the deck of an aircraft carrier. His mouth went dry.

Then the Archangel said, "I quite agree with the Junior Operative. I've heard enough opinions from the Directors. I'm going to project the candidates I feel are the most qualified for the mission. Then we'll take a vote. I need a motion."

Another Director—the spitting image of Eddie Murphy—sprang up. Eddie was dressed in an all-black, skin tight, leather outfit.

"Second the motion," he said with a wide grin that exposed his sparkling white teeth.

No one rose to object for a change.

Darius didn't understand what the Archangel meant when he said *project the candidates*. Did it mean the Archangel would lift the candidates from their seats and line them up in front of the conference table for consideration?

"The voting will be silent," the Archangel told the Directors. "Please project your votes directly to me in order not to embarrass the candidates. It will also save time, which we all know is growing more precious by the minute."

Apparently, the whole nominations and voting process was happening by thought transference, Darius concluded. He assumed there was a great deal of information flying through the ether. His knowledge of how the process of thought transference worked was negligible since his first heavenly class on the subject—Theory of Telepathy—had barely begun.

Darius examined the faces of the other Junior Operatives at the table. They were, in fact, all the same face—a moon-faced white kid who liked to tease Darius mercilessly in the second grade. The twelve moon faces contemplated Darius with what appeared to be a singular intention: cold-blooded murder. They frightened him, which was strange. People usually didn't scare him. He had developed the habit of seeing the good qualities in others. He was used to people responding positively to him after he took the first step, but this was heaven. Apparently, people didn't automatically like each other, and he hadn't had time to make any new friends here. He didn't know anyone. Literally, he didn't know a single soul. No wonder his confidence in himself was slipping along with his beliefs in the way things were supposed to be.

Darius reprimanded himself for being too self-centered with the "Big Emergency" looming, whatever that was, but it didn't help. He couldn't stop thinking about himself and what his future held. What would happen if the Directors selected him for the mission? No, it was impossible. He had to be one of the most inexperienced angels in heaven.

The Directors closed their eyes. An instant later, they opened them. Their minds seemed to work like powerful supercomputers. There had been no discussion about strategy, qualifications, or training for the mission. Maybe the Archangel had included that data in his telepathic thought transmission along with the unlucky souls under consideration for the job. In any case, he had the distinct impression that all of the Junior Operatives were as clueless about "The Big Emergency" as he was. The Directors probably didn't want to alarm his compatriots more than they already were with too much information. It was obvious, however, even to a newly minted Junior Operative like Darius, that a successful outcome of the mission was super critical. He felt a twinge of pity for the poor soul who was about to be stuck with the awful burden of the pending field assignment.

The Archangel lost no time in announcing the results of the vote. Turning to Darius with an intimidating stare he said, "Brother and Sister Directors, I give you Darius McPherson, your overwhelming choice for this…very sensitive operation."

Darius was sure the Archangel had meant to say something like *very perilous mission* before changing his mind.

The room filled with polite applause, as if a piano recital had just concluded. Darius fervently believed the Archangel had made a mistake in mentally counting the Directors' votes.

"Why don't you stand up and say something," the Archangel said with an inviting gesture.

Darius stood. He opened his mouth—and uttered a few unintelligible syllables.

"Thank you, Darius," the Archangel said in an apparent effort to put a good face on a bad situation. Darius figured the Archangel had to do this frequently. The Archangel was in charge of all the angels in heaven. Anyone strapped with such a ponderous responsibility had to put on a variety of faces, Darius imagined.

The Archangel turned back to the Directors. "I ask all of you to keep your schedules flexible. The chances are we'll be meeting frequently without much advance notice." Then he added with a perfunctory nod towards Darius, "I'll see you in my office."

Where, in fact, was the Archangel's office?

An answer to the unspoken question flew into Darius' awareness with the alacrity of a humming bird bearing the relevant information on its shimmering wings. He had just received his first telepathic message, directly from the Archangel, of all people. Wouldn't that be something to tell your grandchildren after they arrived in heaven?

Wait. He wasn't ever going to have grandchildren. The crushing thought hit him like a heavyweight knockout blow to the chin. He hadn't been given time to have children. He thought of Rebecca, her big hazel eyes full of admiration for him, her delicate lips parted, waiting for his kiss. What a good mother she would make for someone else's children. He pushed the memory of her out of his mind. It wasn't easy. He loved her. He longed to be with her. He wanted to hold her hand at this very moment in the most desperate way.

• • •

A moment later, the other Junior Operatives rose to leave. "Don't leave yet," the Archangel barked at them.

The eleven Junior Operatives crashed back into their seats in perfect unison. No one moved a muscle.

The Archangel turned to the candidate-elect, Darius McPherson. "Do you need an engraved invitation?"

With growing concern, the Archangel watched Darius leave the assembly. The candidate held his head high and kept his posture erect. That was encouraging. The bewildered look on his face was not.

"Now then," The Archangel said, returning his attention to the other Junior Operatives. "Here's exactly what I want you to tell your classmates about everything that's gone on here. It's very important that you don't scare them."

THE QUIVERING LEAF

AARON GAZED AT the ball of light that knew itself as Darius McPherson. What could he do to calm this bundle of pure energy quivering like a windblown leaf before his imaginary eyes? He had just telepathically transferred an overview of the big emergency, and it had served to further disorient the candidate rather than focus him.

The Archangel took a few seconds to gather his thoughts. He had the distinct impression the general assembly meeting was going to seem like a joy ride compared to his next task. Where to begin? The boy's history would be a good start. Why did he think of this fine young man as a boy?

Aaron summoned the report. It appeared in front of him an instant later. The pages were as transparent and thin as Saran Wrap. The words jumped off the pages as Aaron absorbed them into his powerful mind. Another part of his agile mind projected a more palatable set of images to the candidate-elect. Darius would see him reading from a spiral bound report with gold filigree covers. Aaron hoped a few opening words of encouragement read aloud from the imaginary report would help brighten the young man's dour mood.

"You are truly a special case," Aaron said while projecting a kindly smile. "The work you were doing before the unfortunate circumstances of your death showed a high degree of compassion and courage."

The Junior Operative listened, unmoved.

Aaron proceeded with a carefully selected excerpt from young Darius' life:

"Subject worked with troubled youth in the inner city. He gave of himself consistently while facing persistent rejection from clients. Despite challenging circumstances, the Subject achieved remarkable results."

The consequences of Aaron's strategy proved to be less than inspiring. Shades of gray as dull as rain clouds hung in the boy's aura. The candidate-elect is not a boy, Aaron reminded himself.

Time was at a premium. So was the Archangel's patience.

"What's bothering you," he finally said.

The Junior Operative made no reply. To call this new arrival a Junior Operative was a stretch. Aaron had included Darius in a group of more experienced, highly promising peers on the strength of his exceptional behavior up to the time of his untimely demise. Under normal circumstances, a newcomer like Darius had plenty of work to do before earning the status of Junior Operative. The Big Emergency had changed everything. The balance of the universe was askew, now that the fallen ones had a slew of new weapons and a frightening plan to use them.

"May I suggest, for the sake of everyone involved, we take another vote and choose a Senior Operative for the mission," the Junior Operative said.

What a promising start, Aaron told himself. He wants to quit. We have never been this deep in the mulch before. I'm sure of that now.

The Archangel was not in a mood for long explanations. "We don't have any Senior Operatives available," he said flatly. "They left on a highly classified mission right before you arrived."

The ether behind Junior Operative McPherson came alive with a trail of question marks. They swam through the effulgent background light of heaven like a school of guppies.

Aaron pressed ahead to dispel the Junior Operative's doubts. "You have deep reservoirs of strength and great possibilities, Darius. You were destined to be a great civil rights attorney, or something along those lines," Aaron added off-handedly. "The Directors have full faith that you are destined for the same greatness here in heaven."

The sputtering ball of energy went right on doubting everything in its imaginary shoes, much to Aaron's dismay.

"Will you PLEASE tell me what's bothering you?"

There was a long pause.

"If the Chief can part the seas or open the heavens and dump fire and brimstone on the bad guys, why doesn't He handle this situation Himself?"

It took all of Aaron's self-restraint not to swoop down on the newborn angel and whack him with several, hard, telepathic smacks on his non-existent behind. In the first few weeks of classes, introductory level teachers routinely answered inane, newcomer questions similar to the one Darius had just spewed up.

"Darius," Aaron practically shouted. "I'm afraid you're going to have to forget about what they taught you in Sunday school. The stories of miracles are merely metaphors."

"You don't have to shout."

The Junior Operative was right, of course. Aaron lowered his tone. "I'll try to make this as simple as possible. The Chief gave every conscious being in the universe free will. It's what makes existence challenging and maddening at the same time."

Aaron waited for Darius to respond. "So, you're saying anything can happen?"

"Exactly," Aaron confirmed.

"I still can't understand how a single pill can threaten the future of the human race?"

The young man had finally managed to ask an intelligent question. Perhaps there was hope after all.

"The ultimate purpose of existence is to discover who we truly are, Darius. It is a challenging and demanding journey. The farther we progress along the path, the more joy, the more peace, the more harmony we experience. The difficulty lies in the considerable investment of good old-fashioned effort the journey requires. It involves a lot of slipping, falling, and getting up again, and the courage to keep going in the face of an uncertain future. Plezenthol threatens to sidetrack the whole process. From the reports I've received from the Senior Operatives following the case, it seems Plezenthol will make it too easy to feel good. People will stop trying to better themselves. The long-term effects will likely be disastrous."

"It will work too well?"

"You heard me correctly. Happiness, real happiness, requires constant attention, willpower, and the development of a clear vision. We do not win genuine happiness, peace and contentment easily, Darius. It certainly does not come in a pill."

Aaron finally had the young man's undivided attention. He was a touch overly serious, but in an oddly winning sort of way.

"How can you be sure?"

"We're never sure of anything. No one can predict the future, not even the Chief. Remember what I said about free will, Darius. We can only calculate possibilities. In this case, the possibilities for disaster turn out to be uncomfortably high." *To put it mildly,* the Archangel thought.

Aaron gave Darius a breather to absorb the information he had just imparted. He wished there was more time to bring the young man along, but...

"There's more to it than the new drug," Aaron continued. "I didn't bring it up in the meeting because the news would have been too upsetting, even for our dear Brother and Sister Directors."

Aaron took a deep breath and continued. "The Exiles have managed to develop a device that enables them to masquerade as human beings."

"The Exiles?"

"That's the name we've given to the angels the Chief expelled from heaven for their stubborn tendencies towards insubordinate behavior. There are bad apples everywhere, Darius. Even here.

The sputtering, popping ball of energy known as Darius McPherson brightened a bit, to Aaron's relief. He sensed the Candidate's concern for others kicking in and heightening his interest level.

"It's all the result of a new energy source the Exiles have developed," Aaron continued. "Our best Senior Operative came back with a report on these troubling developments. I decided to send the entire team of Senior Operatives to find out what the Exiles are up to."

Aaron's expression grew a bit more serious. "I'm still waiting for their reports."

A few sporadic sparks ignited inside the luminous sphere bobbing gently in front of Aaron. He decided on the spot not to burden the new recruit with more information than necessary at this critical juncture.

Aaron brushed aside the previous subject with a wave of his imaginary hand. "Don't worry about what the Exiles are doing for the time being. Hopefully, I'll know more soon. Your job right now is to stop this pill from going on the market. Now, let's move on to the mortal assets you'll have to assemble."

"Mortals?"

"Due to the tight schedule we're on, you're going to recruit a small team to help you after your insertion back on Earth."

"But—"

"Please, Darius. Just listen. I realize working with mortals can be challenging, especially when you have to eventually break the news that you come from heaven. We normally try to keep mortal contact to a minimum, but there's just no way around it in this case."

Aaron paused. "You're good with people, Darius. It's another reason why we chose you. Once you gain their trust, the mortals will get over your angelhood. You'll see."

"But how do I gain their trust?"

"There isn't time for a full-blown discourse on inspiring confidence in mortals. Just be yourself. Use your intuition."

Aaron cringed inwardly. New recruits were notorious for having under-developed intuition. He had to do something quickly to stem the doubts now building up inside the candidate-elect in the form of a purple storm cloud. He drummed his imaginary fingers on his imaginary chin. The perfect answer came to him. He was sure it had come directly from the Chief.

"Here, take this," he said.

. . .

Darius reached for the golden triangle. It felt warm against his cupped hand. A halo of golden light spread around the edges. The circle inside each of the three angles drew his attention. *What was their purpose?*

The triangle's aura held Darius spellbound until the light faded and disappeared. Darius looked up at the Archangel sitting behind an elaborate smoke glass desk. He had seen one just like it when he and Rebecca had gone furniture shopping for their starter home. Something like the elaborate desk and matching chair would have been out of line for their budget, even considering his father had promised to give them a house full of custom-made furniture. They might have splurged on one piece if Darius wasn't so down-to-earth practical. Of course, he wasn't so down-to-earth anymore.

"You'll find it comes in handy when you need it most," the Archangel said, pointing to the triangle. "I'll have my assistant put it on a chain so you can wear it as a necklace. Be sure to keep it with you at all times."

The Archangel rose from behind the desk. He pressed his palms together, reminding Darius of the gesture his fifth-grade teacher adopted when he ran out of time and patience to answer more of his questions.

"We really must get you on your way. Is there anything else you urgently need to know?"

"I just have one more question."

"Fire away."

"How much time do I have to turn the situation around?"

The Archangel's gleaming countenance dimmed.

"I wanted to wait until you were on the ground to tell you, but now that you've asked, the answer is...three days."

"Three days? Are you kidding me?

"I'll ignore that last remark," the Archangel said. "We waited for the FDA to complete the final phase of clinical trials. We don't like to intervene in human affair unless we feel we absolutely have to. When we learned Plezenthol had passed the final phase of testing, we were surprised to learn the drug developer planned to begin manufacturing directly after approval. That's a big gamble. It costs plenty to reserve manufacturing capacity. Most companies wait for approval, and then it takes six months or more to get a new drug into production. It's a highly unusual situation…in a number of unfortunate ways.

"Three days," Darius repeated in disbelief.

"Time enough if you make every minute count."

"How many minutes are there in three days?"

"Twelve thousand, nine hundred and sixty," the Archangel replied without blinking.

It sounded like a nice big number, but hardly big enough for someone who had not even had the time to adjust to angelhood.

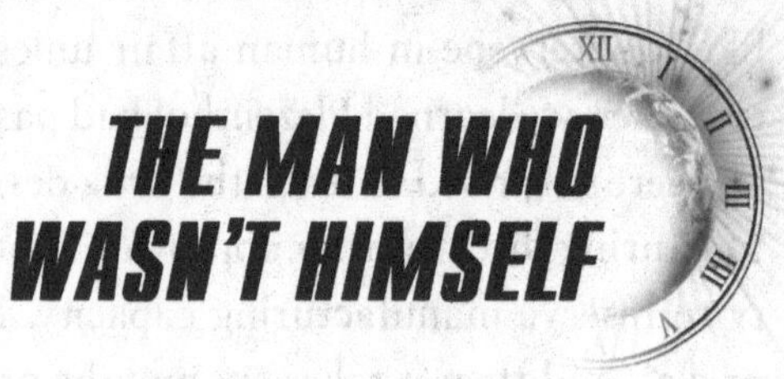

Chapter Three

THE MAN WHO WASN'T HIMSELF

KYLE HUNTILLA'S BLACK Florsheim loafers made a crisp *clacking* sound against the concrete basement walls. He was having another bad headache day. Kyle wasn't about to go belly aching to his boss, however. The five years he had spent in the Marine Corps beginning on his eighteenth birthday had taught him the principles of manhood. Complaining was not one of them. Discipline was. It had propelled Kyle from his trailer park roots to the Mamongen corporate executive suite.

He had spent the last twenty years humping away at a series of bigger-and-better jobs during the day coupled with higher education courses at night to get to where he was today: Chief of Security for a multi-billion-dollar drug manufacturer. Kyle was not about to let a few headaches get in the way of his job performance.

He hated doctors, anyway. His habits included a rigorous exercise regimen, a ramrod-positive attitude, non-smoking and a healthy diet. Kyle's robust lifestyle kept him far away from the dreary confines of over-crowded doctors' offices. He was forty-five and didn't look a day over thirty-two. Who could blame him for cheating with a few touches of black hair dye? The world he lived in belonged to the young.

To be honest, though, he was starting to worry a bit. The headaches were a little more than just headaches. Kyle had periods when he could not remember anything. Chunks of time just walked out the door and went for a stroll down the block. He wasn't having alcoholic blackouts. He enjoyed a few drinks on the weekend. He even got loaded once-in-a-blue-moon when the pressure cooker of his job got to him. To be sure, though, he was light years away from the outer rings of alcoholism.

He was beginning to suspect a brain tumor. It was getting to the point where he would have to face the music and go in for a CAT scan.

Another unexplained phenomenon—He had been having the strangest dreams lately. Some sort of bird-lizard creature ran through his nightly dreamscape. Kyle chalked it up to job performance anxiety. He did not feel entirely settled in his weighty position after only two months on the job. He was confident, however, that he would be firmly in control of his responsibilities before too long. Still, the dreams were weird.

Kyle stopped abruptly and unfolded the triangular sign with red lettering he had been lugging. He placed the sign carefully in front of the restrooms. It was a task normally reserved for an underling. Even though Kyle was a good delegator, he kept telling himself he needed to attend to every detail of this particular errand, including the exact wording on the sign. He had even made himself pick up the sign from the Fedex print, pack, and ship store across the street. The last thing he needed was a lawsuit resulting from an improperly worded warning sign. He stepped back from the sign to make sure the lettering and red stop sign illustration made the desired impact.

"DO NOT ENTER. This facility CLOSED for fire code upgrades until further notice. PLEASE use the restrooms located in the lobby. This also applies to all maintenance personnel. Failure to comply will result in job termination."

Kyle congratulated himself on a job well done. Then he ceased to exist—temporarily.

Glythren the Warrior Lord was now fully in charge of Kyle Huntilla's consciousness. He did not enjoy operating in the Dark Realm and in a human body simultaneously. It made him vulnerable, but it was regrettably necessary. Glythren paid strict attention to details without losing his perspective on the overall campaign. *And what a campaign it was going to be*. Thanks to the advances in camouflage technology made by his mutant son, Prince Strethorne, the dangers of spirit projection into a human body would soon become a fading, unpleasant memory.

A clock above the restrooms struck seven PM, and the overhead lighting in the common areas on every floor of the Mamongen Building faded to an eerie, manmade twilight.

Glythren entered the men's doorway to the restroom. There were no signs of the repair work advertised on the sign outside. The Warrior Lord carefully searched the gleaming tile and stainless-steel bathroom, paying special attention to the toilet stalls. The bathroom was empty. Not even a homeless person in residence, hiding away for a few hours of free heat and clean water. Good. He turned to inspect the restroom next door.

The air-conditioning in the empty bathroom whispered at seventy-eight degrees Fahrenheit—after-hours energy saving temperature. There was no other sound. All of the subterranean compartments of the basement were clear. It was time to begin.

In a matter of seconds, Glythren located the thought stream of the first buried soldier. The Warrior Lord issued a telepathic command.

An explosion in one of the bathroom stalls shattered the stillness. A metal stall door flew into the mirror and washbasin on the opposite wall.

Smoke billowed from a jagged hole in the floor where a porcelain toilet bowl had rested only seconds before.

An overhead light damaged by the explosion flickered on and off as if blinking in disbelief at the preceding events.

A dark, sewage-covered creature emerged from the hole. The beast pulled itself up from the gash in the floor with four muscular arms. The creature clutched a metallic object resembling an over-sized tuning fork in one of its long-fingered hands.

The soldier squinted. The light in the room, though twilight-dim, was too painful for the dark purple eyes set above a drooping beak protruding out of the beast's triangular head. Three sets of horns swiveled toward Glythren like antennae seeking an electronic signal.

Glythren observed the soldier breathing heavily, exhausted from the exertion of tunneling up from the base camp in the cavern a mile below the building.

More explosions shook the bathroom. Four more soldiers squeezed through holes ripped in the tile flooring.

Pointing to the one sink that had survived the carnage, the Warrior Lord spoke to his minions in human tongue. The sooner the soldiers became accustomed to conversing in the awkward human language, the better.

"Wash up before we go upstairs," he said.

Glythren pulled five glass balls the size of a silver dollar from Kyle Huntilla's pinstriped pants pocket. An azure blue light from inside the spheres pulsed like a tiny, beating heart. There was one glass ball for each Exile soldier.

Chapter Four

ALL IN A DAY'S WORK

Javon Quincey aimed the Glock nine-millimeter pistol straight at the pawnshop owner's head. "You deaf or something?" he shouted.

"I heard you, *beeg* man." The middle-aged, ruddy faced, dark haired man behind the counter reminded Javon of a walking jewelry rack. Necklaces, bracelets and rings adorned every body part above his bulging waist.

"You look like you need a good meal more'n my money," the shop owner went on to observe.

"You look like you could go a month without eatin' and no one would see a difference," Javon replied curtly. "I'll take a bunch a' them rings in the case besides the money. My time is valuable. The more time you take, the more it's gonna' cost you. *Comprende*, fatso?"

The shop owner's brown eyes hardened. "Calling me names won't make me move any faster."

Javon waived the Glock to light a fire under the shop owner. The mention of food made his stomach growl. Not a soul in the world besides Javon Quincey knew he hadn't eaten a decent fast-food meal in more than a week. Apparently, it was beginning to show. This was not a good thing. Weakness and drug dealing were a lethal combination on the street.

He had also been scrupulously tight-lipped about the fact his street-drug business had been slowing down for months. Competition was moving in from all sides. He was tired and wired as tight as a piano string.

Javon held the Glock at the end of a long thin arm decorated with a rogue's gallery of angry tattoos. If this Latino asshole didn't come across soon, he had half a mind to bust a cap into him. Only problem was, there were no caps in the gun. His over-stressed, underfed condition had caused him to make the dumb assed mistake of forgetting to load the clip. Javon nervously ran an oversized hand through his bushy, unkempt hair. He had taken out the cornrows an hour earlier to make his face less noticeable.

Javon hated guns. The bigger and more powerful they were, the less use he had for them. If he needed protection, Javon hired a body-guard whenever he could afford one. Guns were for amateurs in the fine art of persuasion. Guns got you locked up. Sooner or later. One way or another.

"Come on already," Javon snapped. "You feel like dyin' today?"

"Take it easy, beeg man. I just gotta' put my hands down to get your cash."

"Real slow," Javon warned. "And quit that 'beeg man' bullshit."

Robbery was for 'bangers with no brains and no motivation, not for smart, enterprising dudes like Javon. But here he was. Robbing a goddamned pawnshop. This had to be a bad dream. It was getting so bad that the risks of selling drugs were starting to outweigh the rewards. What had happened to his free-and-easy, cash flowing lifestyle? All the fun had run. That was the only thing he knew for sure these days.

The pawnshop owner's fingers worked the buttons on an electronic cash register. The muscles in Javon's outstretched, undernourished arm began to throb from the exertion of holding the Glock up rigidly for so many excruciating minutes. He was about to win first place in "The-Slowest-Small-Store-Armed-Robbery-In-Crime-History-Contest." First prize was a twenty-year cruise for one in the 'slam.

Javon told himself to visualize a positive result. He imagined himself strolling out the front door like a rich man walking his poodle. Once outside, he would engage his superior athleticism to make it unscathed and un-captured to his high security crib. There, he would count all the lovely green earmarked for his next drug buy. Wholesale drug buy that is—Javon was a seller, not a dumb-ass-junkie-loser.

While these pleasant thoughts occupied more and more of Javon's attention, the portly owner dipped gracefully below the sales counter. He popped up again with a sawed-off shotgun cradled in both hands.

Javon blinked. The two barrels looked like stacked cannons. The damn thing was an abbreviated riot gun. He cursed himself for breaking one of his cardinal rules, for lowering his standards, for trying a nowhere thing like robbing a shitty pawnshop in his own backyard. He thought it would be easy. One little quickie to tide him over. Bullshit.

The shotgun roared. Javon felt the buckshot rush by him and blow a jagged hole in the store's front window. An alarm sounded. The lanky teenager ducked and ran behind a display case bordering the front door. He waited only long enough to confirm that all of his limbs were present and accounted for. Then he dashed out the shop's front door just before another blast blew a hole in the glass door. Tiny white shards that once spelled HONEST JULIO'S PAWN SHOP AND CASH STOP sprinkled into the street.

Broken glass rained down all around Javon. He focused straight ahead, churning down the deserted street faster than a track star running for a gold medal. As his feet sped over the pavement, the same freaky thought he had been having for the past couple of weeks rushed through his brain. It was simply this. Being broke and hungry was not *really* what was bothering him. He had been in this position more times than he cared to remember in his seventeen years of life. It was something else—the god-damnedest thing—a feeling he never expected.

Javon was growing weary of being on his own.

The idea blew his mind, scared him too. Something was telling him it was time to move on. The lotto jackpot question he posed to himself scared him even more. *To what and where?*

BARRROOOM! Another explosion of twelve-gauge doom whistled after the rapidly diminishing figure of a basketball-tall-would-be-pawnshop-robber.

Chapter Five

THE TERRIBLE TUBE

THREE DAYS. WELL, hadn't the Creator made heaven and Earth in seven days? No, He hadn't, actually. The story of Genesis, Darius had confirmed in his private audience with the Archangel, was only a metaphor.

If only the puny "Window of Opportunity" the Archangel had given him to prevent the dimming of human consciousness was a metaphor as well. The cruel truth of the situation came whirling back to him like a boomerang with scalpels for blades. He had a measly three days to prevent millions of years of conscious evolution from becoming a mudslide into an enormous bog.

After his meeting with the Archangel, Darius had made a gut-busting effort to think positively and stop focusing on his personal problems. Then they had lowered him into the launch chair and catapulted him into hyperspace. There was nothing better than traveling at the speed of light inside a Hyperspace Conveyor Tube to melt your inner resolve as quickly as an ice cube in one-hundred-degree heat.

Boiling stars, multi-colored planets, ghostly moons and splotches of empty, black space whizzed by outside the Hyperspace Conveyor Tube. The walls of the thing reminded Darius of heavy gauge polyethylene tubing. He had seen enough plastic tubing to last a lifetime the summer he had worked in a poly-bag extrusion-plant.

The Archangel had told him not to pay too much attention to what was going on outside the cocoon of the "HCT." Darius was supposed to spend the trip in quiet contemplation in preparation for the big job ahead. What a joke. Darius was too scared to close his eyes for more than the time it took to blink. The Tube kept changing directions. It seemed like the damn thing would suddenly veer off to the left or right, or corkscrew, or oscillate like the needle on a lie detector whenever the spirit moved it. The Archangel had warned him that the Tube's auto adjustments to avoid catastrophic collisions "might be a little disorienting." Darius wondered if the description was a private joke among seasoned HCT travelers.

The absolute worst part, however, was being stuck inside a ten-foot length of tubing that kept disappearing behind you and shooting ahead another ten feet in front as it moved forward. The handler angels in the launch room had explained the effect was merely an optical illusion, "and nothing to be concerned about." He supposed it was easy for them to say that. They didn't have to endure a hyper-space journey during which it felt like someone was constantly pulling the rug out from under you.

Darius was terrified the HCT would forget where it was going and vomit him out in the nuclear inferno of a young star cluster or the baleful light of a dying Red Dwarf.

The HCT swooshed crazily onward; out of one galaxy and into another. Wait a minute. The gigantic planet up ahead looked exactly like Jupiter. A swirling red spot gazed at him like a massive, angry eye. The planet had to be Jupiter. Yes, it was, because movement outside the Tube slowed to a crawl compared to the dizzying forward blur Darius had grown accustomed to.

The Archangel had explained to him the slow down would happen towards the end of the trip. Traveling at the speed of light compressed time inside the Tube. Now, the speed of time outside and inside the HCT would gradually equalize. The analogy the Archangel used was that of a deep-sea diver undergoing decompression in a pressure chamber before returning to the surface. You did not want to interfere with the process, the Archangel stressed, or a resulting case of time-warp- bends would splatter Darius's atoms into eleven different dimensions.

No one knew for sure if eleven dimensions actually existed. It was only a theory proposed by prominent Quantum Physics scientists. The Archangel was quick to point out, however, that Darius should avoid, at all costs, testing the theory first hand.

The idea was to stay inside the Tube until the exact moment when the HCT decided to spew Darius into the world, fully grown, in a brand-new body. In other words, all Darius had to do was entrust his eternal existence to the intelligence of a ten-foot tube that kept disappearing and reappearing. To say the least, the impending conclusion of the trip did nothing to reduce Darius's anxiety level.

Mars, with its twin moons, swung into view. Then Darius saw it for the first time: a tiny blue dot millions of miles away, barely noticeable amid the meteor and dust clouds hanging like shrouds in the ocean of space: Mother Earth!

The HCT suddenly elongated, stretching for what seemed like miles ahead of Darius. A brightness that dazzled like hundreds of high beam headlights awaited him in the distance. He lost consciousness.

• • •

Aaron, in his almost infinite wisdom, had not clued Darius in about the finite details the hyperspace ride's conclusion. He figured the young man's sensibilities would have taken enough of a pounding up to this delicate point. One more jolt like the one that was about to happen could easily drive an inexperienced Junior Operative bonkers. So, Aaron had arranged a short nap for Darius while his pristine body of pure energy was outfitted in a suit of bones, muscles, veins, arteries, a pumping heart, skin—in other words—your basic human body, African American style.

Every angel coming to Earth from the beginning of time had

undergone a similar transformation. It was impossible to operate on Earth without assuming a human body. A physical world required a physical form. It was as simple and as complicated as that. The complications derived from the limitations imposed on the use of angelic powers by the resistance of a human body. Pure energy needed to be tamped down or else the human body would explode—an unavoidable, and in this case, cruel law of nature. The only way for an angel to return to a pure energy state was to step back into the welcoming arms of a Hyperspace Conveyor Tube as it opened for the return trip home.

The number of angel operatives who did not make it home, for one reason or another, was relatively small. Aaron was gravely concerned that Darius McPherson stood a good chance of becoming a member of that unfortunate, tiny population. This concern, like the final leg of the journey to Earth, was something Aaron had gone to great lengths to conceal from his stalwart new recruit.

Chapter Six

A CHANCE MEETING HARDLY

IN THE GRIMY industrial neighborhood of Opa-Locka, Florida, Javon Quincey expertly cut a street corner to avoid a swarming clot of shotgun pellets from slicing him in half. The spray of pellets whined off the pavement just behind him. He turned to see if the pawnshop owner was chasing him. The coast was clear—almost.

With his head turned in the opposite direction, Javon missed seeing a circle of light appear about fifty yards directly in front of him. It would not have mattered if he had seen the phenomenon occur because he would not have believed his eyes. He would have chalked it up to a mind-bending drug flashback. The army of social workers who had long ago given up on Javon called it an RSD: Residual Drug Reaction.

Javon believed deep in his heart he had made another miraculous getaway, a fact that was partially true. A smirking grin spread across the young man's sweat soaked face as he turned his head back around, just in time to see something hurtling towards him like a meteorite.

What the hell?

Javon *zigged left* just as the blur heading his way *zagged* right. The resulting collision knocked the unidentified hurtling object and Javon flat on the sidewalk.

The two bodies lay motionless in the mid-morning sun for a full minute before Javon regained consciousness. He dragged himself up. The first priority was to regain his bearings in case trouble was nearby. The streets were empty at this hour. He knew from experience that all non-violent human life in the neighborhood labored inside air-conditioned, graffiti covered warehouses making products like uniforms, leather belts, parachutes, or plastic hooks to hang packages of salted peanuts from. The streets were full only at the beginning or the end of a workday. It was a bad idea to drive or walk the streets of Opa-Locka at any other time without an urgent reason for doing so.

Javon dusted off his Miami Heat T-shirt and baggy jeans shorts. He looked around to make doubly sure no one had seen him. Anyone who was anybody on the street would needle him mercilessly for falling on his ass while in full flight from a screwed-up robbery. Luckily, it looked like no one had witnessed the spectacle. With a sigh of relief, Javon took an unsteady step, and tripped over the sprawled figure of a black dude dressed inappropriately in a suit and tie.

"The hell you come from?" he asked the body sprawled with eyes closed and a beatific smile plastered across his pretty boy face.

"I'm talkin' to you, bitch."

The body lay there sleeping like a goddamn baby in a plain gray suit and striped tie. Black penny loafers completed the non-fashion statement. Javon snickered at the sight of the brother's bad haircut—not too long or too short, just in-between, which to Javon indicated no personality. He bent over and slapped the sleeping-baby-man across the face.

"Wake up fool."

The eyes fluttered open. The pretty head jerked upwards, butting Javon right above his eye. He galloped in circles, cursing while pressing his long fingers over one swelling eye.

Javon stopped galloping. *The hell with the pain,* he told himself. *Time to get on with the next order of business.* His morning might have been a total disaster, but things were looking up despite his blossoming headache. Things always got better when they could not get much worse. He had no particular reason for believing in this unwritten- law of nature. It was just an attitude he seemed to be born with. And here was another prime example of the adage. The creep he had smacked into looked rich, judging by the gold chain that peeked over his white shirt collar.

The primly-dressed-pretty-faced-baby-man stood. He made a big show of straightening out the wrinkles in his tailored suit. Javon sauntered over.

"Gimme all your money," he snarled. He felt absolutely no fear, even a little giddy. This dude was going to be as easy to take as a nose-full of coke chased by a shot of Tequila.

The man combed through his suit pockets one by one. "It seems they didn't give me any money," he said with muted surprise.

"You mean Daddy forgot to spot you your allowance?"

"I mean…I don't have any money."

That kind of shit was not going to fly. "What's this?" Javon pulled at the chain around his victim's neck. It was a thick neck. The creep looked muscular all over, as a matter-of-fact. It figured. People worked out a lot these days. Javon had no time for nonsense like that. He was always too busy making an excellent living. Until recently.

"You can't have that." The creep grabbed at his chain. He struggled free from Javon's grip while stumbling backwards.

"Where's your car at?" Javon yelled.

"I don't have a car."

Javon rested his hands on his slender hips. "You're the best-dressed-broke-ass-motherfucker I ever met."

"My name is Darius, not motherfucker."

Javon bitch slapped him. "You got any more smart-ass remarks?"

Stunned silence.

"You know where you are?"

"Actually, I don't. What's *your* name?"

"None a' your business. The hell you doin' in my 'hood?"

"It seems I need a ride downtown," Darius answered after some hesitation.

Javon stopped his cross-examination when he spied a police cruiser glide out of an alleyway between two warehouse buildings. It turned down the street in their direction. A dog in the back seat of the patrol car barked loudly from behind a mesh divider. A police officer in the front seat was staring right at him.

He landed two big hands on the pretty boy's shoulders. "You say anything 'bout me to that cop, I'll kill you. You got that'?"

"What cop?"

"The one comin' up behind you. Don't look. Start acting like we's family."

"You don't scare me," Darius said, straight-faced.

"I guess you don't mind dying today. That what you sayin?"

. . .

Threats of physical harm had little effect on Darius. He had already experienced death by drive-by-shooting, after all. There wasn't much left to be afraid of after something like that. What scared the be-Jesus out of him, however, was the possible destruction of his human body. How long would it take to get a new body? He had no clue. Was it even possible to get a new body if someone or something decommissioned the one he occupied? The answers to these questions, and many more, went missing in action from his meeting with the Archangel due to the time crunch.

Darius began gesturing as if he and the obnoxious kid had a long and glorious history together. The idea was about as ridiculous as the three days Aaron had given him to save the human race. The last thing he needed at this moment was a run-in with the Police. He had seen plenty of wayward kids goofing with each other on the street. It was an easy act to produce.

The patrol car pulled up beside them. The window on the empty passenger side of the Dodge Charger opened. The dog barked fiercely from inside. Darius studied the beast. He expected to see a German shepherd. This dog looked more like an Alaskan Husky with his coat cut short for comfort in the tropical climate. The police officer said something to the dog in what sounded like Dutch. The creature stopped barking.

"Nice dog," Darius said in a friendly voice.

"He'll rip you to shreds if I tell him to," the officer replied. "Don't try petting him."

"It sounded like you spoke to him in Dutch?"

"He's a Belgian Malinois. I'd love to chat with you about police dogs, but the thing is we didn't stop you for that reason."

The officer had a thin face and droopy eyes. His face looked as if a good night's sleep had eluded him for more than a year.

"Let's see some ID."

Darius' stomach turned to jelly. He had no ID. They had sent him on his way without anything, apparently, but the clothes on his back and the triangle necklace. It was probably some kind of bureaucratic screw-up related to the rush they were in to shoot him off to Earth in the Hyperspace Conveyor Tube.

"Is there a problem, officer?"

Darius asked the question with sincere respect, something the Police were not used to receiving lately, particularly from young people, he knew. He had dealt with the Police many times before in connection with his youth intervention work. He had become accustomed to respect from police officers. The suspicion in this one's eyes felt as alien to him as the blur of planets and stars he had seen on his return trip to Earth.

The youth who attacked him kept looking back and forth from Darius to the police cruiser. Darius was afraid the kid was going to bolt like a skittish colt at any second. He needed to do something quickly to calm the teenager down. He tossed an arm around the taller boy's shoulders to corral him, even though the smell was unbearable.

"We're canvassing the neighborhood for suspects," the policeman said. "Nothing to be alarmed about, unless either of you attempted an armed robbery about ten minutes ago."

Darius made a show of going through his pockets. "That's funny. I must have left my wallet back at the office."

"Where is your office?" the officer asked, opening the cruiser door. The lack of proper ID had ramped up the tension of the stop.

Darius studied the name shield on the officer's shirt. It read "Juan Gonzales."

"He's employed by a big Miami law firm," the teenager said. "So, I wouldn't mess with his rights."

Oh, my God, Darius thought.

"You look familiar." Officer Gonzales frowned at the kid. "What's your name?"

"Delbert Johnson. I'm this fine, upstanding young black man's driver. We were just on our way to pick up the limo and drive back downtown."

Officer Gonzales glowered at them. Darius surmised Gonzales was in a bad mood to start with, probably from a double shift or a second, off-duty job. Darius had gotten to know quite a few police officers in his time. Many of them worked ridiculous hours to make extra money while staying out of the line of fire of discontented wives who complained constantly about a lack of attention. Darius thought it ironic that the wives complained, since the men worked hard to support their families. On the other hand, women had their own, inscrutable brand of logic as he had learned from his relationship with Rebecca.

Officer Gonzales closed the door of the patrol car behind him. Darius closed his eyes. This was going to be the first time he had ever worn handcuffs. What could he possibly say to Gonzales to avoid an arrest? Then an idea came to him, a longshot, but the best he could do on short notice.

"Do you know Annabel Singerman?"

"Can't say I do."

"I worked with her as a youth counselor in Detroit. She transferred to Miami Dade PD about a year ago." Ask her if she remembers Darius McPherson."

A yawn snuck up and overtook Officer Juan Gonzales. "Excuse me," Gonzales muttered, covering his mouth with a hairy hand.

"I'm with Opa-Locka PD. Miami Dade is a different agency."

Darius had to do something. Quickly. Incarceration, even for a brief time, was not an option if he wanted to stay on Eastern-Standard-Save-The-World-Time. He projected a thought into the police officer's mind. If all went well, the thought would burrow straight down into the Gonzales's subconscious: *Check out Darius McPherson with Annabel Singerman.* According to his heavenly thought transference instructor, implanted suggestions worked quickly if properly executed. There was only one problem. It took considerable practice to hypnotize an alert, human subject. Darius had never tried to hypnotize anyone besides a few angel classmates.

Darius prayed silently for success. He had one thing going for him. Officer Gonzales was practically sleepwalking through his day. It might lower his resistance.

Gonzalez stared at them. He blinked. The fate of the world rested in a single, police officer's hands, Darius suddenly realized. The man had no idea of the enormity of the decision he was about to make. Darius' stomach rumbled. Soon he would have to spend precious moments to fill the gas tank of his brand-new human body. The launch techs apparently forgot to program a square meal into him.

Officer Gonzales stared at Darius with an unhappy look on his face.

Darius noticed the insignia on the rear panel of the Cruiser: "To Protect and Serve."

This is your chance to protect the whole world Darius thought. Let me go.

Glaring at Darius, Officer Gonzales hitched up his utility belt. "Don't let me catch you on the street when I ride back through here." He yawned again. "And keep an eye on your friend, Delbert. I don't like him."

The lawman climbed back into his black and white Dodge Charger. It sped away before Darius had time to breathe a sigh of relief.

The kid who called himself Delbert grabbed his chest and fell straight down on the sidewalk as if he had just suffered a massive heart attack.

Darius immediately knelt beside him, "Are you all right?

Delbert looked up at him. "Man…that was close."

Darius offered the teenager a hand. Delbert reluctantly took it and helped himself to his feet.

"You almost got us busted, Delbert."

"Delbert ain't my name. If it was, I'd change it."

I had a friend named Delbert," Darius said. "He liked his name."

"That's 'cause he's a creep just like you."

"What are you so angry about?"

"Nona' your damn business."

"What is your name?" Darius asked, making a supreme effort to remain polite.

"It's Javon. Javon Quincey. That's confidential information, so don't go blabbin' it all around."

"I know how to keep a secret," Darius said with a wink. "You gave me a start when you fell down. Are you sure you're okay?"

"Bein' a big businessman puts a brother under stress. Gets to me sometimes." His eyes narrowed. "You said something about needing a ride. How much do you pay?"

"I don't know. What's the going rate?"

The teenager scratched the scraggly whiskers on his goatee. "I'd say sixty-five would cover it."

"Dollars?"

"Per hour plus gas" the kid answered, nodding in agreement with himself.

"Is there a car rental place around here?" Darius was not about to pay an outrageous price to someone as untrustworthy as Javon Quincey, if that, in fact, was his real name.

"This is Opa-Locka, man. It ain't Miami Beach. We don't get many tourists, and the locals tend to steal cars if they need one bad enough. Nearest rental car place is too far to walk."

"Then how am I supposed to get downtown?"

"Jus' leave that up to me," Javon drawled.

Chapter Seven

THE CAVERN

A MILE BELOW the basement of the Mamongen Pharmaceuticals Building, a voice that sounded like rustling leaves echoed off the ragged stone cavern walls.

"Our Thinkers have made major breakthroughs that will change the course of history," the voice proclaimed.

Harbot Ankroot, known affectionately to his close friends as "Anky," was having trouble seeing in the blue-gray light. The only object he could make out was a skeletal structure that looked like a scaled-down version of the Eiffel Tower jutting upward and disappearing into the shadows overhead. Anky was beyond caring what purpose the structure served. Amidst the gloom and swirling clouds of mist rising from the cavern floor, it was becoming clearer and clearer that things were not turning out the way Anky had planned. He remembered how all this began.

It was purely a routine Earth mission. Anky first heard about Plezenthol on the Eleven O'clock News. He personally had no interest in the late-night news. The ups-and-downs of human affairs were as predictable to him as precipitation in a rain forest. He much preferred basking in the tranquility of heaven while engaged in sublime thoughts. But a job was a job, and someone who the Archangel Aaron trusted had to do it. His assignment consisted of gathering information on the latest misconceptions, fads and foibles currently floating around in the stream of human consciousness. Human beings never seemed to tire of the detours they took to hide from themselves. Anky used the nightly national news as one of his sources for the latest foolishness that passed as perfectly acceptable human behavior. Anky and his fellow Directors had to be constantly on the alert for human errors of commission, omission, and failures of judgment that could potentially yield world-ending results.

He was putting on his pajama bottoms in his motel room when the last news story of the night turned out to be an exclusive about a new drug in development that promised a major breakthrough in the treatment of common depression. The new wonder drug also promised to be a useful tool in the quest for personal growth as well as the overall enjoyment of life, according to the developer, Mamongen Pharmaceuticals. Anky made pertinent notes on the story before turning off the TV and preparing for a good night's sleep.

Filled with the satisfaction of a day's work well done, the back of Anky's head hit the pillow. He was in the habit of resting his hands behind his head and staring up at the ceiling just before going to sleep to bathe in the ineffable peace that settled inside him after a long day in the uncomfortable restrictions of a human body. At least they always gave him a young body in excellent physical condition and perfect working order. It was hard enough to operate in the dense layers of material existence. It had been eons since he had lived in a creaky old body before passing on.

The spiraling mist that came uninvited through the ceiling startled him. The mist coagulated into a leaden cloud at the foot of Anky's bed. He jack-knifed to a sitting position. His heart rate took flight like a galloping Antelope. The color of the cloud changed to dark purple, then to black, and back to dull gray. Two long-fingered hands with sharp talons reached out from the center of the cloud. It billowed to about ten feet in diameter. Anky knew the apparition was not technically a cloud. It housed a spirit.

Shapes emerged from inside the churning mist. First, a praying mantis appeared, then a goat, then a giant snake, and next a fierce hawk. Only the unmistakable violet eyes of a Warrior Lord remained the same. Anky had learned from his long career as a Senior Operative that shape shifting was a tactic Warrior Lords used to frighten their intended victims before attacking.

Senior Operatives, or any angel for that matter, hardly made a habit of coming face to face with a Warrior Lord, or the spirit of one. There were only eleven Warrior Lords known to exist in the whole of the Dark Realm. They possessed extraordinary powers common only to their rank. One of those powers was spirit projection. Warrior Lords were capable of instantaneous travel to any place in the Dark Realm or the human world above it. A Warrior Lord typically used astral projection to invade the consciousness of a human victim and gradually absorb the unlucky subject's will into its own.

Anky had no time to consider why this particular Warrior Lord had decided to pay him a visit. He leapt out of bed and deployed a high-frequency field of light energy to protect his body. The field matched the frequency of heavenly light so closely that Warrior Lords and their minions rarely came close enough to breach it.

Anky heard a voice that sounded like the beating wings of a thousand locusts inside his head.

"I am not here to fight with you," the voice said.

Anky did not believe a single word the Warrior Lord was telepathically projecting into his consciousness. He summoned light energy from the depths of his being in preparation for the attack he was sure would come at any moment.

"My name is Glythren. I am here to offer you an opportunity."

Anky barely managed to keep a straight face. "Why would little old me want ta' accept an opportunity from a Warrior Lord?"

"Hear me out, angel. I promise it will be worth your while."

Harbot Ankroot had been an angel operative for more than three hundred Earth years. Throughout this time, he had never had the misfortune of confronting a Warrior Lord in spirit or in the flesh. He had heard, however, many tales of heroic angels doing battle with the creatures. Some of these tales ended unhappily enough for Anky to listen carefully to what the Warrior Lord had to say.

"We have the technology now to walk among humans in overwhelming numbers," Glythren said. "I'm talking about battalions of soldiers performing routine, everyday tasks, completely undetectable, until the call to battle is sounded. Before this breakthrough, there were only eleven of us with the capability to operate unseen above ground. Now we can place over two hundred thousand highly trained soldiers into devastating positions."

"That's very interesting," Anky said. "What surprises me more than your claims is that ya' bothered to tell me in the first place."

"I'm telling you to make your side aware that my people will be negotiating from a position of strength."

"Negotiating what?"

"A truce."

Anky's training kicked in. Despite his total lack of faith in Glythren's words, and the deep chasm of mistrust that existed between Angels and Exiles, Anky was duty bound to bring whatever offer the Warrior Lord made back to his superiors. He stood opposite the apparition making a concerted effort not to color the situation with any preconceptions or assumptions that could extinguish the faint possibility that Glythren's presence in his humble motel room signaled the dawn of a new era.

"I gotta' ask you," Anky said. "Why are the Exiles making peace overtures after all this time?"

The apparition began to cycle into all of the colors of the rainbow, one after another. It was quite a lovely effect, actually. Anky interpreted the display as an indication of excitement.

"We want to reclaim our rightful place in heaven," the spirit of the Warrior Lord replied. We are tired of living in these bodies that force us to live underground because humans find us fearsome and repulsive."

"Does this mean the Exiles are ready to cease their rebellion? I hope my use of the word 'rebellion' doesn't upset you, by the way."

"I hope you don't mind this shorthand answer," the Warrior Lord's disembodied voice hissed. "Now that we have the power to destroy you, we think your people will work with us."

Through the ages, Exiles had never gained a widespread reputation for diplomacy in action or speech. Anky knew it was necessary to counter-balance the Warrior Lord's bald statement with a touch of homegrown tact.

"Obviously, our two sides have a lotta' talkin' to look forward to. I'm curious, though. Are the Exiles willing to change at least some of the notions that have kept our two sides apart for so long?"

"The Chief banished us from heaven for disobedience. We continue to view the incident as a difference of opinion, not a breach of faith or conduct. My people will no longer tolerate your harsh judgment. If the Chief and his Board of Directors decide not to allow the Exiles back into heaven, you can expect a full-scale war. It will be nothing like the tempest in a teapot skirmishes our sides tickle each other with now."

"I would hardly call world wars, genocide, and hatred based on racial discrimination 'teapot skirmishes,' to cite a few examples that come to mind." Anky clamped down hard on his anger. "That's not an issue we need to debate now. If you want the Chief and the Board to take your request seriously, I need some assurances from you that the Exiles are willing to change their thinking."

Crossing his arms, Anky calmly awaited the fateful reply, pleased that he had expressed his thoughts smoothly on the first try. He had not lapsed into the old stutter that had beguiled his speech in his human existence and early years as a Junior Operative.

"Naturally, the Exiles are willing to make some adjustments," the voice of the Warrior Lord snapped.

Anky decided the reply was a good enough first salvo in what promised to be many rounds of negotiation. Only an idiot would expect the Exiles to give away the farm right out of the bag. "Hmmm," he said. "It looks like the Exiles have given this matter a great deal of thought. My superiors will want to get a good look at this new technology of yours to get the ball rolling. How can we make that happen?"

"All of the Senior Operatives in heaven are invited to a demonstration of our new technology."

"That's very generous of you, but I'm sure a small group of Senior Operatives would be enough to satisfy our curiosity."

Again, the apparition went through the all-the-colors-of-the-rainbow strobe light thing.

"All of the Senior Operatives must come," the apparition said in a thunderous voice that crashed inside Anky's head. All of you must see, in person, the demonstration of the powerful technology we've harnessed. Second-hand reports are not as effective."

"You mean not as horrifying."

Glythren ignored Anky's remark. "We will hold the demonstration in one of our secret underground locations. For revealing this location to you, we insist that all of the Senior Operatives come unarmed to protect our side from a sneak attack. *Quid Pro Quo.*"

"Hmmm," Anky said. "Let me get back to you on that."

The shape-shifting cloud thinned. "Speak to your people. I will await your reply." With those final words, the spirit of the Warrior Lord spiraled into thin air.

. . .

After returning to heaven, Anky had a private meeting with the Archangel wherein he repeated, nearly word for word, his long conversation with the spirit of the Warrior Lord. He also expressed the strong, intuitive feeling the Warrior Lord's words left with him.

"These claims have a troubling substance to them," he told the Archangel. "I sense real danger. We have to learn more."

Then Aaron asked the hard question Anky knew was inevitable. The imaginary gorilla sitting in the room weighed a good deal more than the standard eight hundred pounds.

"How can we send all of the Senior Operatives at once? Doesn't Glythren's proposal smell strongly like a trap?"

Anky had considered the question carefully during the trip back to heaven in the Hyperspace Conveyor Tube.

"The HCT techs can miniaturize our hand-held homing devices into micro-chips. Then, they can implant the chips under the thumbnail of each Senior Operative. The homing signal will have to be powerful enough to penetrate miles of rock and debris. At the slightest hint of trouble, I can signal the others to slap their knees to activate their chips. The tubes will find us quickly and whisk us away to safety."

"Brilliant, Ankroot. Set up a briefing with all of the Senior Operatives. We'll get on this straightaway."

Anky's thoughts spiraled back to his harsh circumstances in the present moment. The thin burlap robe the Exiles gave Anky to wear offered little protection against the damp, cool air in the cave. He sat there shivering, facing the imposing figure of Glythren, this time in the flesh—all seven feet of the creature. The Warrior Lord hulked in front of a battalion of Exile soldiers and Anky's ninety-nine other comrades-in-arms.

Glythren's head resembled that of a cobra framed by striated strands of long, blood red hair that coiled and uncoiled like the tails of a hundred scorpions. Glythren's torso was that of a yellow-skinned lizard with two sets of arms and a pair of thick, muscular legs upon which the Warrior Lord stood upright. Glythren's prehensile tail undulated like a fat Boa Constrictor sizing up its prey. The muscles of Glythren's body stood out in such sharp relief that it made him look like no skin covered his powerful physique.

A violet aura accented Glythren's body. It pulsed like a heartbeat from every pore in the Warrior Lord's skin. The aura emanated from a vast lake of energy that Anky knew teemed in the depths of the Warrior Lord's body.

To Anky, the most fearsome of Glythren's features were his eyes. They were deep purple with a violet iris and a bottomless black pupil in the center. It was hard to pull your attention away once those eyes fixed on you.

Anky and his brave band of Senior Operatives sat on rows of wet stalagmites hewn into crude chairs. Anky resented the overbearing presence of the Exile Captains standing at intervals throughout the audience to prevent, he assumed, his brother and sister operatives from attempting to assassinate Glythren. Exiles always suspected plots since they enjoyed plotting so much themselves. The Senior Operatives for example, might be wearing miniature, bionic weapons implanted in hard-to-find places in their bodies. Angels, of course, were entirely too honorable to go in for that kind of deception, but try telling it to an Exile.

The Captains had brown skin and stood about two feet shorter than their leader, Glythren. Exiles typically wore brief clothing to intimidate adversaries with their chiseled physiques when not in battle. The only vestment the Captains wore on their rippling bodies, besides a brief loincloth, was a foot-long leather holster with the onyx handle of an energy weapon peeking over the top. Even though they were shorter than their leader and lacked the distinctive aura, only a foolish, inexperienced angel would do anything to draw a Captain's attention without a very good reason.

Glythren spoke in English telepathically to Anky and his confederates. Simultaneously, Glythren spoke aloud to the Exile troops in their native tongue with a cadence that rattled off the cavern walls like the sound of a Gatling gun.

"We have invited some of heaven's mightiest warriors here to begin a process that will literally lead our people out of the shadows and into the light," Glythren said. His words traveled like a dry wind over the sea of expectant faces before him.

The Exile Soldiers, burnt orange in skin color, paid rapt attention to their leader. No one dared speak without permission in the Warrior Lord's presence. Besides Glythren's whisper-rustle voice, the only other sound in the cavern was that of water dripping from the cavern ceiling onto the rocky floor.

The Warrior Lord pointed to a group of Exiles sitting in the front row to Anky's right. He noticed the creature sitting in the middle looked entirely different from the others.

"Rise, Strelthorne," Glythren commanded.

The Exile named Strelthorne obeyed his master's bidding and rose before the assembly. The creature stood about six feet tall with a build similar to a wiry, long distance runner in stark contrast to the other heavily muscled Exiles. His skin color matched the yellow of the Warrior Lord caste. The creature's head was oblong rather than triangular, and slightly larger than average. Strelthorne watched the crowd warily with pitch black eyes interrupted only by a small purple dot in the center.

Strelthorne was a mutant, Anky concluded.

"I have sired the boy standing before you."

There were a few gasps and an undertow of murmurs and whispers from the audience.

"From early on, the boy displayed unusual gifts. One of them is extraordinary intelligence." Glythren spoke these words in a defiant tone. Utter silence reigned once again in the cavern. It was clear to Anky that any further whispered remarks by the rank-and-file concerning the lanky mutant's appearance might be fatal.

"We have Strelthorne to thank for the wondrous new device I am about to show you. It is a product of his brilliant mind."

Glythren nodded to Strelthorne who immediately sat.

The Warrior Lord cradled a small device in one hand. The tiny machine looked to Anky like a child's toy. It was a transparent sphere containing two small, silver pyramids facing in opposite directions. The opposing pyramids joined at the base appeared to be struggling to escape from an uncomfortable relationship.

"Until now, only Warrior Lords have been able to walk freely among humans by infiltrating their bodies in spirit form. With this new invention, Captains and Soldiers can now join us undetected."

A squall of cheers erupted from the Exile audience.

Anky watched as Glythren touched a small semi-circle protruding like a pimple from the back of the sphere. The opposing triangles inside the glass sphere emitted an azure blue halo of light. A yellowish liquid filled the sphere. The halo of light convulsed into a gray cloud that began to pulse like a beating heart. What happened next sent a cold shiver through Anky's temporary human body.

Glythren's violet aura disappeared. The Warrior Lord's tail rolled up into his body. The arms on either side of his body fused together to form one arm on each side. The creature's grotesque head collapsed into its torso and reappeared as a human head. The arms withdrew into the shoulder sockets and emerged again as two human arms.

The skin on Glythren's body bubbled. The bubbles grew in size, gradually engulfing the Warrior Lord's body in a giant, soap-sudsy heap. A throaty roar echoed throughout the cavern. The process was a painful one, Anky was glad to hear. There was at least some justice still at play in the universe.

The bubbling mass expanded to about a height of about eight feet, Anky estimated. After a few minutes, the furious movement of the bubbles slowed, as if an invisible hand had turned down the wash cycle on an equally invisible dishwasher. When the last of the bubbles dissolved, a non-descript man in his early thirties stood before Anky and the assembly, naked as a newborn baby.

"The effect is seamless," the man explained in a clear, masculine voice. "The molecular reintegration of the cellular structure can last for days, if necessary, as long as the energy source inside the glass ball remains viable. We call the process 'reconfiguration.' It is made possible by a new energy source which is a combination of dark and light energy."

Gasps of amazement and then a cacophony of cries of approval spread through the Exile audience.

"Strelthorne isolated a molecule that stabilizes the mixture of dark and light energy. Instead of a destructive explosion, we now have a new, hybrid power source that offers unlimited possibilities."

The cavern filled with a chorus of triumphant cries. The demonstration had exceeded Anky's worst fears. The Exiles had evidently created a potent new form of energy. Who knew what nightmares they might create in addition to the one he had just witnessed? Every moment that passed by was now fraught with potential disaster. Having no desire to waste another precious second, Anky spoke up:

"Lord Glythren. Archangel Aaron has granted me authority to speak on behalf of the Chief and all of the Senior Operatives you have graciously invited here today. I'll hear your proposal and bring your terms for re-entering heaven back to the Chief and the Board of Directors. I'll return to convey their answer to you without delay."

Anky expected to hear a raucous response from the Exile horde. Instead, utter silence reigned. Sensing danger, Anky summoned light energy. He felt a warm sensation rising along his spine. Anky knew the other Senior Operatives were preparing for defensive maneuvers in the same manner. He activated his scanner, as did the others, to bring the HCT's in for an immediate exfiltration.

Glythren turned to a nearby Captain. The Warrior Lord opened his over-sized, long fingered hand before closing it into a fist, a signal to the other Captains.

The Captains quickly surrounded Anky and the other Senior Operatives. They drew their weapons, which resembled u-shaped tuning forks with opposing pyramids about two inches long attached to the end of each prong. Anky figured the Captains were taking the Senior Operatives hostage to hasten the negotiations. Exiles never missed a chance to seize an unfair advantage. What happened next was unprecedented and entirely unexpected.

Just as the homeward bound conveyor tubes pierced the ceiling of the cavern, the Exile Captains opened fire cold-bloodedly.

Anky enveloped himself in a luminous weather balloon of protective light. It was a reflex reaction, born of hundreds of battles fought against the minions of The Dark Realm. Their weapons would be of no use against his shield. Light energy rendered dark energy harmless when they collided. It had been the case for as long as anyone could remember. Why then were the Exiles firing on them? Did Glythren think he could catch them by surprise with this sudden, brazen attack?

Anky heard the screams. He watched in horror as a withering barrage of azure blue energy projectiles from the tuning fork pistols tore into the protective shields of his brother and sister operatives. Their screams subsided only after they dissolved into vapor.

One of the Captains turned his weapon on Anky and fired. The virulent energy projectiles slammed into his shield, tearing it open like a heavy gauge bullet ripping through flesh and bone.

For a few seconds, Anky experienced searing pain, the kind he imagined a person felt in a blast furnace. He heard himself utter a terrible scream. Then there was only darkness and a sickening, swirling sensation.

. . .

Glythren watched the Senior Operatives disappear one by one. The Warrior Lord stood awestruck by the wondrous new power his freak of a son had unlocked. Strelthorne's peers regarded him as a curse and an embarrassment prior to the discovery of the new energy. Now he was a hero, as Glythren always believed the child would become. The Warrior Lord had found Strelthorne's brilliant mind intriguing. It was why Glythren had decided to let the boy live.

The Captains ceased firing. There were no more angels in the cavern. That meant there were no more experienced operatives to interfere with Glythren's plans. The new hybrid energy had done everything Strelthorne had said it would. If the other new weapons coming on stream worked as well, the Exiles would never have to fear the wrath of heaven, or anything else—ever again.

Chapter Eight

A FINE RIDE

JAVON AND DARIUS trudged through the dingy industrial park where half the buildings hulked in various stages of disrepair ranging from barely salvageable to hopeless.

"I thought you said this place was close by," Darius complained.

"Be cool. We almost there," Javon said.

Darius caught sight of six youths smoking and drinking from bottles in brown bags in front of an empty warehouse building partially destroyed by fire. Darius hesitated. Part of him wanted to walk over and talk to the young black men. He wanted to tell them they were inviting disaster into their lives by wasting time. It was so obvious to him. It hurt Darius that the young men could not see it. Doing nothing led to limited choices later in life. It led to unrewarding, dead-end jobs, if you were lucky enough to land a job. Darius saw this with crystal clarity, in 3D digital color. The young men on the corner had very little to look forward to, unless they woke up and mended their ways in a hurry. Apparently, spending even a short time in heaven had a way of sharpening insight.

The tableau of young black men slouching against the building brought back traumatic memories of his recent and extremely premature demise.

"Thought you was in a hurry," Javon called to him.

"Huh?"

"We ain't gonna get anywhere by standin' around admiring the gorgeous scenery."

A few minutes later, Javon and Darius stood in the parking lot of a manufacturing plant housed in a dilapidated warehouse. Darius strained to read the name on the building. It was barely legible under layers of grime and dust: PLUNDER PLATING & MANUFACTUR-ING. In stark contrast to the dreary gray building and the beat-up cars in the parking lot, Darius noticed an expensive red sports car with a lustrous wax shine under a canopy near the front entrance.

"It's a Bentley GT Continental," Javon crowed while eying the car with gleaming brass wheels and dark tinted windows. "That is one fine ride."

The car looked more like a gigantic piece of gaudy jewelry to Darius. "That thing looks like it cost more than a decent house. What are we doing here?"

"C'mon. Just Relax and follow my lead."

Javon walked a few steps and suddenly whirled around to face Darius. "Don't screw this up," he said with a menacing look. "If you do, you gotta' pay me anyway. My time is valuable."

Darius laughed.

"What's so funny?"

"I guess whatever trouble you plan to get into this afternoon will have to wait until after I've overpaid you for my ride downtown."

"'If I wasn't in a financially sensitive situation, I'd bash your head in for sayin' that."

Javon wheeled back around and stomped forward to the entrance.

Darius followed him. The kid was a certified nut job. It would be a relief to end their relationship after the trip downtown.

They entered a tiny room which served as Plunder Plating and Manufacturing's reception area. There were no chairs in the cramped enclosure. *How unfriendly*, Darius thought. "You know what you're doing?" Darius inquired.

"You never got to ask me something like that."

Darius watched as Javon removed a business card from a small tray in front of a sliding glass window protected by wrought iron bars. Darius read the card before Javon palmed it: ROBERT N. PLUNDER, President.

Javon confidently pushed a buzzer on the wall near the window. The window opened revealing a pimply faced teenage girl chewing bubble gum.

"Help you," the girl asked in a bored tone.

"Ashanti," Javon exclaimed. "I can't believe it."

"She don't work for ten dollars an hour," the girl said.

"You look just like her," Javon crooned.

"You a Junkie?"

"Not on your life, girl."

"We don't have any cash or drugs on the premises. What I do have is a loaded gun."

Darius opened his mouth to ask Javon what this was all about when he felt a sharp pain on his thigh. He tried to say something again but felt the same pain. He looked down. Javon was pinching him.

"Ow," Darius moaned.

"Bless you," Javon said to Darius and then turned back to the receptionist: "Do you sing?"

"No, but I can scream real good. What you want?"

"We're here to wash and wax Robert's car," Javon said with a big smile.

Darius was about to say he had no intentions of washing or waxing anyone's car when Javon silenced him with a deadly look.

Meanwhile, the receptionist expertly blew a bubble with her gum and popped it. "What happened to the other two dudes?"

"If I tell you, will you promise not to tell Robert?" Javon whispered.

"It's cool," the receptionist agreed.

"They got a low grade in shine reflection for three straight weeks. Can you believe it? Some people have no pride in their work."

The receptionist blew another bubble and popped it. It was her way of meditating, Darius figured.

"Hold on," she said, picking up the phone.

"I think I'm going to leave," Darius whispered to Javon.

The kid pulled a big gun out of his pocket and pointed it at Darius' groin. This all happened below the horizon of the receptionist's window.

"I was just kidding," Darius whispered again.

"Is your friend okay?" the receptionist asked Javon. "He looks kinda' sick."

"He always looks like that," Javon said.

The receptionist put the phone down. "Robert said you guys are a day early but the car is dirty. I'll bring you the keys."

The girl disappeared through a door in the rear of the tiny cubicle.

"These kinda' dudes are so obsessive about their cars. It's their wild side. Their passion. I just love it 'cause it makes my job easy."

"Why don't you just steal the car without me in it?" Darius said.

"Why should I make one score when I can make two?"

"What do you mean?"

"We're gonna' rob your office when we get downtown," Javon said with a self-satisfied smirk.

• • •

Javon opened the Bentley's door and slid in beside Darius. "You startin' to get with the program. Keep it up and you might live through this. I'm gonna' put the gun down now. Keep your mouth shut or I'll blow your head off. You know what I'm sayin?"

Darius was too angry to say anything. He punched his seat belt into the slot. He had spent barely fifty-nine minutes back on Earth, and already his mission had veered horribly off course.

The engine *varoomed* to life. The car rolled slowly out of the parking lot.

Javon drove the Bentley out of Opa-Locka breaking every local traffic ordinance in the books, Darius was certain. He kept hoping Javon would drive into a speed trap. No such luck. The Rap music Javon insisted on blaring did nothing to quell his mounting nervousness.

"How did you know about the car wash company?" Darius asked.

"I seen two guys cleaning the car in CLEANWAX uniforms a coupla' times. I just filed it away, thinkin' it would come in handy someday."

Javon twirled the steering wheel with one finger and made a sharp right turn. A horn blared behind them.

"Shut up, asshole," Javon said, glaring into the rear-view mirror.

"Look, I'm not quite sure how to put this…I have some really important business to take care of today. Couldn't we put the office robbery off for another day?"

"What kinda' business?"

"Nothing that will make you money. I'm sure of that."

"I can't decide to put off the robbery 'less you tell me about your business."

How could he explain to the sly teenager that there were no financial advantages to saving the world? At least Darius didn't think there were. Javon might have other ideas. Darius decided to try a more direct approach.

"Look, the thing is, if you don't get me safely downtown, and leave me alone after that, you won't have to worry about where your next dollar is coming from."

"Is that some kinda' threat?" Javon said, raising the gun again.

Darius sighed heavily. "I'm not stupid. I understand that you are a very dangerous and tough person. I'm not trying to threaten you."

"Good," Javon said, lowering the gun.

They traveled on in silence for a while. Signs for interstate ninety-five appeared ahead of them. Javon steered the car into the on-ramp for the expressway. Darius watched as they passed one car after another in the fast lane. The pearl clock on the dashboard read twenty minutes to twelve noon. Minutes swept forward as quickly as they sped down the highway, it seemed to Darius. He had to get his mind off the ticking clock before it drove him crazy. Javon had come to the rescue, in an odd sort of way.

"You still ain't told me about your business," he said.

"We have to go to Mamongen Pharmaceuticals. They have a big office building downtown. Do you know where it is?"

"Thought you said we was goin' to your law office."

"No, you said that."

"Oh yeah. Right." Javon turned to Darius with a murderous expression. "I just had a very bad thought."

"I can hardly wait to hear it."

"If you ain't a Lawyer, and you got no money, how you gonna' pay me for this ride?"

Darius had to think fast.

"I'm almost positive my bank has an office on the first floor. We can get your money there." Darius had never told this many lies in a row before. He had never told this many lies in a year. He did not like to lie. Ever.

"You better be able to pay me, or I'll break your arms and legs. Slowly."

"Got it," Darius said.

The sun shone brightly and traffic was moderate. Miami was a beautiful city, Darius thought. He admired a row of stately Royal Palm trees planted alongside the expressway. It was a nice respite from thoughts of what Javon might say or do when he found out there was no bank on the first floor of the Mamongen Building. If by some enchanted coincidence they found a bank on the first floor, what would Javon do when the teller there happily refused to pay Darius a single dollar?

The modern skyscrapers of downtown Miami surfaced on the horizon.

"You got an address for this place we're goin'?"

"I never really made a note of the address. I just know how to get there. Don't worry. I'll give you plenty of warning before the exit comes up."

Javon looked at him suspiciously. Darius smiled while wondering how in the world the Archangel expected him to know where he was going when he didn't even have a street address.

Javon pushed a button on the console.

"Where would you like to go, Mr. Plunder," a friendly voice beamed from somewhere inside the car. Darius jumped in his seat like a startled jackrabbit.

"Directions to Mamongen Pharmacycles," Javon called out."

"Pharmaceuticals," Darius corrected.

"Please repeat the request," the voice said.

"Mamongen Pharmaceuticals in downtown Miami," Javon said. "An' don't take—

Darius clapped a hand over Javon's mouth before the words "all day" came out. He quickly removed the hand before the teenager had a chance to bite off a finger.

The friendly voice gave them directions to their destination.

"Thank you," Darius said.

"They never get it right the first time," Javon grumbled.

"It never hurts to be polite," Darius said. "Who was that person?"

"It was a machine at On-Star GPS."

"That's the first time I've ever seen or heard GPS work," Darius marveled.

"What's the matter with you?"

"I don't buy expensive cars, or make a habit of stealing them."

"I ain't gonna' dignify that with an answer." Frowning, Javon accelerated and changed lanes to pass another car.

Darius eyed the speedometer. "Isn't a hundred miles an hour a bit excessive?"

"You don't want to' be tellin' me how to drive. Know what I'm sayin'?"

"I guess not." Darius closed his eyes. The only intelligent thing to do at this point, he decided, was to meditate in preparation for whatever lay ahead. Maybe being kidnapped in a stolen car was a test to prepare him for the *really* hard stuff to come. The idea, while amusing, did not wash. The sliver of time he had to accomplish his mission did not leave much room for trials. Why then, had fate thrown him together with this street thug like ham and cheese slices in a chef salad? There had to be a good reason. What could it possibly be? Another thought struck him. It was worse than the first one.

What if Javon was supposed to be a member of his mortal team?

He quickly pushed the preposterous idea out of his head.

Javon sang along with the Rap music. Darius meditated. Neither of them noticed the motorcycle cop following a few hundred yards behind the Bentley.

Chapter Nine

HIRAM'S HUMBLE ABODE

HIRAM FYRUM WAS a passionate man. His interests included fine wines, Impressionist paintings, Cubist sculpture, Thoroughbred racehorses, beautiful women (he liked them tall) and most importantly, the pursuit of the elusive, devoutly worshipped, Holy Grail of *Corporate Efficiency.*

No corporation could survive in today's world without efficiency as its highest priority. He often used the term "Corporate Fiscal Fitness" instead of the latter, stale terminology. It was a term Hiram invented. He loved making homey analogies like dieting and staying within budgets. He compared regular exercise for strength and endurance to making cold calls to achieve sales quotas. He peppered his department heads with regular e-mails promoting the parallels of good health habits and financial prosperity. The literal and figurative imagery of these homegrown analogies were not lost on his bright and eager underlings.

Hiram's own contribution to the cause of Corporate Fiscal Fitness came in the form of a twenty thousand square foot penthouse apartment on the top floor of the Mamongen Building. Why waste time commuting to work or flying all over the world for business meetings when you could do it in your own back yard—in a manner of speaking.

Hiram owned many things, but a backyard was not one of them, unless clouds and air space counted.

If business contacts insisted on meeting face to face, they travelled to visit Hiram. It was worth the trip to witness his one-of-a kind world headquarters and listen to his discourses on *Corporate Efficiency* first hand. The penthouse-office concept had come to Hiram while he was enjoying a chateaubriand and champagne dinner on a first-class flight to Singapore. These long-distance business trips cost in excess of ten thousand dollars each with plane fare, hotels, food and incidentals. Travelling less than first class was naturally unthinkable. He'd save more than a hundred-and-fifty thousand dollars a year with the new concept. And he'd save office downtime and the counter-productive effects of jet-lag. The more he thought about the idea, the more benefits occurred to him. He began the plans for his new office/home the first day he returned from Singapore.

The long hours and stressful demands of Hiram's position made time off to recharge his batteries a necessity. This explained the Pace Collection furniture, eclectic, original paintings and sculptures, home theatre, Olympic-sized swimming pool and Dado spa, just to mention a few of the amenities. A healthy, rested body led to healthy business decisions Hiram liked to chirp to his subordinates. Furthermore, a happy executive was a more creative and productive individual. The ideas Hiram's lifestyle spawned made hundreds of millions of dollars for the company every year.

The idea for the "New You" marketing program had occurred to Hiram while sunning himself one afternoon on his three thousand square foot, Italian marble terrace. Hiram was betting that combining Plezenthol with American Mental Health Association approved self-improvement seminars was a sure thing. In an increasingly competitive world, who couldn't use a little more motivation? More to the point, who didn't want a little more happiness?

Hiram expected untold millions of people would be pounding down their doctors' doors for a prescription of Mamongen's revolutionary drug. This new marketing approach was going to beat, by a thousand miles, the established practice of company sales reps calling on busy doctors who didn't have the time or interest to listen to their spiels. The concept promised to be a massive win for pull versus push marketing. The program's half billion price tag would prove to be a drop in the bucket compared to the staggering sales numbers Hiram knew Plezenthol was destined to generate.

There were unanticipated benefits to Hiram's lifestyle. He discovered, by accident, that having one-on-one meetings with Mamongen executives in his study was a highly effective motivational tool. There were no superfluous people around to ask foolish questions, disagree, or fall asleep while Hiram spoke.

At that moment, Hiram and Doctor Simon Worthington III were engaged in one of these private audiences. It was not going, however, the way these meetings usually went.

"The statistical norm for side effects in this product category is in the five to ten percent range," Worthington was saying.

Hiram's Chief Chemist and Research Director held up a copy of the final report from the contract drug testing company Mamongen had hired to conduct the clinical trials on Plezenthol. "The report indicates that only one to two percent of the test subjects reported side effects."

Hiram puffed on his pipe. "The pill works too well. Is that it?"

"I've never seen a report come back this positive before."

Hiram leaned back in a chamois leather chair that was several sizes too big for his diminutive frame. He eyed the bookshelves to his right, stocked to the brim with ponderous texts on Business Management and a conglomeration of best-selling business advice from the shrewdest of Hiram's CEO contemporaries. He made a mental note to remove the one by the poor *schmuck* who had just received a lengthy prison sentence for securities fraud.

"Why, Simon, are you bringing this up at the proverbial eleventh hour?"

"I've been talking to the data entry supervisor at Amcor for the last month. He claims the results have been triple checked. Despite his assurances, I can't help feeling uneasy about these results."

It was entirely possible Simon was experiencing paranoid delusions. Hiram had seen enough brilliant, talented people go off the deep end in his time. Hiram puffed on his pipe some more. Simon erupted into an extended series of sneezes. Hiram dumped pipe ashes into an oversized, lily-pad ashtray in the center of his gilt-edged mahogany desk. He tossed a package of tissues to Simon from a draw in the desk.

Simon blew his nose. He looked around, disoriented. "Where should I put the tissue?"

Hiram pointed to the ashtray.

"What I'm saying," Simon paused, "I know you don't want to hear this, but I have to say it." The Research Director took a deep breath. "We must do more testing to confirm these results."

Hiram held up his hand but Simon wouldn't obey the stop sign.

"We're putting a powerful psychotropic drug on the market with questionable test data to back it up."

"I'm going to chalk that last statement up to oxygen deprivation from the rarified air you've been breathing in your ivory tower, Simon. We have a billion dollars in research, development, and marketing invested in this product. The company is counting heavily on the projected revenue stream from Plezenthol. The FDA loves us. The program is set to launch. The world is watching. Turning around now would be like a bunch of NASA scientists scrubbing the first Apollo mission on the grounds that it might not work."

Hiram tapped more ashes out of the pipe. "What am I supposed to tell the people gathering for the press conference downstairs? Sorry. We changed our minds?"

Simon twisted uneasily in the Art Deco black lacquered chair in front of Hiram's desk. By design, there were no sofas or padded chairs in the study other than Hiram's own *comfy* leather throne.

"It's only normal for someone as close to the project as you to have doubts, Simon. Just look at it like a little bout of post-partum depression. The research has taken a toll on you. I've put you under five years of constant pressure and, I have to say, you came through like a champion. It's time to let your child go out into the world. Relax. Live a little. Take a well-earned vacation. It will do wonders for your outlook. Most importantly, have faith in yourself and the work you've done. Trust the process and enjoy your success."

Simon's hazel eyes brightened. His curly blond hair glistened in the sun filtering through the glass blocks inlaid in the wall below the twelve-foot ceiling. He looked to Hiram like a haggard, unusually tall and thin child hiding behind the mask of a man with a Van Dyke beard and slim designer glasses.

Hiram believed steadfastly in the test results. Regarding his impromptu speech to Simon, there was at least one kernel of truth. The man sitting before him needed a vacation desperately.

Simon extracted another tissue from the small package clenched in one of his fine-boned hands. He blew his nose again.

"I suppose you're right," he said in a soft voice.

Hiram smiled. "Of course, I am."

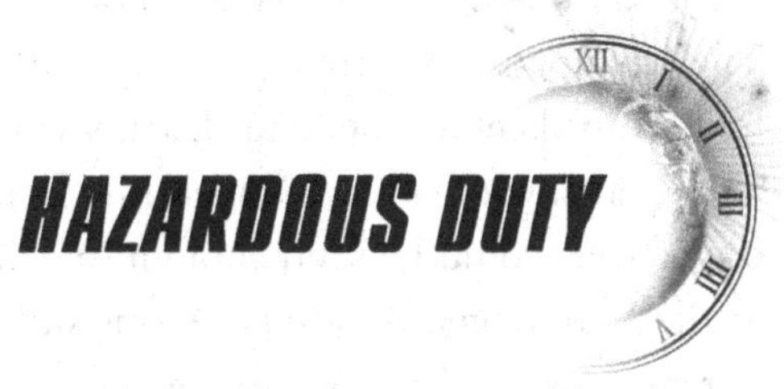

HAZARDOUS DUTY

JAVON SWERVED ACROSS three lanes at once to catch the downtown exit ramp.

"Where did you learn to drive?" Darius inquired, amazed at his sense of calm. It probably had something to do with having nothing to lose.

"From one of the best get-away-dudes-in-the-game."

"Very funny."

"For real," Javon said, as they whizzed off the highway down the exit ramp.

Javon brought the car to a skidding stop at the traffic light near the bottom of the ramp.

"At least you stop for red lights".

"Usually," Javon said.

Darius was about to deliver a lecture on safe driving when he caught sight of a motorcycle cop cresting the top of the ramp in the rear-view mirror. The Policeman came barreling down on them with red and blue lights flashing.

"Where did that mother come from? I must be goin' blind to miss a cop in broad daylight."

Darius felt goose bumps rise on his arms as he watched Javon stroke the scraggly whiskers on his chin. "Whatever you're thinking, forget about it."

I can't be arrested, Darius thought. *The Archangel will kill me.* Then a hopeful thought occurred to him. The kid, in all probability, had a rap sheet a mile long. Darius would simply explain to the officer that Javon had kidnapped him and stolen the car. Maybe then the officer would be kind enough to call someone to give him a ride to the Mamongen Building. Darius suddenly felt grateful for the apparent miracle of the overlooked cop.

"Oh well." Javon said as he tromped on the accelerator and powered the car through the red traffic light.

"What are you doing?" Darius yelled.

Javon didn't answer. He turned left into a one-way street.

"Are you high on drugs?" The misguided kid had steered the car in the wrong direction. It all made perfect sense in a twisted fashion. The kid did everything backwards. Why not add driving in the wrong direction to the list?

A column of cars headed straight for them.

"Shut your uptight ass up. Can't you seem I'm tryin' to concentrate?"

Darius watched the motorcycle cop follow them through the red light and motion for the onrushing cars to stop. Then the officer signaled to them, pointing to the side of the road.

The Bentley languished in the middle of the road with the one-way traffic slowing down and stopping all around them.

"Pull over," Darius shouted into Javon's ear.

"Be quiet or I'll kill you soon as we're outta' this." Javon drove off, deftly threading his way through the obstacle course of idling, bewildered motorists.

Darius turned around to look behind them, just in time to see two police cars come to a skidding stop with their lights flashing.

"The cavalry has arrived. Now we're really dead," Darius said.

"No, we ain't. They gotta' deal with the mess I made." Javon spun the wheel to the right. After the turn, he floored the accelerator.

Darius slammed backward in the seat, feeling like a test pilot on a rocket sled. After the escape, Javon kept the car out of sight on narrow neighborhood streets, all the way downtown.

The kid might be teachable, Darius thought optimistically. He sure had learned a thing or two from *"one of the best get-away-dudes-in-the-game."* Maybe he could learn to do something right for a change.

. . .

Madison Tremane stood with hands on hips next to his Harley Road King Police bike. He surveyed the tangle of cars in the street with a mixture of dismay and righteous indignation. He would have liked to go zooming off after the two idiots in the red sports car with his thirteen hundred and fifty cubic centimeter engine throttled wide open. His first responsibility, however, lay in getting these motorists sorted out and on their way again to avoid accidents and a big traffic tie up. His duty did not prevent him from regretting the necessity of leaving the arrest of the two morons in the stolen Bentley to other traffic units.

As these thoughts went through Madison's head, two police cruisers arrived on the scene. Officers immediately disembarked to help direct traffic. The Police Dispatcher's voice came through the speaker in Madison's crash helmet.

"Subject in stolen vehicle requested directions to Mamongen Pharmaceuticals in Sector One. Proceed to destination and investigate."

Maybe it was his lucky day. Madison hand signaled the other two officers that he was leaving the scene to pursue the stolen vehicle. They signaled back their acknowledgement. He smiled to himself as he mounted the bike. Twisting the throttle, Madison gunned the mighty engine to life. The rear wheel squealed when he engaged the clutch. Steering between the gaggle of cars ahead of him, he whistled as he headed downtown.

Chapter Eleven

THE DOWNTOWN GAUNTLET

DARIUS AND JAVON wandered through the marble and glass lobby of the Mamongen Pharmaceuticals Building. Darius noticed Javon staring at the rounded hills of the "M" in the Mamongen logo on the far wall.

"They make fake titties here?"

"They research and develop psychotropic drugs," Darius answered tersely.

"Psycho what?"

"Drugs that affect the brain."

"Can we get some free samples?"

Darius ignored the question. He was wondering what he was supposed to do next now that the adventure of getting here was mercifully over. He scanned the lobby for someone or something that might strike a responsive chord. Then he saw a tall, red-haired woman standing in a long line at the information kiosk in the center of the lobby. Something told Darius to approach her. He tried moving in that direction but Javon was suddenly tugging on his arm.

"I don't see no bank here."

One look into Javon's hungry eyes told Darius the teenager wasn't going to tolerate any more excuses. He had to pay Javon now, or suffer a hailstorm of negative attention that the wayward youth would undoubtedly call down upon them.

The terrible, unwelcome thought struck him again: *Was Javon supposed to be a member of the team?* This question, along with the urgent money requirement, called for immediate resolution.

Darius had an idea. "We'll use the ATM over there," he said.

"How you gonna' use it without a card?"

"Actually, I have one in my shoe." Another lie. *Ouch!*

"I knew you was holdin' out on me," Javon scowled.

"Can you take a short walk?"

"What for?"

"I need privacy to do this transaction."

"You think I'm stupid? I leave you alone and you're gone."

"You'll have to trust me."

Javon's eyes narrowed to slits. "That word ain't part of my vocabulary."

"You have to leave me alone to do the transaction. It's the only way you'll get paid."

"I ain't gonna steal your *PIN* number. I'll close my eyes."

"Have you given me a good reason to take your word for anything?"

Javon stared at him with what looked like equal parts consternation and surprise.

Darius pressed the advantage. "If you want your money, you'll have to give me a few moments alone."

Javon thought a moment. "Why should I trust you?"

"Because I've learned if you don't go around cheating people, the chances are people won't cheat you."

"Easy for you to say. You got a rich Daddy."

Darius ignored the irksome comment. Every second was precious. He certainly had no desire to argue with a big-mouthed, teenaged felon.

Javon stared at him, searching for the faintest signs of deceit.

"Don't try anything," he said after the longest half minute Darius had ever experienced. "I got my eye on you."

Darius walked the short distance to the ATM on his own for the first time since emerging from the HCT. What a relief. He positioned himself close to the machine to block anyone from seeing what he was doing. Closing his eyes, he focused every atom of his consciousness on the one being in the entire universe he thought could help him. There was a crackling sound like static electricity, and then he heard the words, "Yes, Darius."

His eyes flew open. A smiling, lantern jawed Burt Lancaster look-alike greeted him on the ATM screen, surrounded by an aura of radiant light.

"Thanks for taking my call," Darius said.

"No problem," the Archangel answered. "What can I do for you?"

"This Javon person," Darius began uncertainly, "Am I supposed to work with him?"

"Javon volunteered," the Archangel said through rows of perfect white teeth. "He's just not fully aware of it yet." The Archangel paused. "It's up to you to bring out Javon's better qualities."

"You can't be serious, Archangel. Javon is an accident waiting to happen."

"You have no idea what Javon is capable of, or yourself for that matter."

Darius was dead certain he knew what Javon was capable of and none of it was good. However, he did not want to argue with the Archangel. He had learned during his short stay in heaven that the Archangel had little time for long discussions under normal circumstances—and this was certainly not a normal circumstance by any stretch of the imagination.

He felt something warm against his chest. Pulling on the chain around his neck, he drew the golden triangle out and cupped it in his hand. One of the small circles inside the triangle glowed.

"Trust the people who are sent to you," the Archangel said.

"Most importantly, trust and believe in yourself. Any achievement, great or small, will only rise from a firm foundation of belief in yourself and your abilities."

Darius basked for the briefest moment in the warm glow of the triangle and the Archangel's inspiring words. He looked up. Light poured from the Archangel's face.

"It took you awhile to get downtown."

"Please don't remind me."

"You'd better get a move on." The Archangel's head tilted to one side. "Oh, I almost forgot. Here's some walking-around money."

On the ATM screen, the Archangel's image dissolved into a Northern Trust Bank logo.

Twenty-dollar bills cascaded from the machine. Darius fell to his knees to scoop up the money. He frantically stuffed the bills into his pockets as they fluttered to the marble floor.

Javon instantly dropped beside him, struggling to gather up the money as passersby watched with curiosity.

Just as they were picking up the last few bills, a security guard approached them. He was a gray-haired man in his fifties with a kindly expression set off by the light blue shirt and navy-blue pants of his Mamongen security uniform.

"Can I see your bankcard," the guard said, holding out a well-manicured hand. He was perhaps a retired grade school teacher on his second career, Darius thought.

Javon slipped a hand into his pants pocket—the same pocket that hid the gun Javon had shoved at him earlier. Darius placed a calming hand on Javon's shoulder which he promptly shrugged off.

The ATM clicked and produced a plastic bankcard, just as it seemed Javon was about to shoot the place up.

Darius wasted no time in stepping in front of the ATM to retrieve the card. The Archangel appeared for an instant. His lips moved and the caption "Good Luck" flashed at the bottom of the screen before the page became a bank logo again. Darius' compact, athletic body prevented the guard and Javon from seeing or hearing anything unusual. Retrieving the bankcard from the ATM's slot, Darius turned and handed it to the security guard.

"The cash dispensing mechanism must be broken," Darius said. "The money just came flying out. I'm sorry for the commotion we caused."

The guard examined the card, then Darius, then Javon. "Is there any other business you two have here?"

Darius glanced across the lobby. At the same moment, a motorcycle cop walked through the glass entrance doors. The officer planted his boots firmly in front of the doors and crossed his arms across his chest. Darius jerked his attention back to the guard. "We absolutely have very important business here." *What business?* His mind went blank.

"I suppose you're here for the press conference?"

A funny thing happened. Darius suddenly became aware, beyond the slightest doubt, that he and Javon had come to the Mamongen Building for this very purpose.

"Is it that obvious?" Darius said. "We were just wondering what room it's in."

"The auditorium," the guard answered while looking Javon over. "I'm afraid they won't let you in wearing those casual clothes."

"I'm goin' right out to the truck and change into my cameraman clothes," Javon said. He stuck a thumb inside the armhole of his Miami Heat jersey and pushed it outward. "I just like to stay cool while I can. You know what I mean?"

"It sure is hot out there." The guard handed the bankcard back to Darius. "I'll report the problem with the ATM. Please try not to start any riots while you're in the building."

"Not us, man. We're just tryin' to make an honest living, like everyone else here."

If only Javon's remark were true, Darius thought. It was no fun walking around with the fate of the world resting on your shoulders.

The guard smiled and ambled off.

"Where'd you hide that card?" Javon demanded. "You didn't pull it outta' your shoe. I was watchin'. Very carefully."

"Does it matter? You got paid. More than we agreed on."

Javon's eyes narrowed. Darius wondered what was going on in the criminal mind behind them.

"You got a point. See you around, stiff."

Without another word, Javon strolled away into the crowd.

"Wait a minute," Darius called after him, but the teenager kept walking.

. . .

Javon had things to do and people to see. He had no time for long speeches or creepy dudes like Darius McPherson. He had scored some seed money and had the keys to a brand-new Bentley which he was going to turn into a shit load of cash before the cops found him or the car. Life was about to become very beautiful.

Javon headed for the exit with long, rhythmical strides. In another life, he might have become a pro basketball player. But the people who did stuff like that usually had at least one caring parent and a home to go back to after school every day, not a cold institution inhabited mostly by budding lunatics destined for nothing but trouble.

He was almost at the building's main entrance when he caught sight of the motorcycle cop. Javon wheeled around and quickly got lost in the milling crowd of business people and media representatives.

Chapter Twelve

THE RED-HAIRED REPORTER

VICKY MATTHEWS STOOD waiting impatiently for the woman in line in front of her to understand the directions the Information Attendant was slowly repeating for the fourth time in Spanish. Vicky had to pick up her press credentials soon, or she was going to miss the beginning of the Mamongen Press Conference. That would give Roberta Fernbreath-Larson, a woman who relentlessly pushed the art of being an asshole to new and dizzying heights, the perfect opportunity to fire her.

Half of Vicky yearned to be fired. She hated the rigid confines of the WQES Financial News Division. The other wanted to keep the job that allowed her to continue payments on an upscale, downtown condominium and a BMW sports coup. Staff cutbacks surrounded Vicky on all sides. They were happening to people she knew in her organization and others as media companies merged into bigger and bigger, lumbering giants. This meant two things. One, Vicky's shitty job would be hard to replace. Two, every day Vicky managed not to storm into Roberta Fernbreath-Larson's office and murder her in cold blood was a moral victory.

It was finally her turn in line. Vicky presented her driver's license to the Information Attendant and asked for her press credentials.

"Excuse me," someone said. Vicky's reporter eyes examined the young, earnest looking black man standing next to her. He wore black penny loafers, a department store suit that looked a size too small for his five-foot ten inch running back frame. A neat crew cut framed the square, regular features of his face.

"You have to get in line," Vicky said to the young man. She pointed to the end of the line that snaked behind her.

"Can I speak with you for a minute?" the young man said.

Vicky had experienced just about every pick-up line ever invented. She was tall and built in a way that attracted stares wherever she went. Her intense green eyes, flaming red hair and symmetrical Irish features made it hard to go out socially on her own. Hungry males over the age of twenty-five thought they had the God-given right to walk up and hit on her—anywhere at any time. It was mostly boring, sometimes frightening, and occasionally dangerous. Passing the milestone of thirty recently had not helped to dilute the attention.

The bothersome guy talking to her didn't look anything like your typical pick-up artist, though. He looked like he had just arrived on a Greyhound bus from Omaha Nebraska to sing in a gospel competition. On the other hand, he could be a serial killer. The most innocent, ordinary-looking people could turn out to be monsters. She knew this first hand from years of crime reporting.

With her press pass now prominently displayed from a chain over her peach blouse, Vicky hoisted her knapsack of a pocketbook onto one shoulder and laptop case on the other and started on her way. She still used an older model laptop. Yes, they were harder to carry around, but she liked a large keyboard. She couldn't adapt to the small keyboard of newer models, or the digital keyboard of a tablet. At some point, big laptops would go the way of all flesh, but until then, she would stick to her guns. Vicky was just an old-fashioned girl in some ways.

The Kid from Omaha walked along in step with her. "I'm Darius McPherson," he said.

"If you don't get lost, I'll call a security guard." She was in no mood for a horny country bumpkin who just might be a sadistic rapist in disguise.

• • •

His mind raced. Darius had to think of something to say that would slow the red-haired woman down. He read the name on the press pass bobbing from a chain around her neck.

"I have something very important to discuss with you, Ms. Matthews."

The woman increased her already frenetic pace. Darius, who was several inches shorter than the lanky reporter, would have to break into a jog if she went any faster.

"I'm going to help you write a very important story," Darius said.

His pulse accelerated like the Bentley with Javon at the wheel when he noticed a motorcycle cop prowling nearby. He looked like the same one who had chased them on the highway earlier. The cop was busy scrutinizing every person who came within a few yards of him. He thanked his lucky stars that Javon had had the foresight to steal a car with dark tints on the windows. Vicky cut the moment of gratitude short when she motioned to the officer. He immediately headed toward them with a serious expression.

"I'm going to file a complaint if you don't leave me alone."

"That really won't be necessary, Ms. Matthews."

"You better stop talking and start walking if you know what's good for you," she said.

Darius wondered if the hardest part of the mission was going to be convincing stubborn mortals to cooperate with him. If recruiting helpers was the easy part, he was in big trouble.

The motorcycle cop joined them.

"Can I help you, Ma'am?" The officer's uniform didn't have a wrinkle in it, Darius saw. His leather boots were shiny enough to see your reflection in. The officer's keen eyes examined Darius. He knew that look well. His black skin raised the white cop's suspicion level times two.

The Archangel had warned Darius about using angelic powers around mortals before they were ready for it. The first step of the recruiting process involved building a trusting relationship. Using powers prematurely sent most mortals running away in fear and disbelief. He didn't like disobeying orders. But there seemed to be no other way. Darius drew his attention inward and focused all of his concentration on the words he formed in his mind's eye.

. . .

The motorcycle cop was cute. He had short blond hair and blue eyes. She read his nametag: Madison Tremane. He looked like the archetypical, all-American boy, which made him a rarity, like Vicky, in the multi-cultural city of Miami. She was about to unload the choirboy from Omaha on Madison with a few choice words when a voice clanged into her head.

If you blow the whistle on me, you'll blow the biggest story of your life, the voice said.

Vicky's slender body jerked, as if from an electric shock. The laptop case slipped from her shoulder and plummeted to the floor.

"Are you all right, Ma'am?"

Oh, just fine except for the voice I'm hearing in my head, Vicky imagined telling Madison. He would then Baker Act her on the spot and take her to the nearest mental clinic for psychological evaluation.

"I'm fine," Vicky said, bending down to rescue her laptop.

The voice went off in her head again. *It's me, Darius. I'm not going to hurt you. Just get rid of the cop and I'll explain everything.* This time her over-sized pocketbook hit the floor.

Madison bent down and picked it up. "You sure you're all right?" He handed Vicky the pocketbook. "You don't look so good."

This is bigger than any story you've ever worked on, the voice in her head explained. The only thing keeping her from going mad was her reporter's curiosity. Her curiosity was a drug that propelled her into oodles of weird, uncomfortable, even perilous situations. This one promised to win the Oscar for weird.

"I thought I was getting an attack of Epilepsy," Vicky lied to the cop. "But then I remembered I took my pills this morning. I guess I panicked." She put on a shy smile. "Sorry to bother you, Officer Tremane." Vicky saw he liked the sound of that by his slight smile.

The officer handed her a business card. "I'm looking for a car thief. If you see anyone who looks out of place here, give me a call."

He stood there awkwardly for a minute, hoping perhaps she might write her phone number on the card and give it back to him.

"I have a niece with Epilepsy," Madison said. "I know it's not easy. You have a nice day." Off he went on his manhunt. Maybe she would have given Officer Tremane her phone number if her world hadn't suddenly warped out of joint for no apparent reason. She turned to the choirboy from Omaha.

"How did your voice get into my head?"

"It takes a lot of concentration. I wasn't sure I could do it."

She waved the business card like a yellow caution flag. "You want me to call the cop?"

"I'm telling you the truth. It was actually the first time I tried it."

"You scared the shit out of me."

"I'm very sorry. I didn't want to use thought projection on you, but I couldn't think of anything else to do."

"Thought projection?"

"Yes," the young black man answered with an earnest expression.

Vicky glanced at her watch. She was in danger of missing the beginning of the press conference. She might not even get a seat if she failed to get a move-on.

"We're going for a walk. I'm going to ask you some questions. You'd better have some good answers or I'm going to call the cop and tell him you were molesting me. Is that clear?"

"Perfectly."

She set off at a quick pace.

"What's your name again?"

"Darius McPherson."

"What is it you want from me?"

"I'm going to *give* you something. A story."

"Why did you pick me?"

"You're," he paused, "qualified for the job."

"How do you know?"

"I don't know. I mean, I didn't pick you."

"You aren't making sense," Vicky said.

"Look, if I knew you better, I could probably give you a better answer about why you were picked."

"So, you want to know me better, is that it?"

"Yes. No. Why do you have to be so suspicious?"

"It comes with the job."

Darius McPherson looked innocent and sounded like a lunatic. Vicky's instincts told her the young man wasn't dangerous.

"I'm here to work with you," Darius said. "We have some very important things to accomplish in the next few days. It's an opportunity, a very big opportunity; maybe the chance of a lifetime. Are you going to accept it?"

His sincerity was disarming. Only problem was, Darius McPherson sounded delusional. Now he was putting her on the spot to make a decision, the way any good con man would.

They were approaching a line of people standing in line outside the auditorium. They overheard an announcement coming from inside.

"The meeting will begin in five minutes. Please take your seats."

"I need to get into the press conference with you," Darius said.

Vicky's mind told her to leave Darius McPherson flat-footed. Her intuition was telling her something else entirely.

"You have to be a stockholder or a member of the Press to get in," Vicky said.

"Can't you just tell them I'm your assistant? I imagine we'll be working together quite closely, so it's not really a lie."

She did not like the sound of *working together quite closely*. "I could lose my job and my press credentials for doing something like that."

Vicky walked into line. Darius followed her. "I did not hear myself say we're working together."

She pushed him back out of line.

STRESS PASS

DARIUS HAD LEARNED early on that nothing worth doing in life was easy. Apparently, the same held true for the after-life. A security guard checked the ID's of people funneling through the double doors into the auditorium. Darius had to come up with a plan to gain entrance with Vicky without getting himself arrested or freaking her out. Only one idea came to mind. The idea scared him to death, until he remembered he had already died.

He allowed Vicky and the line to move forward before rejoining it at the rear end. From this vantage point, Darius observed the security guard interacting with the people about to enter the auditorium. The young guard appeared to examine the credentials handed to him as seriously as would a bank auditor searching for signs of financial shenanigans.

Darius understood the theory behind the maneuver he was about to attempt. The problem once again was doing the trick successfully without any practice. He told himself it had gone well enough when he sent his thoughts into Vicky's mind. There was no reason to believe he couldn't do this too. On the other hand, it would be so much easier if a Telepathy Instructor were standing nearby to bail him out if he screwed up. *Wishful- thinking never got things done*, his father always said. It was high time to stop wishing and start doing.

He watched Vicky reach the checkpoint. She pointed to the press pass around her neck. The guard motioned for her to take it off and hand it to him. After staring at the credentials and back to Vicky several times, the guard motioned her through. Five more people went through before it was Darius' turn. The young guard fixed him with a pleasant smile.

"Press pass or stockholder invitation, please."

Darius handed him the bankcard the Archangel had sent through the ATM. He concentrated with all his might, imagining a picture of himself stamped on the card along with his name. He used the triangle with the three circles inside as an idea for a logo. A name for the magazine he supposedly worked for came to him: "The Independent Observer." He mentally projected a composite image of these elements. It took every ounce of his energy to hold the thought image of the fictitious ID in the guard's mind.

The guard stared at the plastic bankcard. He looked up at Darius with a doubtful expression. "This is a bankcard."

Panic gripped Darius. He took the card back with a supreme effort to keep his hand steady. He pretended to fish around in his empty suit pockets for another card. The only thing to do was to reboot and try again with the certain knowledge that another strike would get him kicked out of line, or worse.

"Sorry about that," Darius said, pulling the same card out of his inside jacket pocket. "Life would be so much easier if we didn't have to carry around so many plastic cards." He concentrated once more and handed the bankcard back to the guard.

The guard stared at the plastic card with the corners of his mouth turned down.

Darius quaked inside.

"I've never heard of The Independent Observer," the guard said.

"It's a journal of modern ethical issues. We're based in Atlanta." Pressure from mental exertion was building inside his head.

The Guard peered at Darius with eyes that sought to CAT scan the contents of his brain. Darius had no choice but to stare grimly back, concentrating on the mental image of his bogus press credentials. The guard unlocked his gaze to stare instead at the line behind Darius. Turning around, Darius saw the line had grown behind him.

The guard handed the bankcard back to Darius and motioned him through. Wondering for the briefest moment if he had pulled off trick or the Archangel had pulled some strings behind the scenes, Darius moved toward the open door ahead. His head throbbed, but he was too relieved to care. He entered the auditorium in search of Vicky.

• • •

The press conference was already seven minutes late in starting and the old man had just sent him an emergency text message: "Meet me back stage immediately. Joseph A. Mamon, Chairman."

Hiram Fyrum hoisted his stubby, five-foot frame from a seat on the podium and left the others who were there to address the restless, information-hungry audience waiting on the other side of the video screen.

"Hold for another five minutes," Hiram instructed the event manager in the control suite through the tiny microphone supported by flesh colored tape on his cheek. Joseph, in his typical absent-minded manner, had forgotten to say exactly where they were supposed to meet back stage. Now Hiram would have to waste more time searching for the old man.

Five minutes later, Hiram found the company's founder and Chairman of the Board in the control suite. It followed that Joseph chose the elevated control suite to overlook the press conference through the one-way windows. Joseph was too frail and too important to sit with the general audience, and he always liked to believe he was in control. He sat in a wheelchair surrounded by five empty cardboard boxes used to move audio-visual equipment from another location in the building. Joseph often reminded Hiram of what a great orator he had been in his younger days. These days, his audiences tended to be comprised of inanimate objects rather than people.

Joseph breathed with the help of an oxygen tube, his heart beat with the help of a pacemaker, his ninety-year-old body functions were assisted by a slew of wonder drugs, some of which his company produced. Hiram often thought the sole remaining purpose of the company founder's extended life was to make Hiram's existence as miserable as possible.

"There's something else I want you to say to the audience," Joseph said to Hiram in a breathy, barely audible voice.

"We're already behind schedule, Joseph. I'll barely have time to cover the other points you want me to make."

"This is important," the Chairman declared with a bony finger pointed in Hiram's face.

. . .

"Are you saving these?" Vicky asked the well-dressed man sitting next to the two empty seats in the front row.

"I was until a minute ago," the man answered. "My associates just called to say they can't make it."

Vicky pounced on one of the empty seats.

. . .

Darius had spotted her a few minutes after entering the auditorium. He had rehearsed a few things to say to gain her confidence, none of which felt right. Now there seemed only one thing to do. Striding down the center aisle towards the third row from the stage, Darius inhaled deeply, and plopped into the seat next to Vicky before anyone else grabbed it.

She turned and glared at him.

"Don't be upset," he said. "This is not an elaborate pickup scheme.

I have no desire to harm you." Sooner-or-later, his sincerity had to register with her, unless she had deep-seated trust issues. Perish the thought. He had to believe the people fate threw him together with were supposed to help him in some way. So far, Vicky and Javon had managed to be giant pains in the-you-know-what.

"I'm here to do a job," Vicky said. "If you don't bother me, I won't call a cop."

"Fair enough," Darius replied.

She opened her laptop case and suddenly paused. "How did you get in here?"

"I used thought-visualization on the guard. The technique is similar to the voice in the head thing I did with you."

Her eyes widened.

"I know. It sounds weird."

"Very. Is this big story of yours about mind control?"

"No."

"Give me a one sentence synopsis."

"It's too big for one sentence."

"Then keep absolutely quiet. I have to prepare for this press conference."

She deftly manipulated the keys of her laptop. Darius relaxed into his seat. At least she was behaving somewhat civilly towards him. His direct, simple approach seemed to have captured her interest, at least for the time being. He used the few moments before the press conference began to become familiar with the surroundings. The architecture of the room featured a high arching ceiling reminiscent of the Italian Renaissance and soothing pink walls with aqua accents on the stage risers.

Darius had never attended a press conference before. He estimated there were about five hundred people in the room, most of them from the media, dressed casually with cameras slung over their shoulders and others with thin electronic tablets for note taking. Still others were dressed in expensive business suits. He guessed the well-dressed set were representatives from institutional investment companies with large blocks of Mamongen stock. There was an electric atmosphere of anticipation in the room. Darius also noticed quite a few security guards—maybe fifteen in all.

He massaged his forehead in an effort to subdue the sharp pricks he felt sticking into his brain like hypodermic needles from his earlier mental gymnastics. Vicky turned to him.

"Headache?"

"Yeah. Bad one."

Vicky reached inside her knapsack of a pocketbook and withdrew a small bottle. She shook out two aspirin and held them out to Darius.

"Thanks." Darius dry-gulped the pills down.

"That was a test," Vicky said.

"Hope I passed."

"I don't think you're an alien."

"We're making progress. You can ask me all sorts of history questions if you want me to prove I'm human. History was one of my best subjects."

"I don't think you're dangerous. Delusional is still a strong possibility."

Darius went back to rubbing his forehead.

A small victory. He would take it.

Vicky drummed her fingers on the keyboard of her laptop. She glanced at her watch. "When is this damn thing going to begin?"

As if in answer to her question, the public address system blared:

"Ladies and Gentlemen, please excuse the delay. We've encountered a few last-minute difficulties. We expect to begin in less than five minutes. Thank you for your patience."

"All right then. You're on, Darius. What's this story of yours?"

Vicky's intelligent green eyes locked on his. He had less than five minutes to convince her that the human race was in danger of wandering far away from its evolutionary path to higher consciousness. He decided to begin his pitch in tabloid headline style.

"Plezenthol is a dangerous drug," Darius began.

"And what little birdie dropped this morsel into your nest?"

Good question.

"I'm asking for your sources of information," she said. "You do have sources, don't you?"

"Yes, of course." How could he tell her his only source was an Archangel in heaven? Transparency wasn't exactly an option. He had to measure every word he said to this woman carefully. Her mind was a razor. He could almost feel it. Somehow, his intuition had just become more acute. He remembered the Archangel telling him to expect his angelic powers to increase rapidly after Earth touchdown.

"Now I suppose you're going to tell me you can't reveal your sources."

Darius blinked. Then he remembered one of his critical mission objectives: Meet and gain the confidence of the person responsible for developing the new drug.

"What if I could introduce you to the man who invented Plezenthol?"

"You can get me an interview with Simon Worthington III?"

"That's what we're here for," Darius said. He understood in that instant why he had gone to so much trouble to get a ride to the Mamongen Building, meet Vicky, and find a third-row seat at the press conference.

"How do you propose to get me an interview?"

Darius, of course, had no idea. Then he remembered the line Javon had used on him. "Just leave that up to me," he said.

He felt her skepticism. His explanation hung in the air between them, a wet sheet hanging from a clothesline on a cold, windless day.

"What makes Plezenthol so dangerous?" She asked impatiently.

Darius remembered the Archangel referring to Plezenthol as a "false beacon of light." Following the beacon shed by a Plezenthol lighthouse meant shipwrecking the noble unfolding of human consciousness. How was he supposed to break the news to Vicky without sounding like a raving lunatic? He considered his next words carefully.

"Learning is a process of trial and error," Darius replied. "Expanding awareness requires effort and commitment. It can be painful and there are no guarantees of success. Plezenthol promises to provide an easy way to free the human psyche from pain and suffering. It's a false promise."

"I don't understand," Vicky said.

"What I'm saying is something inside every person pushes them to find answers, to figure out what they are doing here. Without that push, without that quest, we cease to be truly human."

Vicky squinted. "So Plezenthol will affect our natural curiosity about who we are and how we fit into the world around us?"

"That's a good way to put it," Darius said.

Vicky stared back at him as the lights in the auditorium dimmed.

Chapter Fourteen

JOSEPH'S WORDS OF WISDOM

"**M**AMONGEN'S BREAKTHROUGH DISCOVERIES have ushered in a new dawn of mental health and well-being," the narrator said over a panoramic shot of the sun rising out of an emerald ocean bordered by an empty beach in the foreground. "In the Plezenthol era, we will see dramatic productivity increases in the workplace and substantial savings in health care costs."

Darius watched the ocean sunrise shot cut to scenes of contented people at work and play punctuated with shots of happy family gatherings.

"Test subjects report reduced anxiety and enhanced enjoyment of daily life," the narrator continued in a conversational, personable manner.

These images were soon replaced by an illustration of the human brain with cutaway sections revealing a maze of nerve endings that resembled rusted pipes.

"Brain chemistry can be adversely affected by environmental pollutants such as mercury, lead, and cadmium that have been absorbed into the system. Receptor cells clog with these pollutants, preventing neuron transmitters from carrying messages from one section of the brain to another. This condition often causes disorders like depression, anxiety, learning disabilities and obsessive-compulsive behavior.

"Mamongen's proprietary advances in Nanotechnology enable microscopic 'robot sweepers' to cleanse the brain of impurities and rebalance brain chemistry to restore healthy function. I guess you could call it brainwashing…" The narrator chuckled, "…but not the bad kind."

The audience chuckled along with the narrator.

"None of this seems apocalyptic," Vicky whispered to Darius. "Unless the claims the manufacturer is making are false?"

"It's all true," Darius replied.

"Then where's the story," Vicky said, as if speaking to a three-year-old.

"There's a high probability people will become complacent. They will lose the desire to acquire more knowledge; to strive for something better. Plezenthol will dim the light of human consciousness rather than brightening it."

"How can you possibly know that?"

"I can't tell you. Yet."

"Are you saying I'm not ready for the information?"

"Yes."

"Jesus. You are delusional."

"Look at me. Do I seem delusional to you?"

She took a long look at him.

"What makes you think the masses will be dying to go out and buy this pill?"

"Almost twenty-five percent of the American population is on some sort of mood management medication today. If you introduce a new product that promises to makes life easier and more enjoyable and promote it with an effective advertising campaign, it won't be long before most of the population in the industrialized world is on the medication."

Vicky laughed and threw back her long red curls. "I can't believe I'm listening to this."

"I'm not trying to be a comedian," Darius said.

"I get that," Vicky retorted. "I can't accept what you're telling me without facts. I need cold, hard proof."

"You'll get your proof."

"When?"

"In time."

"We're back to that. Listen, Darius, or whatever your name is, I don't waste time. So, don't waste mine. When this is over, go your own way. Or else."

They sat through the remainder of the video presentation in chilly silence.

. . .

The screen in front of the room receded into the ceiling revealing a panel of three Mamongen Executive Directors seated on stage. A glossy mica desk buffered the Mamongen VIP's from the rows of expectant faces in the auditorium. There were signs in front of them: HIRAM FYRUM, CEO—DOCTOR SIMON WORTHINGTON III, PH.D.—PATRICIA FITZWALTER, VP COMMUNICATIONS.

From his seat in the center of the podium, Hiram Fyrum sensed an electric current of enthusiasm running through the murmuring crowd. The excitement pleased him to no end. He loved excitement, especially in conjunction with success measured in money, power, and prestige.

Hiram waved to the audience. "Ladies and Gentlemen, please give us your kind attention so that we can get on with the program."

The room fell silent.

"My name is Hiram Fyrum, Chief Executive Officer of Mamongen Pharmaceuticals. For the past five years, it has been my privilege to serve under the leadership of Joseph Mamon, our company's founder and visionary Chairman of the Board of Directors. Joseph has asked me to convey to you one of the insights that has helped him to achieve miraculous results as a businessperson and community leader. It's a saying Joseph likes to mention whenever my thinking gets a little, shall we say, cramped."

The audience laughed.

Hiram paused. He fervently hoped the audience would interpret the pause as an attempt to build the drama of the moment. In fact, he was using the respite to put the finishing touches on a spiel he hoped would navigate the mess Joseph Mamon had bestowed upon him. He knew Mamon was listening to his every word through an amplified earpiece.

"The sun always shines on those who can feel it," Hiram beamed to the audience.

Joseph Mamon's proclamation sank like a stone in the middle of a whirlpool.

Hiram was quick to fill the uneasy void. "Working with Joseph as closely as I have has made it easier for me to grasp the Zen-like principles our Chairman has developed over the course of his remarkable career. This is not to suggest that any of you aren't keenly perceptive, of course."

Patricia Fitzwalter, Mamongen's Director of Corporate Communication, whispered into Hiram's ear.

"Don't try to explain Joseph's idiotic ramblings. Just make the announcement, please."

Hiram ignored the advice. He was determined to leave the audience with a good impression of himself and the ridiculous pronouncement of his irritating boss.

"To put it in simpler terms, Joseph is reminding us that opportunity only comes to those who seize it." Hiram turned to Patricia Fitzwalter to gauge her reaction. He thought his mini-spiel had saved the day, particularly the part about "Zen-like principles."

Patricia's pinched face reflected too much cosmetic surgery and perhaps impatience with his attempts to adhere to Joseph's instructions. She did not report to Joseph and had no idea what a pain the man was. The worst part was the Chairman liked Patricia's work. This explained the absence of a younger, prettier, more manageable person in Patricia's place. Hiram had no doubt Patricia was, at this very moment, mentally composing an e-mail memorandum studded with the crown jewels of modern corporate communication theory and practice. She would copy all ten of Mamongen's marketing Vice Presidents to ensure the communications fiasco in progress never happened again. Hiram was not in the least bit worried. He was going to make a perfect landing directly on top of the whole situation.

"The point we're making is it took courage on the part of several key Mamongen employees to make the Plezenthol project happen. They seized the opportunity presented to them by the brilliant, pioneering work of our Chief Chemist and Research Director, Doctor Simon Worthington III. It's only fitting that Simon should have the floor for the next part of our presentation. Ladies and Gentlemen, please meet and welcome an extraordinary human being— Doctor Simon Worthington, III."

. . .

Simon rose and smiled weakly at the audience. The applause in the Auditorium was thunderous, deafening, and intimidating. It occurred to him that this should have been one of the most auspicious moments in his always-promising career. People admired him for his awesome intelligence. The newspapers hailed him as a "modern day wizard," a "genius," and most absurdly, "Mamongen's miraculous maven of mental health."

Elation, vindication, pride, and unalloyed joy were the emotions he should have been feeling right now. Instead, he felt like a man with no future, an inmate on death row. Doctor Simon Worthington III had managed to usher his dream into the world—and it had become a living nightmare. Simon fervently wished to be somewhere else, perhaps back on his parents' luxurious estate in Jacksonville Florida, happily trapping grasshoppers at age five and dissecting them to probe the mysteries of their complex construction.

Even better, Simon imagined himself to be as old as Joseph

Mamon, by which time he would have presumably been dead for quite a number of years. Anywhere would be better than this auditorium full of people hungry for the latest tidbit of marketable information and a soaring Mamongen share price.

Hiram was looking at him in a very displeased manner.

"I realize you are terrified of people," Hiram whispered, "but you must try to look more upbeat. You've created something wonderful and we're here to sell it." Hiram turned back to the audience. "He's a little shy. Genius usually has a way of expressing itself through the tender reed."

It was time for Simon to speak up, or slink off the stage in humiliation. He wanted desperately to voice his doubts over the test results. But he couldn't. To question the compilation of the clinical data in public without more proof than an inkling of something being amiss would be completely irresponsible. It would also be professional suicide.

Simon cleared his throat and said, "I'm grateful for Hiram's kind words and honored by your presence here today. I know you all have busy schedules, so I'll get right to the point. Mamongen expects to receive FDA approval to market Plezenthol in North America within the next month. We expect world health authorities will follow suit soon after distribution begins here."

He lost no time in sitting squarely back down in his seat on the sweeping podium. The audience erupted in wild applause.

• • •

It seemed to Vicky that Patricia Fitzwalter deliberately ignored the reporters with the good fortune of sitting in the front rows. She had been delighted to invite questions for the past half hour from every section of the auditorium but hers. Vicky scribbled notes as, one by one, other reporters had their questions answered, mostly by Hiram. Many of the queries were attempts to obtain more specific information on how the drug worked, and how it was different from other anti-depressants. The other typical inquiries were about sales and profit projections.

Vicky had one question no one else was asking. She was beginning to lose hope she would have a chance to ask it as the Q&A session approached the forty-five-minute mark. Finally, the Mamongen Director of Communications decided to turn her undivided attention to the long-suffering reporters in the front rows. Vicky nearly jumped out of her seat when Patricia Fitzwalter pointed in her direction. Her voice cracked from the long wait. She started over again.

"This question is for Doctor Worthington. According to published records, Plezenthol went through clinical testing faster than any drug in this category ever has. Would you care to comment on that, Doctor?"

"What you may not realize is Mamongen spent ten years researching and testing the product ourselves before the clinical trials began," Simon replied.

"But not on humans."

"That's correct," Simon replied tersely.

Patricia Fitzwalter zeroed in on Vicky. "The product was tested exhaustively on humans and in strict accordance with FDA standards. The complete clinical file will be available shortly."

Vicky was about to ask a follow up question when Patricia abruptly invited a question from Darius.

"Thank you, Ms. Fitzwalter. I'm Darius McPherson with the Independent Observer and I'd like to ask Doctor Worthington why he looks so unhappy on an occasion which would otherwise seem to call for joyous celebration."

Vicky could not believe her ears. How could Darius ask such an inappropriate question?

"I don't think my happiness is anyone's business except my own," Simon replied to a ripple of applause from the audience.

For some reason, Simon stared at her from the stage before turning away to answer the next question Ms. Fitzwalter hastily invited.

Did he think Darius was a colleague or a friend of hers? Good luck getting an interview with him now. Vicky slumped in her seat and covered her face with a hand to the forehead. With her other hand, she searched her handbag for the bottle of aspirin.

. . .

Darius noticed three men in tan suits heading down the center aisle towards the front of the room. His heart pounded like a kettledrum. On stage, Hiram Fyrum was ending the program. The audience burst into applause when Patricia Fitzwalter invited everyone to a wine and cheese party next door.

"Why did you ask that inane question?" Vicky wanted to know as they followed the line of people heading for the aisle.

"I had to do something to make an impression on Doctor Worthington."

"You should have deferred back to me when Fitzwalter called on you. Couldn't you see she was trying to avoid my next question? Who's the reporter here?"

"I did what my intuition told me to do. I sensed Simon's discomfort over the release of Plezenthol. I believe he'll talk to us if he feels we're sympathetic to his situation."

Vicky frowned at him. "Or he'll run the other way."

They neared the end of the row. Talking into his hand, one of the tan suits waited for them in the aisle. There was undoubtedly a concealed radio device in that hand. The man was a plainclothes security guard, Darius figured. Something else was unusual about him. He was wearing a bright red pendent under his buttoned suit jacket. The security guard pointed at him.

"You." The tan suit indicated a spot in the aisle next to him. "Come here."

"Let me handle this," Darius whispered to Vicky.

"Like you handled the press conference?" Her green eyes bore into him. "Don't get me involved." She took off past the guard.

"Let's go pal," the guard said to Darius. They walked in tandem up the aisle towards the exit door.

The guard spoke into his tiny hand mic. "Have subject in hand." The other two tan suits stood behind Darius doing nothing besides scaring the crap out of him with their hostile vibes.

"I haven't done anything wrong," Darius declared.

The guard responded by grasping his arm. Darius needed both hands to free himself from the man's grip.

"Let go of me."

The guard stood about an inch taller than Darius. He had neatly barbered, straight brown hair, brown eyes, and plain features. He looked deliberately anonymous, Darius decided.

As the guards "escorted" him up the aisle, Darius closed his eyes. He summoned the awesome power swirling in the subtle depths of his not quite human body. A superhuman nervous system was required to release a surge of light energy. He remembered the Archangel's admonition not to use light energy unless his body was in imminent danger of destruction. He didn't want to unleash even a scintilla of his power on the guards, but he had to be prepared. He also had to be very careful.

Light energy release required practice and a deft touch. Darius was a raw novice in the subtle art of energy projection. A blast of unregulated light energy could easily destroy a sizeable number of innocent bystanders. There was no shortage of them shuffling out of the auditorium.

Darius and the guards approached the exit doors. Ahead, Vicky disappeared through one of them amidst a stream of people. Darius kept the light energy rising along his spinal cord. The lead guard's meaty hand was still clamped painfully onto his arm.

With the main entrance to the building visible in the distance, the guard let go. Darius began to think of him as Lead Dog. The other two guards positioned themselves ahead in the crowd to keep Darius funneled towards the exit doors.

"Make sure you leave the building right away," Lead Dog said.

"Or else?"

"We'll have you arrested for causing a disturbance."

"I haven't disturbed anything," Darius said calmly.

"We saw you harassing the lady reporter."

"That's not true. We're working together. You can ask her. Now, if you'll excuse me, I'm invited to the reception next door."

"Your invitation just got cancelled."

He had no invitation, but that was the least of his problems. Darius' enhanced intuition told him he was in more danger than the unthinkable possibility of missing the opportunity to meet Doctor Simon Worthington III. These guards were certainly nothing like the ones he had encountered in the lobby and at the entrance to the auditorium.

Darius found his attention drawn to the red ribbons the guards wore around their thick necks. Logic told him identity cards dangled at the end of the ribbons concealed beneath their suit jackets. A strong feeling told him he might find something else under those jackets. He was beginning to suspect the worst. It sent a chill up his spine along with the light energy.

Darius doubled over feigning a coughing fit. He staggered backwards to create more space between himself and the departing crowd. He kept coughing and walking backwards. Lead Dog grabbed Darius by the arm and spun him around.

"What's your problem?"

"Asthma," Darius croaked. "I forgot my inhaler."

Darius watched the last stragglers in the crowd filter out through the auditorium's exit doors. He caught sight of the other two guards pushing and shoving their way back into the auditorium.

Now, the only innocent bystander left in the auditorium was himself. If he screwed this up, he wasn't too concerned about the welfare of the three guards. He sensed something about them was way off the standard security guard charts.

He stared into the eyes of the Lead Dog. At the same time, he opened the button on the man's suit jacket in one quick movement.

A weapon with a shiny black handle sticking out of a long holster surprised Darius. It did not look anything like a standard handgun. The glass ball suspended at the end of the red elastic ribbon looked even stranger than the weapon.

Inside the glass ball, Darius watched a small azure cloud beat like the heart of a baby chick inside an egg. Something the Archangel said hit him hard. *Could the glass ball be the device the Exiles were using to disguise themselves as humans? It could be. Very easily.*

"Oh, crap," Darius said.

Before he had time to move, the guard clutched him by the throat and squeezed hard. He coughed, pulling the guard's hand away with one hand while raising his other hand. The guard went for his weapon but Darius fired a mini-bolt of light energy straight into the man's squinting brown eyes.

The guard blinked several times. The other two guards closed ranks quickly. Lead Dog staggered into their arms. Now, they were escorting their comrade away, one in front, and the other behind. Darius saw ripples appear in the back of Lead Dog's jacket. As the guards pushed Lead Dog into a nearby restroom, Darius caught sight of a human hand changing into a long-fingered claw. At least, that's what Darius *thought* he saw. Lead Dog had disappeared so quickly into the restroom it was difficult to tell what had just happened.

The entire incident unfolded in a matter of seconds. Apart from a few curious stares from the self-absorbed business crowd, the unusual encounter went largely unnoticed.

Darius lost no time in moving on. The guard screening guests into the wine and cheese reception turned out to be the same, mild-mannered one he had met in the lobby. Darius pretended to be with two other guests who showed their passes. He walked into the reception without incident, and quickly found refuge in the noisy crowd.

Chapter Fifteen

THE STORY OF A LIFETIME

JAVON WATCHED THE motorcycle cop from behind one of the pillars in the lobby. The dude stood blocking the main entrance with his arms crossed thinking he was God Almighty. That stubborn son of a bitch was the only thing standing in the way of the dream Javon held in the recesses of his conniving heart—an insanely tall pile of cash with his name on it after he unloaded the stolen car. He felt an urge to barrel straight into the cop, knock him over, step on his face, and make a wild run for the Bentley parked in the last space on the top floor of the public parking garage across the street.

He had spent the last half-hour scouring the first floor of the Mamongen building to find another way out. Everywhere he looked, a rent-a-cop seemed to be standing by just waiting for an excuse to bust him. One of the jokers had asked him where he was going. Javon had casually explained to the guard he was in extreme distress due to an emergency bowel movement. The guard had politely directed him to the nearest bathroom. It turned out to be a good idea. Javon used the facility to take a dump, wash up, and tie his bushy hair back with thick elastic bands to avoid attracting attention. He always wore a few of them around his wrists for emergency purposes. In a best-case practice, he used the rubber bands as bill-clips for extra cash generated from drug profits. Present circumstances easily qualified as a worst-case practice.

Get a grip, he told himself. Waiting for the immovable cop to get a move-on was a waste of time. He decided to make one more sweep of the first floor on the off chance he had missed an unguarded exit, even though it might result in being spotted on the security cameras mounted strategically, it seemed, for the sole purpose of screwing up his getaway. If push came to shove, he would have to leave through one of the emergency-exits. Screw the alarms. His instincts and his happy feet would just have to carry him to freedom and a big payday before anyone was the wiser.

· · ·

Wedged into the far corner of the room, Doctor Simon Worthington III watched the people in the room parade back and forth like circus animals. The Mamongen marketing machine had done its job well. The press and institutional investors were high as kites on the Plezenthol story. Many of them were in excellent spirits thanks to an ample supply of free wine and champagne. Simon was in a morose mood despite his third glass of pinot noir. Hiram had warned him against drinking too much at the party. He was supposed to be a good will ambassador—one of the stars of the show.

Patricia Fitzwalter visited briefly with an offer to assist him "in any way she could." Simon suspected Hiram had given her the job of baby-sitting him. Hiram no doubt wanted to make sure his comments were in perfect alignment with the company's recent press releases. Hiram was too busy to attend the party. He told Simon with a wink he would be upstairs reviewing proposals from international companies clamoring for the rights to distribute Plezenthol.

Simon noticed the young black reporter enter the room. Wasn't he the one who had seen right through him, as if he had a view through a window opened directly into his soul?

Another familiar face and figure caught his attention. Heads turned when the tall, sexy redhead came through the meeting room doors. The question she asked in the press conference reflected careful research and intelligence. He remembered her name—Vicky Matthews.

The woman was so attractive it hurt. Simon chastised himself for feeling so superficially drawn to her. Then he wondered if the attraction *was* purely physical. He was a man of science who also happened to have a highly developed intuitive sense. Simon had learned to follow his intuition in his research as well as his personal life. That same intuition told him Ms. Mathews might be the right press person to approach.

He needed to speak to a reporter, someone with integrity and discretion. By raising doubts about the Plezenthol test results through the media, Simon hoped to force the company to re-do the clinical tests on human subjects. When it became obvious someone was leaking highly sensitive information to the press, there was a good chance he might have to resign as Mamongen's Chief Chemist and Research Director. Simon was prepared to make the sacrifice. Naturally, he hoped his misgivings about the human test were groundless, but it was obviously better to be safe than sorry. He would never forgive himself for putting an unsafe drug on the market.

Yes, he thought, Vicky Matthews might be just the right person to get the ball rolling. Standing taller than many of the guests in the room in her high heels, he watched her scan the room, until her eyes found his.

· · ·

Darius feared his reporter's facade would wear thin quickly under the scrutiny of someone as smart as Doctor Simon Worthington III. Then he remembered what the Archangel had told him: *Believe in yourself.* Well, he had made it this far. The Archangel and the Board of Directors believed in him. The last thing he wanted to do was to disappoint them.

Darius gathered his courage, took a deep breath, and headed

toward Mamongen's Director of Research, who was surprisingly alone in a room full of reporters. Then he saw the reason why.

Two security guards wearing Mamongen uniforms stood at forty-five degree angles a few yards away from him. Anyone approaching Doctor Worthington found themselves quickly traveling in the opposite direction courtesy of the blue-shirted guards. The walls to either side of the scientist and the guards in front of him formed an impenetrable fortress. Darius had the impression the tall, Van Dyke bearded man was peering at him from behind the barricade of guards. It was probably his imagination or wishful thing. *Believe,* Darius reminded himself, and continued walking.

Darius wondered if the uniformed security guards were on the same team as the ones who had accosted him in the auditorium. There were no red ribbons sticking out from under their shirt collars. That was a good sign. Their unfriendly expressions were less promising. Darius decided it was best to keep his eyes peeled on his objective. The poor man looked miserable. Darius had always been good at cheering people up when they needed it most. He slapped on a smile. One of the guards held up his hand as Darius approached.

"Doctor Worthington isn't answering questions right now."

"Why don't you tell him I'm here to help," Darius heard himself say. It just popped out of his mouth all by itself.

The guard chuckled. "Try coming back later. The Doc might be in a better mood by then."

"He's having a really bad day, isn't he?" Darius said.

The guard looked more serious now. "I guess that would be Doctor Worthington's business, not yours. Please move along."

Doctor Simon Worthington III strolled up from behind the guards. Darius was close enough to hear everything they said.

"I'll talk to this fellow."

"The guy sounds a little off to me," Darius heard one of the guards say while staring grimly at him.

"I've got to speak to at least a few press people to keep my boss happy. He looks harmless to me. Let him pass."

The guard approached. He did not look pleased. "The Doc says he'll talk to you. Hold still for a minute." He gave Darius the once over with a portable metal detector. The guard then stretched his hand out to indicate it was okay to pass. He kept a straight face as Darius walked by.

"Thank you for seeing me, Doctor Worthington," Darius said. They shook hands.

"I'm Darius McPherson."

"With the Independent Observer," Simon added.

"That's right," Darius said with a smidgeon of self-satisfaction.

"Your question was embarrassing."

"I needed to make an impression on you," Darius countered.

"You succeeded." The scientist drained his glass of wine and placed it on a tray held by a passing waiter. "What makes you think I'm so unhappy?" he said.

"I know you're worried about the Plezenthol test results."

"Who said I have concerns about the test results?"

"We both know it's true," Darius said.

The Doctor's face drained of color like the wine glass he had just polished off. "The test results will be published soon. You can draw whatever conclusions you wish to after reviewing the test data. I have no desire to discuss the subject further with you."

Darius decided it was time to play his trump card. "Your concerns about the long-term effects of Plezenthol are valid."

The scientist did not move or say a thing for what seemed to Darius like a very long time.

"Are you a reporter or a prophet, Mr. McPherson?"

"I'm neither."

Simon Worthington III stood with his arms crossed, massaging his Van Dyke beard.

"Why haven't you held up the tests to verify the data," Darius asked, hoping the genuine concern in his voice would take the edge off the question.

"Are you questioning my competence?"

"Not in the least," Darius said, again with concern. His obvious sincerity kept Simon talking.

"Plezenthol has been in development for ten years. We have been actively testing it for the past five. The final clinical tests represent only a small portion of the work done on the entire project, and, most importantly, the phase IV results surpassed our expectations." Simon paused. "Even if I *did* have a few doubts about the human test results, which you seem to be convinced is the case, I have no tangible reasons to order further testing."

"I believe you," Darius said.

"Then why are you badgering me with annoying questions?"

"Because I want to help you."

"Oh, thank God, I'm saved. Do you know why I told the guards to let you talk to me?"

"You sense I'm trustworthy."

"Wrong. I want to meet the reporter you were sitting with."

Slightly taken aback, Darius motioned to Vicky standing across the room. She waved back with a notebook in her hand.

"She seems to know what she's doing. You, on the other hand," Simon shrugged.

Vicky slipped through the crowd. When she reached the guards, Simon told them, "She can come."

"It's a pleasure to meet you," Vicky gushed. She extended her hand to Simon who ignored it.

"I want to know everything you two think you know about the clinical trials," Simon said.

"I don't have an opinion," Vicky said through a tight smile. "At this point, all I have is a very open mind."

"That's not the impression I get from your partner," Simon pressed.

Vicky sighed. "He's not my partner. I've never seen him before today. If you don't mind, I have some questions I'd like to ask you."

Simon stared at Vicky intently, perhaps deciding if he could trust her. From her brief encounter with Worthington, Darius confirmed, beyond all reasonable doubt, that Vicky was one of his recruits. They needed each other. Vicky had the tools and the experience to deal with a man in Simon's position. Darius had provided the introduction. Teamwork. He saw possibilities opening up.

His optimism was short-lived.

Darius noticed the three men immediately when they entered the room—the same three guards who had zeroed in on him earlier. They had to be Exiles. He had no reason to believe otherwise.

Chapter Sixteen

FIRST LOOK

THE GUARDS MANEUVERED past a table stacked high with over-sized Plezenthol tablets made of cheddar cheese. They continued past the string quartet, down an aisle formed by groups of guests chatting on either side. Turning in unison at the end of the human aisle, they powered straight towards him. Darius noticed the red elastic necklaces underneath the guards' tan suit jackets. Lead Dog, in the middle, appeared fully recovered from the mini-bolt of light energy Darius had delivered earlier. The guards separated. Each one took a singular, menacing angle of approach.

Crooking his arm, Darius lifted his hand just below chin level with all five fingers splayed. He reminded himself of David Carradine as Caine in a "Kung Fu" TV episode. He figured a more experienced angel operative would certainly prepare to attack with more subtlety. Well, subtlety was never one of his strong suits.

"Are you doing isometric exercises?" Simon inquired in a dry tone.

"I know it looks weird," Darius said. "Don't worry. I know what I'm doing."

Simon laughed in a tone that fell somewhere between mild amusement and disparagement. He called out to Lead Dog, the closest of the three guards. "Please escort this young man out of the building. He's bothering me."

Lead Dog walked over, beaming like someone who had just hit the Florida Lottery.

Darius had enough light energy on tap to fire another mini-bolt. He aimed for Lead Dog. Wait a minute. What was he thinking? He could not allow anyone in the dense crowd to catch a glimpse of Lead Dog the Exile after a light energy bolt tore through his human disguise.

Apparently, Lead Dog figured the same thing as he strode brazenly toward the group.

Darius dropped his arm. He waited until Lead Dog reached point blank range before zapping him. His from-the-hip shot struck Lead Dog square in the face with a measured shot of pure light energy.

Lead Dog's face dissolved into a triangular, reptilian head with violet eyes. Although it happened only for the briefest instant, Darius found himself totally unprepared for his first glimpse of an Exile in the flesh.

Vicky dropped her notebook.

In the corner of the room, only Darius, Vicky, and Simon had glimpsed the horror hiding behind Lead Dog's all-American face. Darius grabbed Vicky and Simon by the arm.

"Let's get out of here," he said.

They offered no resistance.

"What in the name of Sir Isaac Newton do you have in that arm of yours," Simon whispered to Darius as they pushed through the crowd with the Exile guards pursuing them.

"Light," Darius answered.

Vicky and Simon exchanged puzzled looks.

"I told you this was going to be the story of a lifetime and I meant it," he said to Vicky as they hustled through the crowd. He turned to Simon. "I'm afraid your concerns about the clinical trials don't even begin to address the problem we have to solve."

Simon squinted back at him through his skinny designer glasses with a look of total incomprehension.

Darius breathed a sigh of relief. He had managed to release the light energy without harming Vicky and Simon. He regretted the necessity of scaring them half to death, but it seemed the only remaining way to shake them out of their disbelief.

Darius closed his eyes and concentrated for a few precious seconds. Where was Javon? He had to be somewhere nearby. The Archangel had said the teenager was part of the team. Despite the difficulty of imagining Javon helping anyone besides himself, he was somehow a key part of Darius's immense responsibility.

. . .

As he walked down one of the long corridors branching off from the lobby, Javon spied Darius walking towards him. His sharp eyes picked out three, mean looking security guards in plain clothes following the group.

Darius walked between an absolute fox on his right and a tall dude who looked like a well-dressed schoolteacher on his left. The fox kept rapping at Darius. She looked a little freaked out. Javon had noticed her in the lobby earlier. She looked like the type who would blow a dude off without mercy unless he had a very good reason to be talking to her. What was she doing with this Darius cat? The dude seemed like someone who could get lost a block away from home.

The three guards trailing them began to close on their position. Darius and his new friends broke into a run. Javon wanted no part of whatever-the-hell was going down. In terms of the big picture, it was way past time to get back to making a living in a world that gave you nothing for nothing. He turned and walked the other way, blending in with the traffic flow in the corridor.

Just as he was settling into a feeling of comfortable obscurity in the crowd, an arm grabbed him from behind. Javon craned his head around. He balled his hand into a fist to smash Darius-the-persistent-creep in the face.

"Leggo my arm. Our business is done. I'm tryin' to lay low."

"Our business is just starting," Darius huffed as he slowed to a walk. The fox and the teacher dude slowed too.

Javon put his mighty fist in the creep's face. "Get lost or I'll cold cock you."

Darius waved at him. The motion was different from a regular wave. It was more like a crowd wave at a football game—only with fingers. Javon's head spun. He was happy all of a sudden. Peaceful like. Something had hit him—not a strong rush, but definitely something nice.

Darius grabbed his arm. "This is our driver," he explained to the other two. They looked back at him with doubtful expressions.

. . .

It took both arms and most of Darius' strength to keep Javon moving along. Vicky and Simon followed close behind. Before long, they reached the lobby and headed for the main entrance. Darius looked back and noticed Vicky was having trouble keeping up with her pocketbook weighing her down. Darius continued to struggle with his burden—a smiling, pacified Javon Quincey who needed guidance every step of the way. He hoped the effects of the soft light blast Javon had forced him to deliver would wear off soon.

"Simon, why don't you help Vicky with her handbag," Darius said.

"Right. I should have thought of that." He held out his hands. Vicky passed him the bag. Simon wobbled for a moment under the weight of it.

"What on Earth do you carry in this?"

"Zip drives, cameras, an extra pair of shoes, and assorted girl stuff. I work out, Simon. I'm stronger than I look."

"I definitely have to get to the gym more often," the scientist said.

Darius caught sight of the motorcycle cop guarding the front entrance, all six foot five inches of him. He was watching business people funnel by with a grim expression. Behind them, the three Exiles who looked to everyone else in the world like clean-cut young men fresh out of college, barreled into the lobby like greyhounds skidding around a turn in a race.

. . .

Madison Tremane watched the gangly black kid come strutting out of the crowd like a drum major leading a high school band. The red-headed reporter he had spoken to earlier made sharp clicking sounds with her high heels from behind the kid. The professional looking young black man he had met in the lobby earlier still accompanied her. What was their connection? A well-dressed bearded man carrying a satchel pocketbook flanked her on the other side. This was going to be interesting.

Madison raised a black gloved hand and pointed at the kid wearing a basketball jersey. "Over here, Mister Miami Heat" he called to the teenager.

The kid ignored the command. The scruffy teenager looked in better spirits than anyone had a legal right to be. Madison thought the kid looked familiar, but he couldn't put his finger on where he had seen him before. The tall fellow with a fancy beard and a giant pocketbook hanging from one shoulder was a total mystery. He looked like the shy, sensitive type. He hoped for the guy's sake the pocketbook belonged to the reporter.

You got a feel for people working in law enforcement. All it took was one look. It was uncanny how often he was right. The sexy reporter looked like she had just seen the dead walking. She had seemed much more sure of herself the first time he met her. Something was definitely up here.

The kid was confident; you had to give him that. So many of the black teenagers Madison encountered came on as if they were the coolest, most untouchable dudes in the known universe. Underneath, most of them were scared shitless. You could smell their fear. It clung to them like body odor. This kid was different. He just came ambling right up without blinking.

"What can I do for you, Officer?"

"Tell me what you're doing here. And while you're at it, why don't you let me in on the secret of your happiness."

"Happiness?" The kid was genuinely surprised at Madison's remark. "You accusin' me of being happy?"

"Are you stoned?"

"Would I tell you if I was?"

Madison looked into the kid's clear, sharp eyes. Whatever buzz the young man was enjoying, it didn't appear to come from drugs or alcohol.

The redhead spoke up. "He's with me. With us," she corrected herself.

He read her press pass. "What's he doing with you, if you don't mind me asking, Ms. Matthews?"

She hesitated. "He's an intern. It's a program WQES is doing with the community."

"Are these two gentlemen interns as well?" Madison said.

"I'm Darius McPherson," the neat young man said holding out his hand unabashedly.

Madison shook the sturdy hand. "That doesn't answer my question," he said.

"Ms. Matthews and I are working on a story about inner city youth," Darius said. "We're on our way to do an interview with Doctor Worthington at Ms. Matthews' TV station."

"We're going to lose our taping slot if we don't leave right away," Vicky added quickly.

The tall bearded guy stepped forward. "I can vouch for these people. I'm Doctor Simon Worthington III, Chief Chemist and Director of Research here."

"Nice pocketbook you got there, Doc."

A silly grin spread across the bearded guy's face.

"Can I see some ID?"

The man who called himself Simon pulled an ID card out of his jacket pocket. He handed it over.

Madison examined the card. Looking up he said, "How do you fit into this feel good story, if you don't mind me asking, Doctor Worthington."

. . .

Darius wondered if Simon had the stomach to add another lie to the pile of untruth they were showering on the police officer. Simon did not strike him as a man in the habit of telling lies.

Simon stared back at the officer for several long seconds. Darius wished he and the others could sink into the floor and find an underground exit from the building. Doctor Worthington had the ball. Would he shoot?

"Mamongen is a big contributor to the youth program," Simon said. "I've kind of been shepherding it along in our organization."

The officer handed Simon's ID back. "You're good to go."

A swirling wave of euphoria swept over Darius. He and the others filed out the blue tinted glass doors, into the bright Miami sunlight.

Chapter Seventeen

THE FUTURE ISN'T BRIGHT

DARIUS GRIPPED HIS seat belt as the Bentley sliced through the dense downtown traffic as if the other cars were only there for decoration.

"Take it easy," Darius said from the shotgun position, the most vulnerable seat in the house. Javon ignored him as usual. The teenager found an expensive pair of sunglasses in the leather console between the two front bucket seats. He exchanged the cheap pair of knock-offs he was wearing for the real thing, taking a moment to admire himself in the rear- view mirror.

"Turn left at the next light," Simon called from the back seat. "We're almost there."

"And slow down," Darius reminded his rambunctious wheel man. Javon spun the steering wheel. The car swerved onto an entrance ramp heading north on I-95.

"Where do you think you're going?" Darius said.

"You said we needed another car. All I'm doin' is turning this one in before we get the new one. I gotta' make a living."

"We don't have time for a side trip," Darius said. "Why does everything have to be a struggle with you?"

"Because you always get in my way," Javon replied emphatically.

"You see. We should have taken a cab," Vicky said from the back seat, looking up from the open laptop resting on her knees.

Darius turned to her. "We don't know how many of these creatures are walking around. For all we know, the cab driver could be one of them. Besides, if they chase us in another car, we need Javon at the wheel in a fast car.

Javon snickered.

Darius turned back to Javon. "We'll lose this car after we're finished at the lab. You hear me?"

Javon turned the radio up and merged into the onrushing, northbound traffic on the expressway.

"Get us back on track or I'll fry you into a cinder. That little jolt I gave you in the lobby was only a hint of what I can do."

"Felt pretty good if you ask me. I wouldn't mind some more a' that."

"I'm tired of your antics. Take the next exit."

"Why should I?"

"Because I know a lot of cops. You remember how I handled Officer Gonzales? I'm the only reason you're still a free man—and that will change if you don't listen to me."

"A'ight," Javon said with a grimace. He cut the wheel to the right. The Bentley eased into the exit lane. Darius relaxed back into his seat.

"I think it's time you told us who you really are," Vicky said. The question hung in the air like a rumble of heat lightning before a downpour. He knew he had to handle the answer carefully or risk losing them. Darius turned to Vicky. She stopped typing on her laptop.

"I have to ask all of you to keep an open mind," Darius began.

"Don't sugar coat it," Vicky said. "Obviously, something very strange is going on here. What is it?"

"Okay. Here goes. I've been sent here to lead you on a mission with far-reaching implications."

"Sent from where?" Vicky said.

"So, here's the part where you have to keep an open mind. Are you ready?"

"Shoot," Vicky said.

"I've been sent from heaven. I'm an angel."

The Bentley swerved slightly going down the off ramp.

Darius watched Vicky sitting in the back seat shaking her head.

"I expected you'd say that," said Simon.

"I'm sure it sounds perfectly ridiculous to a scientist," Darius said.

"It makes perfect sense, actually. First, you show us the monsters. Then you claim to be an angel. That means the monsters are Demons. Am I correct?"

"Not exactly," Darius observed Simon in the seat next to Vicky holding his head up with three fingers splayed around his mouth in a thoughtful pose. "Then who or what did we see back there hiding under the tan suit?"

"We call them Exiles," Darius said, because they 've been banished from heaven for a lack of faith and disobedience, to make a long story short."

"You're saying the stories in the Bible are true?" Vicky asked.

"Some of them," Darius said.

"Why do these Exiles, as you call them, look like monsters," Simon asked. Darius sensed the scientist was genuinely intrigued by what he had said so far. He had expected Simon to be the hardest to convince in the group.

"The Exiles have evolved into monsters after living for eons in dark caves in the depths of the Earth. They no longer belonged in heaven, and they couldn't live as spiritual beings among humans. So, the only place left for them was underground. Living in darkness and cut off from the light, their thoughts turned darker and their bodies naturally grew to reflect their warped thoughts.

"How are you able to exist in a human body if the Exiles cannot." Simon wanted to know.

"I was given a human body by, let's call them, wise beings of light. The Exiles were not granted the privilege of inhabiting human bodies because they couldn't be trusted to use them for constructive purposes. Human beings, on the other hand, come into this world with a constant stream of choices as to how they conduct themselves and live their lives. That's a different discussion. The important point in *this* discussion is that the Exiles have developed the technology to masquerade as humans. It gives them options they've never had before. None of the options appear to be good ones."

Vicky and Simon took a few minutes to ponder this information. Darius noticed Javon appeared to be off in his own world, probably contemplating his next score.

"Pull the car over and park on that side street" Darius said, pointing.

"Why?"

"Just do it."

Javon expertly parked between two cars.

Darius turned around to Vicky and Simon. "Does anyone have change for the meter?"

Vicky dug in her pocket book.

"I've got the pay-by-phone app. There's a sign for it over there. I'll take care of it," Simon announced, opening the back car door.

"It looks like at least two of you are gentleman," Vicky said.

Javon glared back at her in the rear-view mirror.

Simon re-entered the car. "We've got an hour. I sincerely hope it doesn't take that long to do whatever it is we're doing."

"What are the Exiles doing at the Mamongen building," Vicky asked.

"I'm not sure why we ran into them," Darius answered. "I can only guess they want to make sure Plezenthol goes on the market. Somehow, the release of the drug will serve their purposes."

"We've seen a few strange, I'd like to call them, anomalies," Simon said. "Aside from those, you have to admit your story is a lot to swallow."

Darius gulped down a lungful of air and then released it. "I suppose it's time for me to show you more."

• • •

Javon crowded into the back seat with Simon and Vicky in the middle, all of them staring into Vicky's laptop.

In the front seat with the engine idling, Darius took a last look at the storefronts lining the commercial side street where Javon had parked the car to avoid the busy main thoroughfare. Darius closed his eyes. *What would the world look like if a majority of the world population began taking Plezenthol regularly?* The slideshow he meant to show them had to be convincing. The mental images he projected onto the screen of Vicky's laptop had better be vividly imagined and carefully selected.

The laptop floated against a sky-blue screen in his imagination. The black computer screen began to sparkle like a sandy, tropical beach on a cloudless day. Darius plunged into a deeper state of concentration.

In his imagination, Darius sat on the bank of a river lit by a full moon in the middle of the night. The sounds he heard from his audience in the back seat confirmed that he had successfully transferred the scene to Vicky's laptop. The water in the translucent river remained motionless. A mist hung over the river, barely moving, until a water spout formed, spewing a column of blurry images into the air. The images spread out above the river resembling photographs clarifying in developing fluid in an old-fashioned dark room. One by one, Darius sharpened the resolution of the photos.

The first few photos showed nearly deserted streets in Los Angeles, New York, and Tokyo.

Another photo floated forward to fill the screen. It became a video of a news correspondent speaking against a background of graphs and charts illustrating a stock market crash. Shots of shuttered shops and the empty trading floor of the New York Stock Exchange alternated with views of disheveled people walking aimlessly in city streets

The procession of bad news marched onward with images of government leaders arguing bitterly in an emergency session of the UN Security Council.

A high altitude camera angle revealed a grid of city streets degenerating into a lawless, violent jungle. A shocking close up image showed

National Guardsmen joining the ranks of rioters and looters in a plague of urban pestilence.

Television screens, smart phones, and the lights inside majestic office buildings faded to black in the final scenes Darius projected onto Vicky's Laptop.

Darius came out of his trance in time to see Simon slump lower into the cushions of the back seat. The slim designer glasses slid down the bridge of his nose.

They sat for a minute in silence.

"We're a team," Darius said. "We have to work together. What I have shown you doesn't have to happen. It may seem unlikely that three people can stop a worldwide catastrophe, but the simple truth is we can, otherwise they wouldn't have sent me."

"Tell me again. Who are they?" Vicky queried.

"Angels with a lot more experience than me," Darius said. He regretted the explanation immediately.

"Does that mean you aren't very experienced?" Simon interjected.

"It means I'm the best available option."

Darius made a concerted effort to speak with an air of authority. Again, he realized, it came down to believing in himself. His team of mortal helpers had to have confidence in him or the mission had no chance of success. Darius suddenly felt quite alone.

"Count me out," Javon announced. "You all can get out at the next corner and I'll be on my way."

"You really want to take on the monsters without my help?" Darius said.

"All I seen was a bunch of pictures. Ain't no such thing as monsters."

Vicky said, "We saw one, Javon. He came after Darius just before we met you. I don't think you want to run into one of those creatures by yourself."

Javon snapped the elastic band on his wrist. "They'll pay ten large for this car, no questions asked. I'll give you some of the cash to buy guns to fight your monsters," he said to Darius, and raised a hand. "Swear to God as my witness."

"Who are you kidding? The last thing you'd do is share your money with anybody," Darius said. "I wasn't born yesterday."

"I ain't so sure about that. Look, nothin' says I got to hang with you people if I don't want to."

"You could be ripped to shreds before the end of the day if you don't," Darius said. The odds were a hundred-to-one against it happening, but it worked. Javon finally quieted down.

"How much does all of this have to do with Plezenthol?" Simon groaned.

The look on Simon's face matched the rings of despair Darius was surprised to see radiating from the scientist's head. Apparently, he was now capable of seeing what he was sensing as his awareness continued to expand like an inflatable rubber raft.

Simon was obviously in no condition to receive more upsetting news. Darius soft-pedaled his answer.

"I can't say for sure. This whole situation caught every one upstairs off guard. It just crept up on us without warning. And now we only have three days to stop your boss from setting up a worldwide distribution network for Plezenthol."

Simon moaned closing his eyes and massaging them. Then he sat up abruptly. He focused on a billboard overlooking the highway in the distance. "I remember that sign. We're not far from the testing lab. I've been meaning to go there, but Hiram has kept me in non-stop product launch meetings."

"Where's this place at?" Javon grumbled.

"It's about five minutes south of here."

Darius decided a little motivational speech was in order. "I'm feeling better about our chances. We've come together as a team. We're close to the lab. The pieces are falling into place. This is happening."

Javon snickered.

"Can't you try to be a little more upbeat?"

"Naw."

Darius brought his palms together in a mock prayer gesture. "Please. Just drive where Simon tells you to go."

Chapter Eighteen

IN CASE OF FIRE THERE ARE NO STAIRS

THEY ENTERED THE outer offices of Amcor Research and Development. Simon gave the receptionist his ID and credentials. He introduced the entourage with him as research assistants with the exception of Javon. He introduced Javon as a scholarship student. With Simon's credentials verified, they were allowed into the offices.

Darius used his arms and hands to scan the employees in the outer office. He had used the same technique at the wine and cheese reception to detect and expose the Exile guards. A zephyr of light energy would do no harm to an innocent employee. It would only bump up the old mood level a notch or two—no complaints in that department, Darius assumed. He pointed at a secretary standing at a document copier making a stack of reports. Darius camouflaged the move by scratching his head. He pointed at another employee doing accounting work at her desk. This time he blew his nose into a handkerchief. The receptionist stared at him.

"I'm having a bad allergy day," Darius explained.

He pointed to a third employee and covered it up with a big sneeze.

"Bless you," the receptionist said.

The outer office was Exile-free, Darius concluded.

After they each had signed in, the receptionist led Darius, Simon,

Vicky and Javon to the data entry pod. They passed through a tunnel studded with air jets to blow the dust off them. The air jets looked like high-fidelity speakers to Darius. The shiny, metal walls full of holes made Darius feel like he was walking through an alien spacecraft. The receptionist called it a "wind shower."

"The supervisor will bring you back whenever you want," she told Simon. "He's at lunch now but we expect him back shortly. It's an honor to have an important client like you visit us, even when it's a surprise."

She laughed nervously. "Sorry we can't give you the guided tour. As you can see, we're a little short-handed right now. We've had some layoffs due to an unusually slow season." She brightened. "It's either flood or famine around here. Too much work or not enough. Might as well enjoy the quiet." She smiled again.

"We prefer to be on our own," Simon assured her.

"Oh well, then," she said, clasping and unclasping her hands, "just tap on the safety glass when you're done and one of the techs will let you out." She paused. "We've been working round the clock to get your project wrapped up, Doctor Worthington."

"And I appreciate it," Simon replied with a polite smile.

"Oh, I almost forgot." The Secretary handed Darius and the others a pair of paper slippers. "Please put these over your shoes to keep the dust out. Sorry for the bother, but it's policy, even for someone as important as you, Doctor Worthington."

"Please stop apologizing," Simon remarked. "Thank you for letting us in on such short notice."

"I hope you find everything to your satisfaction," the secretary replied with a toothy smile.

"I'm sure we will," Simon said, putting the paper slippers on. "I hope we don't upset the work flow."

"The techs won't even know you're here. You can see them but they can't see you. Their work area is soundproofed as well."

"It seems you've thought of everything," Simon said.

The secretary swiped a security card through the outer locking device and the electronic door slid open. "In you go," she said cheerfully.

No other sounds except the low hum of the particle filtering air conditioning filled the spotless yellow room. The walls and ceilings gleamed with the shine of high gloss enamel paint. Stainless steel ceiling fixtures lit the room brightly. The front portion of the room where they stood served as an observatory. Through safety glass windows, Darius and the others watched five data entry technicians working with precise movements at a row of computer workstations.

"They're converting raw data from test subjects into statistical tables and charts using a proprietary software program specially designed for the Plezenthol study," Simon explained. "It's one of the reasons I chose Amcor to do the testing for us."

"They must be highly trained and experienced," Vicky remarked.

They looked more than highly trained to Darius. They looked superhuman. The technicians' fingers flew across the keyboards as if they had small brains in each hand. Their heads seemed to work independently from the rest of their bodies. Their eyes scanned a rotating roll of paper held in place by metal sprockets.

"What are those rolls of paper for?" Darius asked Simon, pointing at one of the foot wide rolls unwinding onto an empty spool below. The mechanism reminded Darius of film going through an old-fashioned projection camera.

"That's the raw data," Simon answered. "It's a new method Amcor developed. A scanning device converts individual case files into a single roll of paper. It saves time and handling and reduces human error. The process allows raw data conversion into electronic files in one, continuous process, replacing the inefficiency of manila folders stuffed with papers. The operator can set the turn rate at whatever speed works for them. They can stop the roll any time they need to if they want to take a break."

Darius glanced up at a row of monitors attached to the shiny ceiling. The monitor screens were blank. Simon stepped forward to turn them on. Two monitors displayed the workflow of each technician.

One showed a close up of the raw data on the paper roll and the other displayed a close up of a tech's data input screen.

Darius read from the monitor on the ceiling directly above him. PLEZENTHOL DOUBLE BLIND STUDY—PHYSICIAN NOTES: "SUBJECT PRESENTS SYMPTOMS OF A LACK OF MOTIVATION AT HOME AND AT WORK."

His eyes traveled across to the next monitor where the tech typed in the following: "SUBJECT REPORTS A GENERAL SENSE OF WELL BEING AND NO SIDE EFFECTS."

Vicky removed a digital camera from her pocketbook and snapped off shots of the monitors.

Darius turned to Simon who stood tall with legs spread and arms folded over his light gray pinstripe suit jacket. The matching breast pocket handkerchief seemed to droop, reflecting his facial expression. "I knew there was something wrong with these results. But this...." His voice trailed off as he threw an arm out towards the monitors and shook his head.

Javon, standing behind Darius, tapped him on the shoulder. "How long we gotta' stay here? I had to park the car in the lot next door. A cop could spot it."

Darius kept his attention on the monitors where he observed every third or fourth data entry altered by the technicians.

"Stop worrying about the car. We're going to leave it here when we're finished."

"Ah man, that ain't right."

"Can you have a car dropped off to us from Mamongen?" Darius asked Simon.

"I doubt cell phones will work in here," Simon commented while watching the overhead monitors along with Darius. "The walls are heavily insulated."

"Give it a try," Darius said.

Simon pulled out his smart phone and attempted to make a call. He frowned. "No luck."

Darius turned to Vicky who was snapping pictures crisply from vertical and horizontal angles. "How much longer will it take to wrap this up?"

"This is dynamite stuff," Vicky said, smiling and clicking. "I'm almost done."

The door slid open behind them. In walked a young man with a shaved head and a pair of slim black glasses. He wore a blue lab smock made of disposable paper and a matching set of slippers. The young man circled around them and stood in front of the glass windows. "How did you get in here?" he asked.

"I'm Doctor Simon Worthington III from Mamongen Pharmaceuticals."

The young man brightened. "Doctor Worthington. What a pleasant surprise. I'm Dennis Johnson, team supervisor. If I'd known you were coming, I'd have invited you to lunch. Today was my turn to eat out. We allow ourselves that luxury when we're on schedule with our work."

"Either your work is incredibly shoddy or your data input technicians have instructions to deliberately falsify my test results," Simon shot back.

"Doctor Worthington, how can you make an accusation like that? Amcor is one of the most respected names in our industry. Now please. I'm afraid we can't allow photography." Johnson held out a hand. "I'll need your camera to delete the digital images you've taken."

"We're keeping the pictures." Simon said, red faced.

Simon's remark seemed to have no effect on Johnson. He stood there smiling. His eyes blinked twice. The Amcor team supervisor was unimposing physically, about five foot ten, not more than a hundred and seventy pounds, Darius judged. Simon virtually towered over him. Darius wondered how he could remain so calm in a situation like this.

"I can't understand how you might have gotten such a wrong impression," Johnson said. "We'll certainly provide you with all of the individual case files if you request them." He grabbed something out of his breast pocket and held it tightly in one hand. Darius caught a glimpse of the man's pupils dilating. Johnson took one threatening step towards Vicky.

Javon rushed forward and punched the supervisor hard in the face. The man hit a glass window and bounced off like a volleyball. He didn't bleed. Not a drop. His nose should have been all over his face, Darius thought.

Javon reached back to launch another shot. Johnson ducked in time to avoid the second blow. Javon's fist hit the glass. "Damn," he shouted, shaking his big, bony hand.

Darius summoned light energy. It was something he should have been doing the moment they stepped into the room. The excitement of their discovery had distracted him.

Slowly at first, Johnson's face rippled. It began to bubble as if giant pimples were erupting underneath his skin. The supervisor hunched over and cried out in pain. It sounded like the screech of a giant bird.

Darius and the others watched in terror as an extra set of arms grew out of Johnson's side. A muscular tail burst from the seat of the smock. The chest inflated, ripping the shirt into pieces like an eggshell that had outlived its usefulness. The triangular head of a brown-skinned lizard bloomed from the expanding torso.

The power inside Darius swirled from the depths of his being. The peaceful warmth of the energy kept him from jumping out of his skin. Vicky and Simon moved for the door. Javon did not budge. He kicked the transfiguring monstrosity in one of its thickening legs. The beast spun around and roared.

Javon backed against the wall. The creature whirled around to face Vicky. It hopped on feet that looked to Darius like they belonged to an Ostrich. Vicky screamed. The creature stopped and canted its head as if bewildered by the sight of a woman or the sound of her shrill cry. With a sweeping motion, the Exile whipped the camera out of Vicky's hands. It happened so fast it was a wonder her hands remained attached to her wrists.

The power continued to rise inside Darius, along his spinal cord, branching out along nerve endings, coursing through his torso. *Hurry, before this creature tears one of us to pieces,* Darius told the force gathering inside his body.

The Exile crouched in the middle of the room. Powerful arm and shoulder muscles worked in unison with huge hands to grind Vicky's camera into tiny lumps of metal that scattered on the rubber flooring.

The creature looked up at Vicky. It bared a mouthful of teeth that would have made a Tyrannosaurus Rex jealous. Vicky inched away.

Somehow, Darius knew his batteries, in a manner of speaking, were fully charged. He was good to go. Without a moment's hesitation, he released a bolt of high intensity light energy. His entire body shook with an adrenaline rush.

"Aarrrghhhh." The sound poured out of his mouth involuntarily.

The Exile burst into flames. Not ordinary fire, though. Darius had no idea what was happening. This was the first time he had released light energy at full force. The monster roared as the flames knit together to form a three-dimensional triangle hanging in midair. The triangle glowed brightly. There was no heat. No sound. No odor. Darius watched in awe as the triangle began to pulse for several seconds before it collapsed into its base like a blazing, wooden "A" frame. Only a luminous line in the air remained. Then the line disappeared.

"Man, if this ain't some weird shit," Javon observed.

Darius watched two of the techs leave their stations on the other side of the glass.

Simon ran to the exit door. Pounding on it, he cried, "Let us out."

Javon sauntered over to the scientist. Balancing on one spindly leg, he unleashed a barrage of Karate kicks against the door. It didn't budge.

Vicky collapsed to her knees. She appeared to be shocked out of her wits, crawling like a child, scooping up the pieces of her shattered camera into a small pile. Darius zeroed in on a glass ball rolling to a stop near her. The light energy hadn't quite taken everything with it. The glass ball was the size of a large marble with an azure cloud of something swirling inside. Darius bent to pick up the strange object. It burned his thumb and forefinger.

"Ouch," he cried, dropping the ball. It raised a blister on his thumb.

The electric door leading into the data processing area slid open. Two techs walked in pushing Simon rudely back into the room. The automatic door closed behind them.

"The room is sound proofed," the shorter one said to Simon. "It's no use to struggle."

"They know we're in here," Simon said defiantly, referring to the front office employees. The taller tech produced a glass ball from his breast pocket. Gripping it in his fist, the tech's features began to change. It didn't take long for his face to become a clone of Simon's.

It was clear to Darius what the four remaining techs were planning. They were Exiles, just like their fallen team supervisor. They intended to murder Darius and his mortal friends and then impersonate them leaving the office. Darius didn't know what they would do with the bodies, but he figured they had a plan. It would be a tidy cover up, as if the rubber floor had swallowed them in one large gulp.

The door behind the two techs opened again. The other two techs walked through in light-blue smocks. As soon as the door closed, one of them raised a weapon that looked like a foot long tuning fork with joined triangles pointing from the ends. With ten fingers outstretched, Darius was about to fire light energy bolts in succession at all four of the techs when Simon decided to be a hero.

The scientist tackled the gun-wielding tech directly in Darius' line of fire. Simon missed becoming toast by a nanosecond. The tech, who was much smaller, struggled against Simon's grip. The weapon discharged three energy projectiles. The exit door buzzed and crackled. Jagged purple lines sawed the white door into ragged pieces. The energy consumed the fragments until there was nothing left except the door frame and the noxious odor of burnt plastic.

The armed tech flung Simon against the far wall where he crashed in a heap. He turned and leveled the weapon at Darius.

Darius opened fire before the Exile had a chance to squeeze off a shot. He ducked and rolled like the heroes he'd read about in his books while squeezing off more light energy bolts. Soon, all four techs were burning like hearty campfires.

"Get Simon," Darius called to Javon.

Darius helped Vicky out the door. The people in the front office were going to think World War III had just begun in their own back yard. Maybe they had already called the police. Maybe trained guards from Amcor's private security service were on their way to the building.

They reached the outer office. It was empty. The receptionist and three office workers had vanished, probably on the advice of a 911 operator. Lights were flashing on and off on the alarm unit next to the front door.

"Looks like we're back to using that stolen car of yours," Darius called to Javon.

"I don't want to hear no more talk about leaving it behind," Javon crowed. "That car is lucky and it's my ticket to a better life."

Javon's last comment struck Darius as odd. He made a mental note to talk to him about it, if time ever allowed.

Simon had an arm draped around Javon's wide shoulders. The teenager held the scientist up with an arm around his waist.

"Help me with this dude," Javon said to Darius.

They carried Simon out to the parking lot. Vicky followed, still holding a few pieces of the digital camera the Exile had shredded as easily as an incriminating paper document.

Chapter Nineteen

AN EXPENSIVE BATTERING RAM

THEY RACED THROUGH the sunlit streets of Miami.

"Where to now?" Javon drawled.

"Back to the Mamongen building," Darius said.

"If you think you can convince Hiram Fyrum to pull the plug on Plezenthol, you're sadly mistaken, Darius. I know him much better than you do. We'll need undeniable proof to convince Hiram of anything. All we have are uncorroborated stories. If we go to him now, he'll think we're experiencing some kind of weird, shared psychosis. He'll have us carted off in straight-jackets."

Javon peered into the rearview mirror. "Damn. We're being followed."

Darius whirled around to see who was behind them.

A black Maserati with dark tinted windows closed to within inches of the Bentley's rear bumper. The Maserati's logo had always reminded Darius of a devil's pitchfork.

Javon stomped on the accelerator. The Bentley GT's five hundred and fifty horses kicked in with the jolt of a rocket sled. An exit ramp for I-95 northbound loomed a block ahead.

"Let's get back on the highway," Darius said. "We don't want to run into a red light and what's inside that Maserati."

Javon zoomed onto the highway ramp. The Maserati lost no time in taking up the chase. In an instant, both cars were now ducking in and out of traffic, at speeds in excess of one hundred and twenty miles per hour over the expressway.

Javon changed lanes with the gritty expertise of a dirt track stock car driver. The Bentley, with its low center of gravity, wove between and around slower moving cars like a graceful leopard running at full tilt across a South African veldt. Darius observed Javon checking the rearview and passenger side mirrors every few seconds to make sure they were staying ahead of the Maserati and any representatives of the Florida Highway Patrol that might pick up their trail. Up ahead, Darius noticed, with a sinking feeling, the traffic was slowing down.

A wall of cars stretched across the highway, moving like a school of pregnant manatees. Javon tromped on the brakes to avoid ramming into an elderly couple in a Dodge minivan. The wall of cars was comprised of minivans and RV campers, Darius realized, probably a travel club crawling their way up the highway for a weekend at some State Park. He saw the Maserati bearing down on them. The passenger side window rolled down. A tan-suited arm holding the same kind of weird pistol they saw at the Amcor lab was pointing directly at the Bentley. Javon saw it in the rearview mirror. He jerked the wheel. Darius felt the seatbelt tighten automatically. The Bentley dove across several lanes and burst through the rubber dividers into the express lanes.

A bluish-gray burst exploded from the weapon, smashing into a section of the retaining wall to their left. A chunk of the wall splintered into fragments. The concrete particles disintegrated into grains of fine sand. Then the sand disappeared into thin air, leaving behind a jagged hole. Darius hoped the knot of traffic they had just managed to avoid would delay their pursuers. Then the Maserati careened into the express lanes speeding after them.

"Maybe we should try to lose them in local traffic," Darius suggested to Javon.

"What about the red lights?" the teenager replied.

"I guess we'll have to pretend they're stop signs."

Darius and Javon broke out laughing.

"I don't find any of this amusing," Simon complained. He sat slumped next to Vicky in the back seat. Darius thought they looked like two rag dolls tossed into a corner with their heads touching. It was perfectly understandable given the ordeal they had just been through at Amcor. Vicky hadn't said a word since the monster swiped her camera.

They were coming up to the exit for SW 8th Street. Javon accelerated. The Bentley burst out of the express lane and virtually flew towards the exit ramp at ninety miles an hour. Darius closed his eyes and meditated. He breathed a sigh of relief when the traffic light turned green at the bottom of the exit ramp. Something actually went right for a change. He looked behind them. No sign of the black Maserati.

Javon nudged the Bentley into the mid-day crush of traffic streaming up and down the street. "Calle Ocho. That's what they call this street," Javon said. "It means Eighth Street in Spanish. It's famous, but I neva' come here. Don't speak Spanish."

"Good to know." Darius hoped the flashy Bentley would be less noticeable wedged into the dense snarl of traffic on the street, but he knew it was only a matter of time before a patrolman spotted it. He craned his head from one side to the other, looking for an inconspicuous place to abandon the car and continue their journey on foot.

Calle Ocho was an odd mix of small, family-owned shops and restaurants sporadically interrupted by modern malls composed almost entirely of chain retail stores. Here, it seemed to Darius, the past and the present existed side by side in an uneasy truce. Street vendors could be seen everywhere hawking wares from brightly colored brooms to food snacks made from corn bread. Musicians played classical guitars, flutes and woodwinds in front of the shops to small, appreciative crowds. Artists painted pictures on the sidewalks. Sketch artists offered caricatures to tourists. Pots and pans, small appliances, and a cornucopia of home-made products like jewelry, belts, and clothing beckoned to prospective buyers in the vibrant, open-air market that was a world of its own only a few miles from the down-town area.

Darius didn't want to see the color and vitality of a unique world like this one brutally destroyed. This vibrant outdoor market was a single petal on an endlessly diverse flower of life. It was a tiny spec of paint in the Creator's glorious, multi-faceted work of art, now threatened by an all-consuming dark cloud.

"Let's drop the car over there," Darius said, pointing to a side street blocked by two wooden barricades.

Javon turned to him with a remorseful, resolute face. "I don't want to leave this car, man."

"I'm sorry," Darius said, placing a consoling hand on his shoulder. "We'll get picked up by either the Police or the Exiles if we keep riding around in this thing."

"How come I never jacked a car like this one 'fore I met you?"

"Maybe I make you feel brave," Darius offered.

"Naw."

"Being part of something makes you feel stronger. The trick is you want to be part of something good, something that has a good purpose behind it."

Javon looked bewildered. Darius wondered what to say to make Javon feel better. *Don't worry. We'll get out of this.* There was no way a watered down platitude was going to help at a time like this. He gave Javon a playful punch in the arm. "I'll get out and move those barricades," he said.

"Watch your ass," Javon said, snapping the elastic band on his wrist.

Darius heeded the advice. He kept a watchful eye out for police cruisers and a certain Black Maserati while he moved the barricades over to one side of the road. He motioned for Javon to bring the Bentley through, which Javon promptly accomplished. Darius immediately set about replacing the barricades.

He wiped the sweat off his forehead with a handkerchief that was now soaked and soiled. Sweat poured down from inside the suit jacket he had forgotten to leave in the car in his haste to hide the Bentley.

He cast one more look down the broad street and caught a glimpse of the Maserati behind a pickup truck a hundred yards away. He had a feeling the Maserati had been using the truck as camouflage. Darius quickly disappeared into the shadows of the deserted side street. He ran to the dead end of the street where Javon was neatly executing a K-turn to park his beloved Bentley.

Behind him, Darius heard the squeal of tires. He turned just before reaching the Bentley. The Maserati motored straight through the barricades, slowly but surely. The Bentley and the Maserati faced off with their powerful engines purring. Darius noticed there were no windows in the buildings overlooking the street—just bare concrete walls climbing three stories high—probably the back end of a small warehouse. At least they were out of sight of the circus of life on the main thoroughfare.

Darius grabbed Vicky by the hand and pulled her out of the car. Simon followed.

"Get out of the car," Darius screamed to Javon.

Javon sat stolidly in the Bentley, grimacing. Darius flung the front door open. He pulled at Javon's T-shirt. "What's the matter with you?"

Javon pushed Darius' arm away. Didn't he realize the Bentley was about to become a very expensive coffin?

"Get out of here," Darius called to Vicky and Simon.

Vicky took a quick look at her laptop and handbag before bolting away without attempting to rescue them from the back seat. She turned back to Darius with a plaintive expression before running back to the relative safety of Eighth Street. She reached the street corner and fled out of sight with Simon matching her stride for stride.

Javon revved the Bentley's engine in what Darius knew was an extremely foolish attempt to scare the two Exiles in the other car.

· · ·

From inside the Bentley, Javon watched the black Maserati idling menacingly. Suddenly, the engine roared to life in answer to Javon's challenge. Something bad was about to happen and he wasn't about to wait around to find out what it was. He gunned the engine and rammed the Bentley head first into the Maserati. The elegant front ends of the two luxury automobiles crumpled like discarded cigarette boxes with a metallic *crunch.*

If he was going to die, Javon had decided to do everything in his power to take the ugly-ass-motherfuckers in the other car with him. If that wasn't possible, he was going to cause the bastards as much pain and misery as was humanly possible before it was all over. He backed the Bentley up and rammed the Maserati again before the assholes inside had a chance to think twice.

Javon watched the Exile driver step out of the car. The creature had already morphed into a fully mature Exile body. Chiseled muscles rippled with its slightest move. The bushy hair on the monster's head crawled like a nest of cobras. It stared at Javon with limpid black eyes punctuated with violet pupils.

Powered by its muscular tail and haunches, the Exile leaped through the air, landing with a *thud* on the hood of the Bentley, denting it. The creature proceeded to pound the Bentley's windshield with crazed abandon, delivering blow after blow with its four claw-hands, spreading cracks across the sturdy Plexiglas.

Inside the Bentley, Javon slumped behind the steering wheel, unmoving. He had no doubt this was the end of the line for him. The windshield was now a spider web of fractures. The only thing holding it together were the space age fibers forged into the glass to prevent it from shattering. A few more shuddering blows and there would be nothing but fresh air between Javon and the monster. Javon clenched both fists. He was determined to bash the shithead's face in before it tore him to pieces.

• • •

Darius closed his eyes and felt a refreshing rush of warmth course through him from the pit of his stomach to the crown of his head. A wave of ineffable calm swept over him. He raised his arms and aimed at the Exile pounding the Bentley's windshield with maniacal rage. The monster seemed intent on one thing only—breaking through to its human prey behind the brushed metal and leather steering wheel.

Darius waited for the charge to build up inside him. He finally accumulated a lethal charge and released a high intensity light energy bolt. The Exile burst into flames. The other Exile jumped out of the Maserati from the other side. Darius fired again, this time with only enough energy to stun the creature. It stood upright, gasping for breath, shaking all over from the shock of the blast.

He needed time to accumulate more energy for a lethal shot. His system wasn't renewing itself as quickly as it had in the struggle with the Exile techs earlier. He had to find a way to train his body to become stronger, assuming he could manage to stay in one piece.

The Exile shook itself like a bear coming out of a stream.

The Bentley's tires squealed as Javon backed the car away from the clutches of the Maserati. Expertly changing gears, he smashed the damaged front end of the car into the remaining Exile before it had a chance to fully recover. Once, twice, three times. Javon used the crumpled front end of the car to knock the Exile senseless.

Darius heard Javon scream *shithead* from inside the car each time he plowed into the tottering beast. The front end of the Bentley collapsed with the third blow. A gusher of steam blew from the ruptured radiator. Javon threw the low-slung door open and dashed from the car in a blur of skinny arms and legs.

Javon's offensive gave Darius enough time to reload. He fired another light energy bolt. The Exile wailed as flames engulfed it in a triangle shape, sending it to God knew where. Darius didn't especially care. It only mattered that there was one less monster to deal with. He felt sluggish, as if his body had suddenly become as dense as a block of carbon. He sat down on the ground, exhausted. Javon ran over to him, his head darting in all directions, checking for signs of more creatures, Darius assumed.

"Thanks," Darius said.

"For what?"

"Saving my bacon."

"I was just savin' mine. I see what you mean about bein' on your own against these ugly-ass-monsters. It ain't smart."

"I'm glad you understand."

"What we gotta' do now?"

"Some errands," Darius said mysteriously. "But first we need to get out of here before anyone shows up to see what a mess we made."

"I'm down with that," Javon concurred.

Javon helped Darius up while glancing woefully in the direction of the ruined Bentley languishing at the end of the desolate street. He shook his head. Then they started walking.

BREAKING BREAD

THE SUN WAS setting in a symphony of pink pastels above the sweep of modern office buildings arching across the downtown Miami skyline.

Javon stared into the rear-view mirror and frowned at the reflection looking back at him. His once beautiful, long, bushy hair had hit the floor at Super Cuts, shorn like sheep's wool, replaced by a horrible crew cut. Instead of the long-breasted suit he wanted to buy, Darius had purchased the three-button standard model—in boring gray, no less. It got even worse. He was wearing penny loafers. The last straw had been the car they rented. Instead of something respectable like a Cadillac SUV with tricked-out wheels, Javon found himself driving a powder blue Chrysler Sebring. There was no end to the humiliation a brother had to suffer to stay alive in an unfair world.

Javon ran a brush through what was left of his hair as they waited in line for their order at the Burger King drive-through.

"Never met a 'B' didn't like a Whopper. You sure you're black?"

"All of your Brothers *and* Sisters aren't going to be enjoying hamburgers, or anything else for that matter, unless we get on with our work."

"Can't do nothin' if I'm hungry."

Darius slumped back in his seat. "I thought you were beginning to understand."

"Understand what?"

"What we're involved with here is a little bigger than your immediate needs."

"Listen. Nobody ever gave me nothin.' When I's eight years old, my old man got stoned an' tried to set me on fire. They put me in a bunch of foster care places after that 'till I got sick of those places and went off on my own. Eva' since, I been takin' care of myself. I come first. That's what works for me. I'm a self-made man, you know what I'm sayin?"

Darius rubbed his eyes and forehead. "All *I'm* saying is there's a certain sense of urgency here you fail to grasp."

The car moved up to the pickup window. A beautiful girl with a head set, about twenty, waited for them with two brown sacks peeking out of the window. Darius thought she looked more like the store manager than a regular employee. She was probably filling in for someone who was on break, or helping out with the dinner rush. The girl had the look of someone who was wise beyond her years—and something else—the most lovely, hazel eyes. Those eyes reminded Darius of his lost love, Rebecca. Strong and independent, she had the courage to defy her rich, white father who didn't approve of one of his daughters dating a black man. Rebecca was the kindest person he had ever met. He let his mind wander back a few years.

Darius and Rebecca laughed as they walked hand and hand amid the rolling hills, statues of saints, meditation paths, and austere halls of higher education. Rebecca's cascading raven black hair danced with each lively movement of her head. Darius had spent the whole week waiting for just the right moment. Something told him this was it. His heart pounded with excitement. "I'm finding it hard to let go of your hand," he said.

"Then don't, silly," she said.

"I guess what I mean is I don't ever want to let go of your hand."

She laughed, but then her expression turned serious. "Are you feeling insecure about us?"

He pretended to think about her question deeply. Then he said, "Not in the least."

That was when he handed her the tiny box with the ring inside and asked her to marry him as casually as if he were asking for a Kleenex.

"Darius, you awful person," she shrieked, and hugged him tightly. She opened the box to admire the engagement ring with a tiny diamond in the middle. Tears of joy streamed down her cheeks. Her hand shook as Darius slipped the ring on.

"Twelve forty-seven, please."

The words fractured the world Darius was in like a bulldozer knocking down a house. The girl in the window was holding out two brown paper bags of fast food in both hands. Javon took them. Darius rummaged in his pants pocket for some money. It reminded him again of reaching for the ring. How had his life changed so drastically in such a short time?

The powder blue Sebring slid into a space in the Burger King parking lot. Javon attacked the brown bag cradled in his lap. He tore a chunk out of his hamburger like a hungry Rottweiler. He stuffed a handful of fries into his mouth and irrigated the food with a gulp of chocolate malt. He sat next to Darius chewing like a cement mixer with a look of profound satisfaction on his face.

Darius ignored the spectacle of Javon inhaling his dinner. He was deep inside himself. He removed the lid from a cardboard cup of hot tea and broke off a piece of English muffin. He stared absently across the street at a van with two lift chairs protruding out of the top like the arms of a praying mantis.

"That all you gonna' eat?"

"I'm not that hungry," Darius replied, almost in a whisper.

"Man, what's wrong with you? You're actin' like some kind of love sick fool."

Darius whirled around. "Don't say that."

"What'd I say?"

"What do you know about love?"

"Look at you. All blowin' your cool like that. Don't tell me you got a girlfriend? Excuse me, had a girlfriend, unless a' course angels have bitches."

Darius glowered at Javon. "How dare you call her a bitch?"

"Take it easy, man."

Darius turned away. A tear spilled down his cheek.

"Ooeee," Javon crooned. "Whateva' it is that's bothering you—you better tell me."

"Why, so you can continue to ridicule me?"

"What do 'ridicule' mean?"

"It means to mock or make fun of someone."

"Stop bein' so damn sensitive."

"You want me to be just like you, which is to say, without feelings for another person."

"Okay," Javon prodded. "Lay it on me."

Javon Quincey was the last person on Earth Darius felt comfortable telling his story to. But it was way too close to the surface now. He couldn't stop it from pouring out.

He told Javon about Rebecca Donahue. How he had almost married her. About how deliriously happy they had been together. How they had shared everything from the smallest detail of their lives to their grandest hopes and dreams. While telling his story, Darius re-lived the horror of the drive-by shooting. He felt the pain of waking up in heaven without Rebecca; without his mother and father; without his friends from college. He talked about his plans to go to law school at the same school Rebecca attended.

"I can't understand why it all happened to me," Darius said at the end. He felt a sickening emptiness, as if a sump-pump had sucked all of the energy out of his body. It was the first time Darius had talked about his feelings since the horrible day he died.

"Listen up," Javon said, resting an arm on the back of the passenger seat. "Some dumb gangbangers too drunk to aim straight snuffed you out. God was probably takin' a nap at the time. Face it, man. You was in the wrong place at the wrong time. Shit happens."

Darius glared at his first recruit with rising anger. Then a voice told him to temper his indignation. What did he expect from Javon? Solace? Scripture quotes?

"Sorry to burden you with my troubles," Darius said.

"You gotta' forget about the bad stuff that happened to you," Javon said. "I had to do it. You can too."

"What happened to you was terrible," Darius said. "No one should have to go through what you did. It's just that what happened to me still hurts. Badly. It's hard for me to put it out of my mind."

"It's like you keep tellin' me," Javon persisted. "We don't have a lot of time. You gotta' let it go."

Darius couldn't argue with that.

"I'm counting on you to get me outta' this mess," Javon added.

"At least we have one thing in common," Darius said.

"Yeah, what?

"Desperation."

Javon snickered.

Across the street, Darius noticed two men in lift chairs finishing the installation of a billboard advertisement. It depicted a beaming young mother and father holding a smiling infant in a sun-drenched modern kitchen. He squinted through his rimless glasses to read the caption at the bottom of the family scene:

"Are You Enjoying Life to the Fullest? Ask Your Doctor about Plezenthol—Developed by Mamongen Pharmaceuticals. For more information, visit us at: *www.mamonpharm.com*."

Darius closed his eyes to think about what to do next. In less than a minute, an idea came to him.

Chapter Twenty-One

THE ANTHILL OF NEWSGATHERING

"**THE MAMONGEN STORY** is bigger than you can imagine," Vicky said to her boss, Roberta Fearnbreath-Larson.

"You make a laughing stock of yourself and this news service at the press conference and you have the nerve to come in here talking down to me,"

"Plezenthol is a dangerous drug," Vicky said.

"Can you prove it?" Roberta said, breathing heavily, something Vicky's chain-smoking, overweight, diabetic boss was in the habit of doing. "Who was that joker sitting with you in the conference?"

Vicky's mind was spinning. Her adventures with Darius McPherson haunted her. She had yet to summon the courage to speak to anyone about the incredible events that had unfolded before her unbelieving eyes earlier that day. How could she explain to Roberta she was working on a story with an angel?

"He's a source," Vicky answered vaguely. "He introduced me to Mamongen's Chief Chemist, Simon Worthington III. We visited the testing lab today." Vicky paused for dramatic effect, "and we uncovered proof that the Plezenthol test results are being enhanced to cover up for some of the side effects."

Roberta's pudgy face folded into the semblance of a Saint Bernard dog. "I want to see this proof."

Roberta stood abruptly and waddled over to the picture window of her corner office. She pointed outside—to the hulking shadows of what were, by day, giant skyscrapers.

"Those are our customers, Victoria. The people who run the corporations in those buildings are very serious people. The information we report to them has to be a hundred percent accurate."

"Are you saying you don't have confidence in me?"

"Can I tell you something, Dearie? I took you on because the city editor couldn't stand you anymore. He called you an obsessive-compulsive, high-minded-pain-in-the-ass. He didn't have the heart to fire you, so the man prevailed upon me to give you a chance in the financial news division." Roberta paused. "I owed him a favor."

Under normal circumstances, this information would have been devastating news to Vicky, but normal was no longer a part of her vocabulary. A young black man who claimed to be an angel and backed it up by doing things that were nothing short of miraculous had changed her life forever. Where was he now? She had to find Darius.

"You rub people the wrong way," Roberta carried on. "And you certainly lack the passion necessary to be a success in this department."

Passion? To feed money hungry business people with the information they crave to cut each other's throats?

"You'll have my resignation on your desk before I leave," Vicky said.

"I'm sending someone to your office to download your notes on the story," Roberta said without the slightest hint of emotion.

"I left my computer in my car. I'm going right back to it after I leave here. Doctor Worthington wants to meet me face to face to talk about something. I only came here because you insisted that I report to your office. *If only the part about meeting privately with Worthington were true.*

"Your notes are the property of this news organization." Roberta sneered. "If I don't have them on my desk first thing tomorrow morning, you'll never find another media job in this town after I put the word out on you."

Back in her office cubicle, Vicky stared at the resignation letter displayed on her desktop computer. She had purposely neglected to update it with the notes from her laptop. Fernbreath-Larson would personally take her to the nearest psych ward if the bitch ever laid eyes on her observations of the day's events.

All around her, in tiny cubicles like her own, drones laboring in the anthill of newsgathering continued pushing grains of information up the steep incline leading to the printing presses. Vicky was in a different world now. She experienced a fleeting sense of relief. She was free of the WQES Financial News Division and of Roberta Fernbreath-Larson. She would have no problem selling her story to the highest bidder. The only little thing standing in her way was the real possibility of the world ending. And if the world survived, there remained the challenge of finding concrete proof to back up her first in a series of Plezenthol articles.

Her smart phone chirped. A friend of hers had downloaded the sound of a cricket as a joke earlier in the week. She was not in a mood for jokes. The call came from Simon.

"I can't talk for long," he said. "I'm searching through my computer records to find enough anomalies in the test results to prove that they're unreliable. So far, all I can tell is that Amcor did a masterful job of faking their reports. How are you doing?"

"Good as gold," she said. "I just quit my job before my lovely boss had a chance to fire me."

She heard Simon laugh on the other end of the connection. "Should I be sorry to hear you're out of a job?"

"The short answer is no."

Under normal circumstances, she would have proceeded to ply Simon for more information with whatever it took short of offering up her body. She wondered if anything would ever be normal again.

"Hey, Simon. I just thought of something. What if we called a press conference to report our findings? We could say our research on the test results is preliminary and subject to further investigation. Wouldn't that be enough to delay the product launch and give us more time to present some solid proof?"

"We'd get sued. I'd lose my job. And every monster on the surface of the planet would come after us."

"Got it. It was just a thought."

"I'm acting like nothing unusual is happening to avoid starting a panic."

Vicky sat through an awkward silence in the conversation.

"Can you meet me tomorrow at the Conrad Hilton downtown, eleven AM, in the Tarpon Springs room?"

"Wait a minute, where?" She grabbed a pen.

He repeated the instructions.

"Why are we meeting there?"

"I have to be there for a marketing function."

"Why do I have to come?"

"According to what Darius said, we're supposed to be a team. I don't think it's a good idea for you to be running around all by yourself."

Vicky couldn't help smiling.

"That's Hiram calling me back on my other line. See you tomorrow at eleven."

Simon broke the connection. Vicky sat there holding her smart phone. Simon cared about her. She liked that. There was only one thing to do, she decided. Go home and start working on her story. A few hours of sleep wouldn't hurt either.

It was sweet that Simon felt the need to protect her, but he was no match for those horrible monsters. They needed their guardian angel. *Where was Darius.*

Chapter Twenty-Two

SUPER SAM'S

THEY STROLLED THROUGH the merchandise-laden aisles of Super Sam's Discount Outlet. A sign on the back wall of the big box retail store painted in rainbow colors shouted: *EVERYTHING FOR THE HOME AND OFFICE AT THE LOWEST PRICES UNDER THE SUN.*

"Oooeee," Javon exclaimed, pointing to a row of sleek computers on display in the next aisle.

At six o'clock on a weekday evening, the store was not very busy. *Most people are at home with their families eating dinner,* Darius thought. He missed his mother and father terribly. He missed his older brother and younger sister too. His older brother had joined their father in the cabinet making business. The business was blossoming with the two of them working together. His younger sister was studying to be an English teacher. She looked up to Darius. He loved her dearly. He needed his family. They needed him. Why was this happening?

He pushed these thoughts out of his head. The first precious day of his three-day mission was almost over. This was no time to feel sorry for himself. He was grateful to Javon for setting him straight on that issue.

While these thoughts went through his mind, Javon was busy

checking out a laptop with a seventeen-inch screen loaded to the gills with expensive audio-visual features. He was clicking and typing away at a furious pace when Darius grabbed his hand.

"We don't have time to play with the machine. Can you get on the Internet?"

"The browser won't open. How do they expect to sell these things if you can't take 'em for a test drive?"

A rotund salesperson came up to them. His face was aflame with a type of acne that had lingered beyond adolescence. Darius often wondered if afflictions like these were punishment for some hidden, unclean sin. He was beginning to doubt it. The reason was probably nothing more than unfortunate genes.

"Awesome machine," the salesperson boasted, sidling up to Darius. "It's on sale, you know. Take an extra twenty percent off—today and today only."

"Can you show us how to try out the Internet features before we buy it?" Darius inquired.

"The machine comes with our iron clad, thirty day, no questions asked return policy. You can try it all you want once you take it home. Can I tell you about super Sam's insane lay-a-way plan?"

"Why don't you talk into his head and make him do it?" Javon whispered to Darius.

"I can't make anyone do anything they don't want to do," Darius whispered back.

The salesperson regarded them with a curious expression.

"You can tell me how to get on the Internet," Javon declared, "or get your head broke."

"Excuse me while I call Security."

The salesperson pirouetted and marched away indignantly.

"We'll be happy to buy the machine...or maybe one a little more reasonably priced," Darius called after him.

The salesperson whirled back around. "Now that sounds like a much better idea," he said with a broad smile of instant forgiveness.

• • •

"I've seen the data being falsified with my own eyes," Simon finally shouted across the desk to Hiram. The room suddenly felt as warm as the hot yoga class he had promised himself never to attend again. Why had he decided to go against the solid advice he had given to Darius? Deep down, he knew the answer. He could no longer live with the horrible truth he had witnessed.

Hiram stared back at him from the throne in his study. He spread his hands on the desk palms up. "How could a company like Amcor afford to do something like that? They have too much to lose. Why would they do it?"

Simon knew the answer, but he held on to the impulse to blurt it out with his last smidgeon of self-control. "They're doing it," he said evasively. "Come down there with me and I'll show you. Just make sure we take a bunch of security guards that I hand select with us."

Hiram's expression instantly changed from wonder to suspicion. Simon immediately wished he hadn't added the part about the security guards.

"I'm not paranoid, Hiram. I know what I'm saying sounds off-the-wall, but it's true. I saw it. You have to believe me."

Hiram slumped back into his overbearing executive chair. A look of dismay crossed his face. It was a remarkably smooth face for a man in his fifties. *It was the face of a man who simply refused to worry*, Simon thought.

"I'm too busy to go running over to Amcor right now," Hiram said. "If you want me to believe you, you'll have to bring me some very convincing proof."

Simon saw the look in Hiram's eyes. The man was losing confidence in him by the second. He should never have tried doing this on his own. Staring down at an expensive Persian rug, he tramped out of Hiram's study feeling worse than when he had come in.

Chapter Twenty-Three

A SMALL CONFESSION

EVERYTHING ABOUT THE economy-sized motel room made Darius feel uncomfortable. The wooden desk pinched his muscular thighs. The garish green and gold colors of the carpet and bedspreads did nothing to calm him down. And, the room smelled from cheap cleaning fluid.

Javon, sprawled asleep with his basketball sneakers hanging over the end of the bed, snored so loudly it distracted Darius from his research. The tiny table lamp cast a feeble circle of light. Force of habit made him choose this place. He wanted familiar surroundings rather than something new—like a luxurious suite—courtesy of the unlimited expense account the Archangel and Board of Directors had given him. Big mistake. From now on, he was going to enjoy the finer things in life on Earth, even though there were only two days of said life left.

Darius squinted at the screen of his new lap top computer. He was weary and ached all over from the drain of summoning light energy to fend off the Exiles in the street battle earlier in the evening. His first day back on Earth almost seemed more eventful than his twenty-five years of mortal life.

Darius stared at the Mamongen home page. It was a simple design, clean and functional. He thought the understated web design indicated the company's confidence in its dominant market position.

Underneath the seductive curves of the Mamongen logo, he read the corporate slogan: *BETTER HEALTH WITH THE LEADER IN BIOTECH RESEARCH AND DEVELOPMENT.*

Darius clicked on the *PLEZENTHOL* link. The screen displayed a series of images accompanied by short, persuasive captions extracted from the video presentation Darius and Vicky had seen in the Mamongen auditorium. At the bottom of the page, the linked words *THE NEW YOU* appeared. Darius clicked on the link.

Now the screen displayed photos of individuals, couples and groups enjoying professional success and recreational activities. He read the sparse promotional copy on the web page: *IF YOU FEEL LIFE HAS MORE IN STORE THAN WHAT YOU ARE EXPE-RIENCING, COME TO A FREE SEMINAR SPONSORED BY MAMONGEN PHARMACEUTICALS. ENTER YOUR ZIP CODE FOR THE DATE AND LOCATION NEAREST YOU.*

Who could resist an offer like that? Darius noted the motel's address on the complimentary message pad lying next to the computer. It was one of the few free amenities in the spartan room. He entered the motel's zip code and discovered the nearest "New You" seminar was scheduled for 11:00 AM the following morning at the Conrad Hilton, a swank hotel in downtown Miami overlooking Biscayne Bay. He chuckled. Javon was going to hit the ceiling when Darius broke the news that they were going to a self-improvement seminar.

As if he was tuned in to Darius' thoughts, Javon awoke with a start. He watched Javon shuffle off to the bathroom grumbling to himself. He heard the toilet flush. Javon lurched unsteadily back into the room in the general direction of his narrow bed, still mumbling to himself.

Darius expected to see Javon flop into bed in a tangle of skinny arms and legs. Instead, Javon stopped by the side of his bed. "Cain't do it," he whimpered, frowning, weaving in a circle, eyes half closed.

Darius shook Javon hard. "Can't do what?"

Javon opened his eyes wide and looked at Darius as if seeing him for the first time. He slapped Darius' hands off his shoulders and sat on the edge of his bed. "I'm finished with this shit," he said.

"Our *job* isn't finished. I need your help." They sat facing each other, their knees almost touching in the economy-sized room.

"I got my own business to worry about."

"You won't have *anything* to worry about if most of the people in this world go off their train tracks."

"Why should I give a shit 'bout other people? Nobody eva' looked out for me."

"What do you think will happen to you if you go back on your own? You think the Exiles will let you rob stores and party?"

"I got better things to do than rob shitty-ass stores."

"Like what?"

Javon contemplated the question. It seemed to have him stumped.

"What's really bothering you."

Javon massaged his sleep-puffed face with the palm of his hand. "I'm scared," he said.

"Congratulations," Darius said.

"Fer what?"

"Joining the human race."

Javon straightened. "Hunh?"

"I'm scared too. I'm sure Vicky and Simon are scared out of their wits. It's not a crime."

Javon stared back at him with a pitiful expression.

"It's nothing to be ashamed of. You're allowed to have feelings."

Javon turned to look out of the room's only window. There was nothing to see except another wing of the motel not more than twenty feet away.

"We're in this together for a reason," Darius said. "Someone thinks an awful lot of you to put you in this position."

"Yeah, well, I'm talented, you know."

"Something tells me there's more to it than that." Darius paused. "You want to be more than just a bad guy, don't you, Javon?"

Javon didn't answer. He waved an arm dismissively, then curled up on the bed. Shortly after, he was snoring again.

"I guess that means yes," Darius said to his sleeping friend. He hadn't thought of Javon before as a friend. Now he did.

Day Two of the mission promised to be a higher mountain to climb than Day One. Darius needed rest. He closed his eyes and emptied himself of all thoughts. A feeling of ecstatic serenity welled up inside him. In seconds, he was fast asleep.

Chapter Twenty-Four

SUNBEAMS WITH GOSSAMER WINGS

THE SEMINAR ROOM turned out to be a dimly lit theater shaped in a semi-circle. Soothing images of beaches and Art-Deco hotels and motels appeared on the white wall that served as a screen in the front of the room. The images swam through a small slot, Darius noted, in the center of the back wall just above him. Sound absorbing acoustical carpet on the walls gave the room a cozy, secure feeling.

Javon sat next to him cautiously surveying everything and everyone in the room.

"I don't think the Exiles will be joining us," Darius assured Javon. "The sight of security guards in this small a space would make people feel uneasy."

Darius watched Patricia Fitzwalter enter the room from a door on the left. Patricia wrung her wrists and cleared her throat.

"Let's try to get everyone seated," she asked the crowd in her nasal voice. The back rows quickly filled with eager audience members.

Simon and Vicky entered the room. Darius had called Vicky first thing that morning from the motel. He was delighted to learn she and Simon were already planning to attend the seminar. It saved him the trouble of convincing them to come when he was not entirely sure why he was here himself. He was operating purely on intuitional prompts that grew stronger by the hour. His inner GPS told him he needed to gather as much information as he possibly could about Plezenthol before doing whatever was required to stop the drug from going on the market. At least his team would be together. Everything else was up for grabs. He waved to Vicky and Simon and pointed to the seats he had saved for them.

"Our presentation is about to begin," Patricia Fitzwalter said in a whining voice. "Please enjoy the program and don't forget to complete our short questionnaire on your way out." She smiled thinly before exiting the room with her narrow shoulders square and sharp chin held high.

Simon and Vicky took seats next to Darius. He shook their hands. Javon peered at the reporter and the scientist warily from the seat on the other side from Darius.

The lights dimmed to darkness. The video portion of the program began. The same friendly spokesperson who appeared in the press conference video strolled through a research laboratory. He looked and sounded to Darius like the ageless announcer Hugh Downs who had recently died like many of his famous contemporaries.

"It is estimated that ninety-nine percent of us are under-achievers," The narrator said. "The reasons for this are as varied as the differences between human beings. The demands of daily survival have made the goal of self-discovery a necessity rather than a luxury. Self-actualization is no easy task, but today, remarkable advances in the fields of Pharmacology, Nanotechnology, and Psychology have made the realization of human potential a more accessible and achievable goal for everyone. You can spend thousands of dollars to change your outer appearance. But if you remain the same old you underneath, your chances for happiness in life will remain as limited as your ideas of who you are and what your potential is..."

A small flicker of light above a woman to the right of Darius caught his attention. He watched it glide lazily through the air like a butterfly, then gather momentum and disappear through the projection slot above his head. Then another swirling sunbeam burst from the head of a young man seated farther to the right in the second row. The young man sank slightly in his chair, like a tire that had just lost some air.

Darius watched the same thing happen to an old woman in the third row. Then it happened to a young woman right in front of him. Soon after, tiny glimmering lights were bursting out of more and more people in the audience. The sunbeams moved like a swarm of lightning bugs towards the back of the room. The lights then abruptly swooshed out of sight through the projection slot in the back wall.

"This is cruel beyond words," Darius said in a barely audible tone to Simon who sat next to him.

Simon turned to Darius with a perplexed expression. "What do you mean?"

"It wouldn't make sense if I told you," Darius said. "I'm not even a hundred percent sure of what's happening myself."

"It's a promotional film," Simon said with a pained expression. "What's the mystery?"

"Can't you see the light coming out of those people?"

"What are you talking about?"

"I must be tuned to a different wavelength than you and everyone else in the room. I guess that makes sense. I'm an angel, after all."

"You aren't making sense," Simon whispered.

"I'm seeing something you can't. I have a very bad feeling about it. We have to find the projection room. I need all of you to come with me."

"Are you sure?" Simon asked.

"Yes," Darius said. At least he felt sure of himself, despite not knowing the reason why. Intuition was like that. Fortunately, his kept getting stronger.

"...In addition to priceless, life enhancing benefits, you can earn ten thousand dollars if you qualify for a three-month test program available in your area," the narrator continued.

One by one, they slipped out of the back row through the exit door and out into a hallway. Darius led Simon and the others along the corridor wall behind the theater. He motioned for them to stop next to a door marked "Projection Room." He heard a low, electronic hum coming from inside the room.

He tried the door. The darn thing would not budge. He focused his mental energy on the doorknob. The simple locking mechanism opened easily in response to the kinetic energy Darius applied. If there were Exiles inside, would they react to an intrusion with force and risk disturbing the audience members on the other side of the wall? Darius didn't think so. He opened the door and held his breath.

The electronic hum became louder. He listened more carefully. A subtle, intermittent clicking sound accompanied the low hum. Darius turned to the others. "Wait here 'til I see what's inside."

With his heart in his mouth, Darius entered the projection room. It was pitch black. The only signs of life were the mechanical humming and clicking sounds. The faint light of the computer projector in the center of the room provided insufficient illumination. Darius waved his arms in front of him like a drowning swimmer in search of the nearest wall and a light switch. His hand struck a cold, metallic object. The object fell to the floor with a dull thud. The humming and clicking sounds stopped. Thank heaven for thick carpeting, Darius thought, grateful not to have made a ruckus.

Darius managed to find a light switch in the darkened room. He flipped it on, half expecting to find several Exiles frozen in place waiting for the first opportunity to bash his brains out with their bare hands.

With an audible sigh of relief, Darius saw the room was empty of monsters, or monsters disguised as humans, or even real humans. Simon appeared at the door. His scientific curiosity had gotten the better of him, Darius assumed. Vicky and Javon followed Simon into the room. Darius motioned for Javon to close the door behind him. There was no sense in broadcasting their presence here.

The object Darius had knocked over lay on its side on the floor next to the projector. It was nearly six feet long, Darius judged, and oblong, reminding him of the body of a praying mantis or some similar, giant insect. A tripod of three spindly legs extended from one end. The other end tapered to what looked like a short, reed-like neck, then bulged out into a bullet shaped head about two feet long.

Darius bent down for a closer inspection. The object was as black as a starless night with the sheen of a polished gem, similar to a cat's eye or black pearl. He touched it with a forefinger. The object was cold as ice.

"Don't do that," Simon called out. "It might be dangerous."

Darius ignored the warning. Gingerly, he picked up the object and stood it upright on its three legs. Immediately, the humming and clicking sounds started up. The dead, black cylinder had suddenly come back to life. Darius jumped backward away from it.

The lights went out in the room.

Darius began to summon light energy to fight off the Exiles he was sure would come pouring into the room any second from now. It was likely to be a losing battle.

Instead of Exiles, light beams fluttered into the room through the square opening in the wall. It seemed like the humming sound drew the lights to the stick figure-like machine like the dulcet tones of a seductive pied piper. Darius observed the light beams flickered out one by one in the center of the room like lightening bugs devoured by a carnivorous plant.

The lights in the room winked back on. They were alone in the room with the humming machine.

"Guess I knocked the lights off by accident," Javon said in an indifferent tone with his finger still on the switch.

Darius figured the machine had scared Javon to death when it turned back on. He would never say that out-loud in front of Vicky and Simon. Javon had admitted to Darius he had feelings, and was indeed, a human being. Even though the teenager was half-asleep when it happened, Darius considered their brief exchange a watershed event. He would not do anything to betray Javon's confidence.

Simon walked up to the slender machine and examined it closely. "It appears to be some sort of collection device," he said.

Vicky joined the two of them by the machine. She pulled a digital camera from her handbag and began clicking pictures.

It all suddenly made horrible sense to Darius.

"The Exiles are stealing light energy from humans and storing it inside this machine."

"Why would they do that?" Simon asked.

"Good question," Darius replied. "It must be part of the Exile plan to weaken human consciousness, and probably something else. I wish I knew what the 'else' is."

"What do you mean by stealing light?" Vicky asked.

"I mean they are siphoning off positive energy, the foundation of what we experience as creativity, wisdom, and positive emotion."

"That sounds like a pretty tall statement."

"Light energy exists," Darius said to Vicky, "even though the most sophisticated instruments aren't able to measure it. Light is at the core of everything we see, hear, feel, touch, and smell. The physical world is only a thin layer of a much deeper reality."

Simon stared in deep thought at the spindly machine in front of them. "I'm obviously very familiar with psychology and the latest research on human consciousness as a result of my work. The thing that fascinates me about this machine is that it seems to be capable of capturing the essence of awareness. I'd love to take this thing back to the lab with me."

Simon pointed to the top end of the machine that swelled into a wider cylinder like some sort of head on top of a torso. "There's some sort of trigger or valve on the side there. You see?"

Before anyone had a chance to see what Simon was talking about, footsteps sounded from the corridor outside. Darius searched the room for another doorway, a closet to hide in, maybe an empty air-conditioning duct to crawl through.

Nothing. Nowhere to go. The room was barren except for a notebook computer hooked up to a projector and the alien machine to keep it company.

A German shepherd guard dog stuck its head in the door. It growled, baring rows of sharp teeth. Wild fury poured from its coal black eyes. Vicky and Simon eased their way behind Darius. Then Vicky dropped her camera. The sudden movement sent the beast into a fit. The dog strained against its sturdy leather leash forcing a set of powerful shoulders and half of a rippling flank into the room.

Darius fixed on the glass ball hanging from the dog's collar. He pointed his right arm at the animal and released a stream of low voltage light energy. The X-ray effect revealed a hellhound hiding behind the disguise of a police dog. Bony plates covered the hellhound's body forming a grotesque suit of protective armor. The creature growled. The animal's teeth reminded Darius of a picture he had once seen—an artist's rendition of an ancient wolf with foot-long teeth.

Two men in tailored suits entered the room behind the hellhound. One of them controlled the beast with a leash made out of a mesh of leather and chain links. Darius had no doubt the two men were Exiles in disguise.

The Exiles and their hound circled them. Vicky held on to Darius tightly. Simon stood right behind her.

The Exile handler removed the leash from around the hound's neck. The creature circled Darius, sizing him up, ready to attack. Then, he heard a familiar, strident voice from behind.

"I'm goin' straight back into the theater and tell all the people about you assholes."

Darius spun around. Javon loomed in the doorway, skinny arms and legs spread-eagled like a scarecrow. A second later, the doorway was empty.

"I'm already gone," Javon taunted from somewhere down the corridor.

The hound rushed Darius and leaped with open jaws at his head.

Darius closed his eyes. In a second, the creature would tear his head off. He stood there with his eyes closed and his heart pounding.

Nothing happened.

He opened his eyes.

The hellhound had leapt over him to reach the doorway. It crashed into the wall, shook itself after rising from the floor, and scampered into the corridor after Javon.

The two Exiles ran past Darius out of the room.

Chapter Twenty-Five

GUEST SPEAKER

JAVON BURST INTO the theater. Patricia Fitzwalter stood in front of the audience, beaming with manufactured joy. "For those who want more information about The New You test program, please remain in your seats and a representative will stop by."

He hesitated for a moment. The meeting in the theater was in full swing. "The hell with it," he muttered to himself before running right by the old hag before she had a chance to say another word. Then he realized the entrance to the theater was down the hall on the opposite end from the projection room. If he tried to leave the theater, the security guards and their mutt would be on him. He figured they were Exiles in disguise. The monsters would drag him politely out of the room, kicking and screaming, to some dark and silent place where no human eyes could see the horrible things they did to him. Sweat trickled from his armpits and bloomed in pools on the outside of his neatly pressed, light gray sports jacket.

Patricia Fitzwalter's face screwed into a knot. "What exactly are you doing here?" she sputtered in Javon's direction.

Where was Darius? He needed some slide time. No. He needed to step up and improvise.

Javon sidled up to Patricia Fitzwalter, extending a friendly hand. "Didn't they tell you, Ms. Fitzwalter? I'm one of the people whose been benefitting from your wonderful program. I'm here to tell these fine people about the amazing changes I've been goin' through."

Patricia took Javon's hand limply. One of her eyelids began to twitch.

"Are you sure you're in the right place?"

"Oh definitely," Javon crooned.

"Well then...why don't you...just go right ahead," Patricia said. "I'll just fire the person who forgot to tell me you were on the program."

The audience laughed at her joke which wasn't really a joke.

Patricia yielded the floor to Javon. She was on her smart phone before taking a seat in the front row.

Javon smiled broadly at the audience. They looked at him, droopy-eyed and slack-jawed, as if the gathering had turned into a high-grade heroin party. They looked about as interested in self-improvement as he was. But the show had to go on.

"This may sound a little goofy," Javon began, "but the truth is... since I stopped takin' street drugs an' started dropping Plezenthol an' listening to the self-improvement tapes, I feel like I just found God in a bottle."

Javon noticed Patricia Fitzwalter straighten in her seat. She looked like someone had just pumped three thousand volts of electricity into her body. Her face twisted into a death mask. She dropped her phone on the floor.

Javon was just starting to get warmed up.

"Now it might be hard to believe someone who looks as together as me was all messed up in his mind and his body, but I'm standin' here to tell ya'll that I really and truly was."

A German shepherd guard dog pulled two men in tailored suits into the theater. The muscles in the pit of Javon's stomach twitched.

Patricia Fitzwalter rose from her seat. "I think we've unfortunately over-stayed our allotted time," she said, looking at her watch. "There's another group scheduled to come in at any moment." She smiled sweetly to the two security men. "Can you help us out here?"

The monsters-in-disguise were more than happy to oblige, Javon could tell. They rambled towards him. Their eyes were aflame with the same wild fury he had witnessed in the blows the Exile had landed on the Bentley's windshield only yesterday.

"I just remembered I got a group therapy meeting to go to." Javon announced to the audience. "It's been real. See ya'll."

He walked away from the oncoming Exiles. He planned to lure his pursuers away from the single door entrance—then double back and make a break for it before they could respond. It wasn't exactly a brilliant idea, only the best he could come up with on painfully short notice

"Get him out of here," Javon overheard Patricia whisper loudly to the guards. Did she know they were monsters? One of the guards split off to block the only way out. Javon froze. He was out of options. The situation was beyond desperate. There was only one thing left to do. He had not tried anything like it since his abbreviated childhood days.

Javon gulped down a mouthful of oxygen. He began to pray for help to the nearest benevolent being or force that might be listening.

Chapter Twenty-Six

THE DANCE OF LIFE

TO **HIS MASSIVE** relief and utter astonishment, an answer came to Javon's hastily uttered, barely audible cry for help.

A section of the far wall opened. Daylight streamed into the theater from another section of the Tarpon Springs room.

"The room is being prepared for the next event," Patricia said jovially to the audience members. "Please gather your things and be on your way. Thank you for coming. We'll be in touch with those of you who have expressed an interest in the New You program."

The audience began filtering out of the room. Javon regretted stuffing himself on the free food during the reception prior to the video portion of the event. The next time he found himself in a dangerous situation, he resolved never to over eat again.

He was getting ahead of himself. The first order of business was to make sure a next time came.

Javon sprinted past the startled audience members into the open end of the room.

There was no one in the former reception room except a man in a maintenance outfit watching the dividing wall retract itself automatically. Javon rocketed past the man like an Apollo space capsule on its way to the moon. He turned his head to see if anyone was following him. A half-second later, he crashed into the food table. The force of the collision knocked Javon's legs out from under him. He collapsed in a heap on the floor. Bite size roast beef and turkey sandwiches decorated his new suit.

He crawled out of sight underneath the skirt of the food table. His left thigh was throbbing. He reached down to feel for broken bones. It hurt like hell. After a cursory examination, he determined the pain came from a bruise about the size of Kansas somewhere south of his knee. The good news was he had no broken bones. The trick, of course, was to keep his legs and the rest of himself in the same condition until he could make the guards lose track of him.

Javon picked up a corner of the silvery fabric. The skirting probably cost more than his suit. Why did he have to be born poor? Poverty had led to all of his troubles. Ironically, hustling the mean streets of Opa-Locka seemed like paradise in comparison to his current predicament. He promised himself never to take anything for granted again—especially the luxury of breathing without the fear of certain and immediate death staring him smack in the face.

The guard dog scrabbled into the expanded room followed by the two security men. With its snout to the floor, the leashed animal pulled the men straight towards the food table. The small glass ball the animal wore on a chain around its neck dragged on the carpeted floor. Javon wondered what the dog really looked like. Then he decided it was better not to know.

He lay there quivering as one of the guards opened his suit jacket revealing an elaborate leather holster. The holster bore a series of interconnected triangles embossed in the leather. It occurred to Javon the intricate artisanship was an indication of the high regard the Exiles held for their weapons. He had seen what those weapons did to inanimate objects like doors and concrete dividing walls. He had no desire to discover what they did to flesh and bone.

The dog eagerly dragged its Exile handler closer and closer. The pseudo-guards were only about ten feet away. Javon figured the Exiles would not start shooting until the last of the audience members left the theater. It was time to make his move, or forever rest in peace.

Javon jumped up from under the table. He grabbed one of the trusty elastic bands he always wore for emergencies on his wrists. He stretched the band wide and fired it at the dog. The elastic projectile slapped into the animal's nose. The dog wailed.

With the dog and its handler momentarily distracted, Javon joined the tail end of the line of audience members stumbling in a daze towards the exit elevators.

"What's wrong with you?" he asked a young woman in a black business suit and ponytail who looked like she hadn't slept in a week.

"I've got to get off coffee," she replied with a yawn. "It's just killing me."

Whatever her problem was, it looked to be more than too much coffee. Someone or something grabbed him by the arm. Javon whirled, ready to throw a sucker-punch, but the guard caught his arm and twisted it. The dude was as strong as Superman. Javon tried to wrestle free as the guard dragged him back to the food table in the middle of the room where the other guard and the dog waited.

The last of the audience members trickled by without showing the slightest concern for Javon's plight. They looked and acted like zombies. What was up with that?

The Exile guard threw him to the ground and kicked him hard in the ribs. Javon figured it was standard monster operating procedure for ornery prisoners. Or maybe they just had bad tempers. Whatever the reason, Javon had the opening he needed. These dudes had no idea just how tough he was. One little kick in the ribs was not gonna' keep Javon Quincey down for long.

He pushed up from the floor, twirled in the air, and took off for the elevators. One of them was just opening up. Only a few hundred yards and he would be home free. Then a thought struck him: *What about the others?* Then another thought: *Why worry about them?* Well, for one thing, he was dead meat without Darius. Habit made it hard to wrap his mind around the idea that his survival depended on another person or persons. And there was the other side of the coin— maybe the others were depending on him!

Javon jerked around in a small semi-circle.

The elevator closed behind him.

He was alone in the room with the two Exiles and their guard-dog-monstrosity.

The Exile handler turned to his companion. The other one drew one of those weird pistols. Javon bolted in the general direction of the theater, pausing only to cartwheel three times, roll on the floor, pirouette in the air, and otherwise try to convince the Exiles he was too fast and too much trouble to catch or shoot. His strategy seemed to be working perfectly, until he started to run out of breath.

Javon devoutly wished he had spent less of his precious youth in a single-minded quest to pickle his bodily organs in poisonous substances. His breath came in short, rasping gasps.

His head felt woozy thanks to the alcohol, weed, and other mind-altering substances he had used to escape the mean streets of his harsh reality. His legs wobbled. His arms felt like lead.

Javon stopped dancing. He decided he was not about to die jerking around like a puppet on strings.

"YOU GOT NOTHIN'," he screamed at the Exiles. "I AIN'T AFRAID OF YOU." The tuning fork gismo the guard without the dog held in his hand ceased bobbing back and forth. Now it was aimed squarely at his heart. He thought of zigzagging his way over to the dude, grabbing it with a shake-and-bake move, and then blowing the two shit-heads and their mutt into space dust.

What a dumb-ass idea. He was getting desperate if the best plan he could come up with had a ninety-nine percent chance of turning him into a super-sized French fry.

He grabbed another elastic band from his wrist and fired it at the Exile holding the gun. The elastic band bounced off the dude's cheek leaving a red mark.

"Ouch," said the guard, rubbing his wounded cheek. The two Exiles and their dog closed on him. Javon gaped at the weird pistol aimed at his head and the snarling face of the pissed-off guard dog.

Then Javon spotted a lectern in a corner of the room where Patricia Fitzwalter had addressed the crowd at the reception prior to the video presentation in the theater. He made a run for it. Skidding behind the lectern, he screamed into the microphone. "SOMEBODY HELP ME."

The lectern splintered into nothingness at the same time Javon bolted for greener pastures.

Patricia Fitzwalter stormed into the room followed by Darius, Vicky and Simon.

Javon pointed to the two Exiles standing awkwardly in the center of the room. The Exile shooter had quickly holstered the tuning-fork-pistol-thing at the first inkling of human presence. The dog knelt beside its Exile masters—a picture of obedience.

"THEY TRYIN' TO KILL ME," Javon shouted across the room to Patricia Fitzwalter.

Patricia's face crumpled. "What on Earth is going on out here," she demanded of the security men. They continued to stand uncomfortably. Neither one of them said a word.

· · ·

Darius stepped forward. It had taken several minutes to calm Vicky and Simon down in the projection room after the hellhound incident. Now, here they were in this mess. His father had encouraged him from early childhood to tell the truth regardless of the consequences.

He was about to once again break this deeply ingrained habit into smithereens.

"I'm the boy's legal guardian," Darius called to Patricia Fitzwalter. He moved with long strides towards Patricia who was shaking like a palsy victim. Darius felt waves of panic streaming from the woman. With the seminar turning into a sideshow, Patricia Fitzwalter looked like she was going to blow as high as Mount St. Helens any second.

Darius placed a calming hand on Patricia's shoulder. She jumped as if jolted by an electric shock. Then she smiled in an odd manner as the healing energy Darius released worked its way through Patricia's tense body.

"Javon had a very difficult childhood," Darius said to Patricia in a soothing tone. "He suffers from hallucinations resulting from illegal drug-taking. I believe they call them flashbacks."

Darius waited for a response from Patricia. None came. Something had caught her eye. Darius followed her gaze to the center of the room. There he saw what had captured the woman's attention: the splintered remains of the lectern.

Patricia pointed a quivering finger at the smoking pieces of wood scattered like leaves on the expensive woven carpet. "Someone had better have a good explanation for that." She turned to the two security men with pleading eyes.

"Those two are monsters who look like people," Javon said, pointing to the guards. "Take a look at their guns if you don't believe me."

Patricia turned to Darius. "I'm going to call the police and have your ward locked up."

The thought of having Javon as a ward was about as revolting as Patricia calling the police.

"Like I said before, the boy suffers from residual drug reactions which sometimes border on psychotic episodes," Darius said. "I've been through this before with him. Just let my friends and I leave quietly. I promise Javon won't cause any more trouble."

Patricia pondered the proposal for several long seconds. "I suppose you have some sort of mental health training?" she demanded more than asked.

"I have a Master's Degree in Social Work," Darius lied.

"If I get word of one more incident involving that boy, I'm calling the police," Patricia said. "Now get out of here. All of you."

She turned to the guards. "What happened to the lectern?"

"The boy blew it up with a cherry bomb," one of the guards answered.

The dog barked, as if in agreement.

"Clean up that mess," Patricia barked in response. "And get your animal out of here. The last thing I need is that creature pooping all over the carpet."

Chapter Twenty-Seven

CONTROL ISSUES

THEY STOOD IN a group at the top of a steep bank of granite steps. Hotel guests of every conceivable nationality gushed in and out of the brass and glass doors of the Conrad Hilton's front entrance.

"We have to set up a meeting with your boss right away," Darius said. "Simon, snap out of it. I'm talking to you."

Darius sensed his companions had been preoccupied with their own thoughts while walking through the lobby, either in shock, or in an effort to reconcile themselves to their new circumstances. Even Javon had been unusually quiet. Darius had been on high alert for any signs of Exiles-in-disguise lurking in the shadows. He had not seen any suspicious-looking characters following or watching them, which made no sense.

"What's your purpose in meeting with Hiram?" Simon wanted to know.

"To convince him not to put Plezenthol on the market," Darius replied.

Simon broke into a laugh which sounded somewhere between panicked and hysterical. "Hiram Fyrum would rather jump from his penthouse balcony without a parachute than agree to something like that. Besides, I've already tried."

"You went to mister Fyrum on your own?"

Simon's shoulders sagged. "I went against my own advice and made things worse."

"I understand, Simon. You've witnessed terrible events and learned some awful truths about Plezenthol. You over-reacted. That's history. Now, if we work together, I think we can win Hiram over to our side."

"I can't imagine how," Simon said bitterly.

"I can put on a demonstration the likes of which Hiram's never seen. I gave you a sample in the car on the ride over to Amcor."

Simon frowned. He pushed his glasses higher on his long, straight nose. "I'm fairly certain Hiram won't be taking any of my calls for the foreseeable future."

"Really?"

Simon nodded morosely.

Darius squared his shoulders and held his chin in a contemplative pose. He inhaled deeply. "All right. We'll have to find a safe place to stay and figure out what to do next."

"Together?" Vicky said.

"We can all stay in the Lab," Simon said. "There are cots and showers and separate cubicles for privacy. My staff and I are used to working late. The walls contain two feet of solid steel for extra security. I can lock us in."

Javon made a sour face.

"It's a safe house, not a jail," Darius said, patting Javon on the shoulder. He turned to the others. "It's settled, then. We're off to Simon's lab."

• • •

The old woman saw the stunning ring on the security guard's finger. She stopped abruptly in a partially hidden alcove of the lobby designed for resting or impromptu meetings. She had never seen an onyx stone in such a peculiar shape. The opposing triangle design was positively arresting—a real trompe l'oeil, as the French liked to say.

She walked over to a rather handsome guard standing at an oblique angle from her in the alcove.

"Excuse me young man," the old woman said cheerfully. "I couldn't help admiring that ring of yours. Would you mind telling me who the designer is?"

The guard, who was staring intently through a wall-to-ceiling plate glass window overlooking the street, whipped around to face her, scaring her half to death. She managed to recover from the shock and smiled sweetly.

"My husband owns jewelry boutiques," she went on to explain. "We've bought and sold jewelry all over the world and I have to say, I've never seen a stone in that shape before. It's really quite beautiful."

Flattery of this sort always brought a torrent of useful information, she knew from long experience.

The handsome young man continued to stare back at her in stony silence. She wondered if the robust young man had a hearing problem. He finally spoke.

"My ring is none of your business. Please go away."

The insensitive reply stunned the woman all the way down to the soles of her biometric walking shoes. She had a good mind to report the impudent young man to his supervisor. Such rudeness would no doubt earn a harsh reprimand in these times of scarce jobs and high job performance expectations.

"I'd learn some manners if I were you," said the woman.

"I'm very busy at the moment," the guard said without even a grace note of apology in his voice. "Move along."

She lost no time in walking away and resolving to find the hotel manager's office. Glancing back over her shoulder, she almost shouted to the rude guard that he didn't look very busy when, what she saw, stopped the words from coming out of her mouth. Holding his hand up close to the window, the guard squeezed both sides of the ring. She thought it looked like he was pulling some sort of a trigger.

. . .

"We'll wait for you in front of the Mamongen Building," Darius called to Vicky and Simon through the open window of the powder blue Sebring convertible.

Vicky waved to Darius in confirmation. Darius buckled his seat belt in preparation for the roller coaster ride he knew lay ahead of him, courtesy of his faithful chauffeur. He turned to Javon. "Did you hear that?"

"Hear what?" Javon replied.

"A beeping sound."

"The monsters got you spooked. I don't hear nothin'."

Darius listened. He heard nothing but the familiar sounds of the engine idling and the air-conditioning blowing. Maybe Javon was right. Cars made plenty of weird noises these days with all the electronics the manufacturing companies loaded into them. They drove off into the teeming mid-day traffic.

...

"Where's your car," Vicky asked.

Simon fidgeted. "I don't own one."

"I know. You don't want to contribute to global warming. Right?"

"Not exactly. I spend a lot of time going through chemical equations in my head. I have a tendency to ignore traffic signs and other cars."

Vicky laughed. It just came out before she could do anything about it. Simon smiled awkwardly.

"I'm not laughing at you, Simon. Really, I'm not."

"It's all right. Everyone laughs at me. Everyone always has. Why should you be any different?"

Vicky took Simon's hand and squeezed it. "We can take my car."

A valet pulled Vicky's emerald green BMW coup up to the curb. Simon tipped the valet before Vicky could fish a dollar out of her wallet.

Inside the car, with Simon safely buckled up, Vicky gunned the engine. "I like being in control. I'm happy to drive."

It was the first time they shared a laugh, and Vicky enjoyed it immensely. The BMW roared into traffic.

. . .

Darius checked the speedometer. For some reason, Javon had been driving at a reasonable speed since leaving the Hilton.

"You're only ten miles over the speed limit and you haven't changed lanes once. What's the matter with you?"

"This car ain't handling right."

"How can you tell?"

"I can feel it. I'm an expert. Remember?"

Javon slowed the car and drove to a stop on the shoulder of the road. Within minutes, he was investigating the underside of the car with his skinny legs sticking out from beneath the chassis.

"Goddamn...what the hell is that," the teenager exclaimed, loud enough for Darius to hear.

Darius stood by the passenger door nervously scanning the cars whizzing by on the highway. He was prepared with a friendly smile and a phony story in case a State Trooper rolled up.

Darius crouched next to Javon. "What's the problem?"

Javon shimmied out from underneath the car. He stood and meticulously dusted off his new suit pants. "There's some kinda' weird doohickey on the axle," he said.

Darius tore off his suit jacket and practically dove underneath the car. The yellow blinking light on the ominous looking device caught his attention immediately. The shape resembled a series of octahedrons stuck end to end. Darius watched an oscillating yellow line jump from one section to the next. The process kept repeating from one end of the device to the other. He sensed the device was communicating electronically with a control device, presumably in Exile hands. If it was a bomb, there was no time to lose. Darius grabbed the device with one hand and pulled hard.

The device stuck to the axle as if it was factory installed. The thing felt warm in his hand. He grabbed it with both hands now and pulled with all his might. A clamp sprung loose. It smacked into the side of his head, just missing the eye socket. He winced in pain—and felt the device loosen on the axle.

Darius twisted the thing some more. He pulled harder. Another clamp sprung free, bounced off the concrete shoulder of the highway. The mysterious object seemed to die in his hand the minute he freed it from the axle. Darius struggled out from under the car. He hurled the alien device into a runoff canal running parallel to the interstate.

"We have to catch up with Vicky and Simon," Darius told Javon. "There isn't a moment to lose."

. . .

"Every muscle in my body freezes when I have to look at those creatures," Vicky said.

"I'm sorry," Simon said. "All of this is my fault."

"You can't possibly be responsible for those monsters,"

"Somehow I brought them here by developing Plezenthol."

"You didn't falsify the test results. Don't overthink it. We just have to get on with...whatever it is we have to get on with."

Vicky glanced at her passenger slouched in the bucket seat beside her. Simon looked deeply troubled.

"We have cars and airplanes to get us to our destinations faster," he said in a low voice. "We invented the Internet for instant worldwide communication. Cell phones to make sure we stay in touch every moment. We have pills for accelerated weight loss and better sex." He paused, then blurted: "why was it so terrible to make a pill to help people find a little more happiness in life?"

"Calm down, Simon."

"You know why people only use ten percent of their brain capacity?"

"Stop shouting."

"Because they're too ignorant, lazy and scared to use the other ninety percent."

"You're hyper-ventilating."

"Well, guess what?" Simon babbled. The man refused to be consoled. Vicky gripped the steering wheel, waiting for what came next.

"When it comes to higher awareness, there is no elevator. You have to take the stairs!"

She gave that last comment a moment to breathe.

"Do you feel better now?"

At first, Simon didn't respond. Then he said, "Yes."

"You're out of your lane," he went on to observe dryly, his emotions apparently spent in the tirade.

The car was suddenly difficult to control. The steering system felt to Vicky like it had suddenly come down with Parkinson's disease. "There's something very wrong with the car," she said, struggling against a steering wheel that had a mind of its own.

• • •

The blue Sebring swerved from lane to lane on the expressway. Javon had lowered the convertible top for greater visibility. Darius and Javon craned their heads, desperately searching for a green BMW sports coupe.

"How we gonna' find those two in all this traffic," Javon shouted against the swooshing air rushing over the windshield.

Javon had a point. What was he thinking? Providence was not going to send the green BMW his way just because he was trying so hard. He had to think of a better, faster method of finding Vicky and Simon.

Darius closed his eyes and concentrated. He imagined a circle spreading out in all directions from a single point in the center of his forehead. He began to hear conversations. A couple argued about where to eat dinner. He heard more voices, music, static, someone singing—a rising cacophony of sounds as his awareness expanded. It became deafening, overwhelming.

Opening his eyes, Darius let his mind go blank. He was alone again, with only his own thoughts and the sights and sounds around him to process. He felt a momentary sense of relief before returning to the knotty problem of locating Vicky and Simon telepathically without blowing his mental circuits in a universe of extraneous noise.

It occurred to Darius that he had tuned into Vicky's thoughts yesterday in the lobby of the Mamongen Building while projecting his voice telepathically. He had Vicky's thought frequency stored in his memory somewhere. Every person had a unique thought frequency. Darius had learned that much in class. Every thought frequency was as individual as a fingerprint. Theoretically, he should be able to tune into Vicky's frequency just like tuning into a radio station. Darius closed his eyes again and concentrated.

Darius pictured himself in the lobby projecting his voice into Vicky's mind. The moment in time appeared to him with crystal clarity. He re-lived the event in his mind as if it were happening for the first time. With a tiny part of his mind locked on the memory, Darius sent his awareness outward again in an expanding circle. There was no interference this time from other thought frequencies. There was instead a sublime stillness. It was sweet, joyful, a complete respite from the turmoil Darius had experienced pretty much non-stop since his summons to the emergency meeting in heaven where all of this had begun. Then Darius flinched. The sudden movement spooked Javon.

"Whas' up?"

Darius was too busy concentrating to answer Javon. The stillness he had experienced for a few, short, blissful moments was shattered when Darius connected with the jumbled, frightened mind of Vicky Matthews.

Chapter Twenty-Eight

THREE HANDS ON THE WHEEL

VICKY JUMPED WHEN she heard the voice. She barely avoided smacking into the car speeding alongside in the next lane. She was having enough trouble wrestling the car over to the break-down lane without hearing someone else's voice in her head.

She struggled with the steering wheel. Simon leaned over. He grasped the wheel with his left hand.

Despite three hands struggling to control the stubborn steering wheel, Vicky was close to losing control of the car. A horn blared behind them.

You must get out of your car right away, the voice in her head insisted for the second time.

"No kidding," Vicky said. She checked the rearview mirror. A black Mercedes sedan had pushed up on her tail.

"Watch out," Simon yelled, as a car in the next lane swerved to avoid the fishtailing BMW.

It's Darius, the voice in her head said.

"Where are you?" Vicky said.

"Who are you talking to?"

Vicky was too preoccupied to answer Simon. The steering wheel was trying to push them back into traffic—and it was succeeding. There was only one thing left to do. She tromped on the brakes.

The black Mercedes smashed into the BMW's rear end. Horns blared and then Vicky heard another *crunch*. A third car had plowed into the back end of the Mercedes. She felt sorry for the third driver. The tailgater could go to hell.

Vicky helped Simon maneuver his lanky body over the console out onto the side of the road closest to the shoulder. They scampered over one lane to the breakdown lane. Passengers were beginning to emerge from the other two cars.

Wait right there. We're coming. She was amazed Darius was able to communicate with her telepathically without being anywhere in sight.

Vicky observed one of the accident victims reach into his Dodge Charger. He pulled out a six-pack of Miller Lite, walked over to the embankment, and calmly dropped the beer into the ditch. Everyone knew the Florida Highway Patrol would be arriving on the scene any minute. She imagined herself explaining the accident to one of the officers. *Well, I was driving along when my car stopped responding. That was just before it attacked me.* Something along those lines would earn them an immediate Breathalyzer test closely followed by an arrest for reckless driving.

Vicky went back to the car to collect her handbag and laptop. She liked to call her handbag a "mobile office" with all the stuff she kept in it. The pictures of the alien machine taken in the projection room would be extremely useful as background evidence for the incredible story she was almost ready to file. The story was the only thing she had to keep her grounded.

· · ·

Javon wove through traffic like the Formula One racing drivers Darius had witnessed during a summer trip through Europe. It was the summer he had decided to go to law school while sitting in quiet contemplation near a beautiful lake in the countryside of France. He was proud of Javon. Darius now realized what a vital member of the team the teenager had become. He also realized he had practiced only a fraction of what he had learned as a part-time youth counselor in his former life. He had judged Javon harshly without seeing the boy's potential. Fortunately, a byproduct of becoming an angel was the growing ability to view human nature from a broader perspective. Feelings of compassion were becoming a more common occurrence. *Was he beginning to appreciate his angelhood?*

The sight of cars slowing down in front of them dashed these high thoughts. Darius frowned.

"Not to worry," Javon said.

The teenager maneuvered the car into the breakdown lane.

Only one day ago, Darius would have had zero patience for the move Javon was about to make. Now he just shook his head and laughed.

The blue Sebring streaked along the breakdown lane, passing a multitude of stalled cars on the highway.

Darius kept a sharp eye peeled for any sign of Vicky's car. "Slow down," he said.

"You see them?"

"I hear them. Vicky's thoughts are coming through more clearly. They must be nearby."

Javon slowed the Sebring to a crawl.

"There they are," Darius said, pointing to the two figures standing on the side of the road. With their business suits and erect postures, Vicky and Simon contrasted sharply from the six casually dressed people leaning or standing near the three damaged cars joined in a crooked chain on the highway. Simon held his pinstriped suit jacket in one hand and had wrapped the other around Vicky's shoulder. She wore the same light blue blouse and conservative navy skirt outfit from the morning's activities at the "New You" seminar.

Javon eased the car to a stop. Darius jumped out. Simon saw him and waved.

"You made it," Vicky called out.

"Let's get out of here before the Highway Patrol shows up," Darius said.

"Amen to that," Javon agreed.

"We'll be cited and fined for leaving the scene of an accident," Simon said.

"Doesn't matter," Darius said.

"Amen again," Javon said.

Chapter Twenty-Nine

THE ABRIDGED EXILE ENCYCLOPEDIA

DARIUS AND THE others entered the Mamongen laboratory behind Simon. The company's research and development department occupied two entire floors. Here, on the sixth floor, the expensive business of combining chemicals to treat the ills of the world went on seven days a week. Mass spectrometers, microscopic scanners, measuring, assay, purification, and chemical combination devices of every size and description filled the room. The equipment lined ten aisles with enough space in between to allow lab-coated research teams room to maneuver.

Simon stood in the center of the room and clapped his hands to get the attention of the thirty odd technicians working deliberately at their tasks.

"I'm afraid we have to shut down early today," he announced.

The technicians looked up from their work, many of them with stunned expressions.

"It seems marketing scheduled a last-minute photo shoot for a publicity release. Naturally, we're the last ones to find out about it."

Darius watched the research technicians begin the meticulous process of closing down their workstations. Simon walked back to the three of them. "It will take them about a half hour to clean up," Simon whispered to Darius. "We'll have the run of the place after that."

Javon stood gawking at a bank of computer workstations.

"You're looking at about five million dollars-worth of equipment right there," Simon told him.

Vicky and Simon took seats at adjoining computer consoles.

Javon walked over to another console, ready to take a powerful imaging computer for a spin.

"Better not touch," Darius called to him. "I doubt they have any games stored on those machines."

"What we gonna' do for fun while we wait?"

"Maybe Darius can give us a better idea of what we're up against," Simon suggested.

Darius took a deep breath. He was no expert on the Exiles. The Archangel had provided a radically abridged version of Exile history during their briefing after the general assembly meeting. He had also spoken to a Director angel named Joshua to supplement the Archangel's overview before shipping off to Earth for the mission. After these briefings, he was only slightly more informed on the subject of Exiles than his eager audience. However, he wanted to share whatever he knew about the Exiles because then, he figured, they would be less afraid of them.

The Exiles, Darius explained, descended from a band of thirty-seven angels expelled from heaven for the high crime of willful misconduct. The severe punishment, it turned out, derived more from the nature of the misconduct rather than the willful aspect of the misdeed itself.

Before the human race emerged from the primordial ooze, angels of every rank had the attention and the affection of the Chief all to themselves. The trouble began when the Chief brought Mankind into the picture. Proud of his new creation, the Chief announced to the heavenly host that it would be their job to minister to the needs of human beings in their fumbling attempts to find the joy of heaven while living an Earthly life in a physical body.

Why the Chief would bother to set this game in motion struck the insubordinate angels as incomprehensible. The dissenting angels considered the creation of Mankind an act of pure folly. Why, they reasoned, turn an ignorant creature like Man loose in a world fraught with innumerable pitfalls, detours, blind alleys, wrong turns, and every other imaginable danger to chase after, of all things, the elusive goal of Self-realization? Obviously, the Chief, in his infinite creativity, had simply given birth to a very bad idea—on a grand scale.

The difference of opinion, however, did not contribute to the ultimate fate the dissenting angels suffered. What roused the Chief's righteous indignation happened to be something else entirely. While it is fair to say that the heavenly host in general found it difficult at first to adjust to the idea of competition for the Chief's attention, this gang of thirty-seven simply could not accept the idea. Their jealousy precipitated their undoing, to make a long story short.

Darius paused to take an emotional and intellectual inventory of his audience. Simon, Vicky and Javon stared at him with expressions and postures reflecting wonder, awe, and exhaustion. The events of the past two days had taken a lot out of them, Darius observed. They were like boxers sitting in their corners after eleven rounds of a twelve round fight.

Vicky asked the obvious question. "How did the angels become monsters?"

"Good Question." Darius was happy to provide the answer, and relieved to have covered the topic during his abbreviated angelic education. He continued to relate the story that had held him spellbound when he had first heard it from Joshua.

At first, the Chief threatened to transform the dissenters into humans with the most elemental level of consciousness—a total ignorance of their divine origin. Incredibly, the dissenters added the ugly trait of arrogance to their jealousy. Having enjoyed the exclusive attention and affection of the Chief from the beginning of time, the rebellious angels refused to take the Chief's threats seriously.

"Fascinating," Simon murmured.

"Dumb asses," Javon observed, and yawned.

"It's easy to judge with 20-20 hindsight," Darius said with a level stare in Javon's direction. "Anyway, the Chief decided to make an example of the dissenters."

Darius glanced at the electronic clock on the wall above his audience. The time reflected in the clock's twenty-four-hour readout startled him—twenty minutes past six PM. His allotted time on Earth was rapidly dwindling. He had to finish the story and wrap up the meeting. They all needed to rest up for day three, whatever it might bring.

"The Chief," Darius told his audience, "condemned the dissenters to live underground in monstrous bodies so that they would be unable to mix with humans and infect them with their wrong-headed ideas. He thought the punishment would teach the wayward angels a lesson, but He was wrong."

Darius paused, remembering what Joshua had said towards the end of their meeting. He passed the information on to his pupils. "I shouldn't say the Chief was wrong. The insubordinate angels simply refused to learn their lesson. No one can predict the future, not even the Chief. He gave us all free will. The Exiles have lived a miserable existence underground for more than seven thousand years because they have stubbornly chosen to stick to their warped way of thinking."

"That's the whole story?"

"The highly abridged version," Darius responded. "I can tell you have a slew of follow up questions, and I wish we had the time to answer them, but the priority now is to eat and get a good night's rest. We have one day left. Let's make it a good one for humanity."

Chapter Thirty

THE GOOD—THE BAD— AND THE MIND-BOGLING

THE ROOMS IN the dormitory section of the lab complex reminded Darius of the economy cabins aboard *The Celebration,* an ocean liner he had chosen for his honeymoon with Rebecca. He wondered if the pain of separation from her would ever go away. It was still hard to accept the idea that their honeymoon dreams of a lifetime spent together had vanished as quickly as the smoke from the gun that had extinguished his mortal existence.

Darius forced his wandering mind to concentrate on the problem at hand. How was he going to get an appointment to speak to Hiram Fyrum without Simon's assistance? If he somehow secured an appointment with Fyrum, what was he going to do to convince the strong-willed CEO to pull the plug on his prized billion-dollar Plezenthol project? Would nightmarish visions of the future be enough?

Javon snored loudly in the bunk bed above. The teenager stirred, pulling his covers up. Within seconds, he was sawing away again. Darius felt a sudden chill in the room. With a start, he noticed a gray mist rising out of the beige carpeting. His first thought was the room had caught fire. Then he realized there was no smell of smoke.

Darius sat up, bashing his head into a metal rib supporting the upper bunk. His head swam. He touched his bruised forehead. The mist congealed into what looked like a mass of potter's clay. The clay then modeled itself into shapes: a fierce leopard, a prehistoric pterodactyl bird, and an angry Minotaur. If the shapes were supposed to scare him, they were doing an excellent job of it. Then, he heard a voice.

"I am Glythren."

The mass of clay became a giant beetle before the voice spoke again. It sounded like rustling leaves.

"What sort of a being are you?" Darius managed to ask.

"I am a Warrior Lord."

Darius was now certain the apparition had not shown up for anything remotely resembling a polite conversation.

The voice quickly became irritating, scratching across Darius' eardrums.

"I am here to warn you against meeting with Hiram Fyrum tomorrow."

"Why is my business with Hiram Fyrum any concern of yours?"

Darius had been busy charging himself with light energy from the moment the apparition had identified itself as a Warrior Lord. He did not know if the vaporous clay cloud tumbling around in the air was capable of attacking him, but only a fool would underestimate the powers of a Warrior Lord.

The clay cloud changed into a beautiful white heron. The change in imagery from frightening to friendly surprised Darius.

"You cannot change the course of history with your limited experience and an army of three frightened mortals," the white heron said.

"My orders are to try," Darius replied.

"Did you know that the Exiles and your brothers and sisters in heaven are discussing a reconciliation?"

The statement rocked Darius with the force of a tidal wave. Why hadn't the Archangel mentioned anything to him about it? He steadied himself.

"Even if that were true, how does it affect what I'm here to do?"

"The Exiles believe that angels should inherit the Earth after the human race finally succeeds in destroying itself with this new drug.

We are discussing with your superiors the allocation of the Earth's land masses and seas to each of our sides

The sound of the Warrior Lord's voice had changed from rustling and scratching to something more akin to a gentle breeze caressing the tops of trees. Still, Darius found the content of Glythren's statement troubling, but he deliberately took the edge off his next remark to avoid a confrontation.

"How can you expect me to believe the word of someone who has been the sworn enemy of my superiors for centuries?"

The white Heron changed into a giant, laughing bullfrog.

"I wasn't trying to be funny," Darius said.

"I am laughing," the jolly bullfrog said, "because all of that has changed."

"In two days?"

"Yes."

"And my meeting with Hiram Fyrum will somehow upset the reconciliation talks you mentioned."

"Yes again," the bullfrog said with a sunny smile.

The idea, of course, sounded ridiculous, but there was a slight chance it was true. Perhaps the Exiles had created the "Big Emergency" to drive the Chief and the Board of Directors into accepting the Exiles back into heaven. In that case, Darius did not want to be responsible for derailing the peace talks. He had to find a way to connect with the Archangel…but how, with time so short?

Darius watched the bullfrog change into a multi-colored bird of Paradise. "I have to get in touch with my superiors to see what happens next," Darius said.

"Yes, do that," came the reply. "Don't do anything rash until you speak with them."

The bird of paradise dissolved into a cloud of clay which in turn dissipated into vapor. The vapor disappeared into the carpet, as if sucked down by an intake valve somewhere beneath the floor.

Darius sat in the darkness of the small room with only the sound of Javon's snoring to keep him company. He slumped down on the hard bunk. The strain of the last two days overwhelmed him. He slipped into a deep sleep. The golden necklace Darius wore moved up and down with his regular breathing. The circle inside the right-hand angle on the triangle's base glowed brightly. Darius turned on his side without awakening. Seconds later, Darius awakened in an unfamiliar setting.

Chapter Thirty-One

A FEW TIDBITS OF TRUTH

AT THE TOP of the Mamongen Building, the Archangel sat with his legs dangling over the ledge of Hiram Fyrum's penthouse backyard. He wore a broad smile along with his gray flannel suit and red tie emblazoned with a white cross. Darius sat next to the Archangel wondering why he had summoned the image of a hypocritical Evangelist to represent the dignified Archangel. It was probably because he felt betrayed by everything he believed in after the drive-by shooting. Disoriented and full of mistrust, Darius had subconsciously made the Archangel a symbol of corruption. Now, he wanted to change the image, but he wasn't sure which actor to choose. Then it came to him. Paul Newman was the man for the job.

Immediately, Burt Lancaster morphed into a middle-aged version of Mr. Newman without the sharp edges of the characters the actor had portrayed earlier in his career. His eyes were soft and kind. They were the eyes of a man who had seen a lifetime of good and bad. Near the end of his life, the mind behind those eyes had decided to make salad dressings for his friends and then give the profits to charity when the idea became a big business.

Darius gazed down through the space between his dangling penny loafers. He cleaned his wire-rimmed glasses and replaced them on his nose. He could barely make out the streets and buildings below. It seemed like they were sitting miles above the city. People and cars scurried about appearing like the particles of matter Simon had shown Darius under the electron microscope just before they had all turned in for the night.

"What's your name?" Darius inquired.

The Archangel tilted his curly-haired head. "I suppose you've earned the right to know. It's Aaron."

It made Darius feel more comfortable to be on a first name basis with the Archangel. Now, maybe he could ask him the question that had been troubling him since he arrived in heaven. He needed to ask the question. He couldn't live with it inside him any longer.

"Why was I killed?" There, he said it.

Aaron fixed his soft blue eyes on him. "I'm not sure you're ready to go there."

Darius straightened. "Anything you can tell me will help."

"All right, let's begin with a rather extreme example, because I'm already late for another meeting with the Directors. Here we go." Aaron inhaled deeply. "Do you think the Chief wanted Christ to die on the cross?"

"He died for our sins," Darius said.

"Do you really think the Chief is that cruel, Darius?"

"I didn't until I woke up in heaven," Darius admitted.

"Human beings decided to crucify Jesus. It was an ignorant, brutal act of free will. Christ didn't have to die on the cross."

"But, how can that be?"

"The simple truth is human beings are given more choices than most of them want to take responsibility for."

"But I was shot to death for helping people."

"You weren't shot because you were helping people, Darius. Your life on Earth ended in a violent, wrongful act of free will. As long as people have the choice to exercise their will in the wrong way, innocent people like you will be victims. Your death was obviously *a tragedy. No one in heaven wanted you to die. Unfortunately, there was nothing anybody could have done about it except the people who shot you."*

Darius sat perfectly still for a while with his hands in his lap before speaking again. "I'm confused," he said with a solemn expression. "On the one hand, you say everything that happens to a man or woman is the result of free will, but on the other hand, you send me to Earth to stop a pill from going on the market. Why am I interfering with the free will of the people who want to sell Plezenthol?"

"Good observation, Darius. It sounds like a contradiction, but it's more like a distinction. We have to pick our fights carefully. We try not to interfere with the operation of human free will. We sat by and watched in horror, for example, when Roman soldiers crucified Christ and terrorists flew commercial airliners into the Twin Towers. But there are times when we must take action, when a worldwide catastrophe could result from human failure. We intervened during the two world wars and the Cuban Missile crisis, to cite a few recent cases. We have also been involved when the psychological, moral or spiritual evolution of the species is at risk. A literal example of such a case was our influence on the outcome of the famous 'Scopes Trial.'"

"Tell me more."

"Alas, as you are well aware, time is not our friend. We have much to do before your education can continue."

A covey of birds appeared in the sky with their graceful wings spread, wheeling effortlessly on the breeze.

"You can't allow what happened to you to extinguish the light within you," Aaron said. "You can't allow it to blind you to the light that shines all around you."

The Archangel leaned a bit closer. "Think of all the good you'll do if you succeed in your mission. Human consciousness will have a chance to evolve in a positive direction. Consider the miracles waiting to manifest from the intelligent, creative use of free will."

"Wait a minute," Darius snapped. "I've just had a visit from the spirit of a Warrior Lord who said if I complete my mission it will ruin the peace talks between heaven and the Exiles."

The Archangel drew back. "Glythren spoke to you?"

Darius nodded.

For once, the Archangel Aaron seemed to be at a loss for words.

Darius broke the silence. "You didn't tell me about any peace talks with the Exiles."

"There was a lot I didn't tell you because I didn't want to load you up with too much information. As I told you in our meeting before you left for Earth, your job is to deal with the Plezenthol situation."

"But my job is interfering with the peace talks," Darius objected.

Aaron frowned. It was the first time Darius had seen Aaron wearing a glum expression. "I'm afraid there won't be any peace talks," he said.

Darius couldn't imagine how the affairs of heaven and Earth could be any more jumbled. Aaron's expression told him otherwise. "What do you mean," he asked, not really sure if he wanted to hear the answer.

"Glythren visited our oldest Senior Operative to request a truce to discuss reconciliation between the Exiles and ourselves. The Warrior Lord claimed the Exiles had discovered a new form of energy, and were using it to create new weapons that could result in… well…let's just say a radical change in the balance of power. I mentioned some of this to you in our briefing before you left on your mission."

"Yes, I remember."

"I've known the Senior Operative who made the report since he was a Junior Operative. I trust his judgment implicitly. We both agreed there had to be some substance to Glythren's claims. The Warrior Lord would never try to blackmail us into peace talks without something truly dangerous to back up his threats. Glythren said we had a choice between peaceful reconciliation and facing the Exiles' new weapons in an all-out war. We sent all of the Senior

Operatives to a demonstration to check out a new device he said would allow Exiles to walk among humans undetected."

"It's true," Darius interrupted. "I've seen the device. It works. I fought with Exiles disguised as humans."

The Archangel hung his head. "We thought we had taken all of the necessary precautions to safeguard the Senior Operatives…but we have lost touch with the entire expedition."

"They're lost?"

"I don't know what happened to them. What I do know is that we are at war with the Exiles. The fact that Glythren lied to you about the peace talks confirms it. We never agreed with the Exiles to back off of our efforts to stop Plezenthol from going on the market."

"So, we're dealing with an all-out war with the Exiles in addition to the Plezenthol situation," Darius said.

Aaron sighed. "I admit, it's a bit overwhelming, but you have to stay focused on your job and let me deal with the other issue."

"You make it sound easy."

I gave you the golden triangle to help you, but it won't work unless you practice the principles it embodies. The first principle is to foster a deep belief in yourself and your abilities, and to believe similarly in Javon, Vicky, and Simon. Are you doing it?"

Darius nodded.

"The second principle is hope, Darius. You have to believe in the positive outcome of your efforts. Hope is a creative force. With effort and the power of hope, noble intentions pass from ideas into physical reality."

Light streamed from the face of Paul Newman. Aaron held an upturned palm out to Darius. Darius took it. He closed his eyes. Warm, radiant light filled his body. A mantle of peace settled upon him. He felt confident and secure in himself and in his expanding angelic powers.

When Darius opened his eyes, Aaron was gone. The carefree birds had disappeared as well. In their place, the sun was setting into an ominous black hole punched into the light blue sky.

He woke up with a start and found himself back in the cramped room accompanied by Javon's loud snoring. Staring at the bedsprings supporting the mattress above him, Darius wondered if the meeting with Aaron on top of the Mamongen Building had been a dream. It had all seemed incredibly real. The feelings of peace mixed with confidence were still there.

He closed his eyes, and this time fell into a deep, dreamless sleep.

Chapter Thirty-Two

THE PROOF IS NOT IN THE PUDDING

HIRAM FYRUM FELT the same kind of elation he had experienced on his graduation day from Harvard Business School. He had just received word that the first batch of Plezenthol tablets was tumbling off the production line of a low-cost pharmaceutical manufacturer in western Canada. When the news broke on Wall Street, the price of Mamongen stock would match Hiram's soaring spirits.

The phone buzzed on the desk in his study.

"How are you this glorious morning," Hiram chirped into the phone. There was a long silence at the other end, then:

"Why, I'm fine. "It's nice to hear you in such a good mood, sir."

"Today is a very auspicious day, Glenda my dear. I've dreamed about days like this since I was a little boy. What have you got for me?"

"Simon is here to speak with you."

"Since when is Simon in the habit of coming to my office without an appointment?"

"I don't know, sir. He's here." There was a pause. "With some friends," Glenda continued.

"Friends?"

"That's what he calls them."

"How many friends?"

"Three, sir."

Hiram thought for a moment. "Tell Simon to come in. Without his friends."

"Yes sir."

Hanging up the inter-office phone, Hiram picked up his smart phone and punched in a private number. After a short conversation lasting fifteen seconds, he moved to his comfy interview chair, rumored to be called "The Throne" by his jealous subordinates. Waiting for Simon, Hiram composed himself.

Simon entered Hiram's inner sanctum through one of the twelve-foot-high black lacquered double doors. Without a word, he sat in a hard backed black lacquered chair with minimal cushioning opposite Hiram.

Hiram held up his right hand in the manner of a cop stopping traffic. "Before you say anything, I want to advise you of a decision I've come to after many hours of careful, and, I should add, painful thought. "I've decided to dismiss you as the Director of Pharmaceutical Research, effective immediately."

"You're making a huge mistake, Hiram."

"Your behavior is erratic, to put it mildly. You are a danger to this company and to yourself. You will have an opportunity to review said behavior in a copy of the release documents which will be sent to you. Is there anything you wish to say before I have you escorted out of the building?"

"Yes. I have substantial proof that Plezenthol is a dangerous drug. Do you want to be known as the man who unleashed a catastrophic plague on the human race?"

"You're not well, Simon."

"What have you got to lose? Take a look at the proof."

"Where is this proof?"

"It's not in the pudding. It's outside with my friends. Come out there with me."

Inhaling deeply, Hiram stared at the sound-proofed ceiling. "All right, Simon. This had better be good."

. . .

The sweeping burgundy sofa resembled an inflated horseshoe. A matching leather chair sat squarely at the opening of the sofa's two ends. Darius examined the plump, low-slung chair with a puzzled expression while his friends gawked at the artwork on display in Hiram's living room. Darius noticed a console with buttons inside one arm of the chair. He concluded the swept-back chair doubled as a therapeutic massage device for dissolving stress.

Beige textile wallpaper adorned the walls providing a rich, warm background for the eclectic collection of original oil paintings hanging throughout the room. The Mamongen logo bloomed in the center of the room, stitched into the expensive carpeting.

Hiram Fyrum entered the room with Simon trailing him. He hardly made the impressive appearance Darius expected. The room's high ceilings and over-sized doors made Mamongen's CEO look like a child who had gotten lost in the woods and wandered into a giant's castle. Fyrum, for his part, looked perfectly at ease amid these grandiose surroundings.

"Sit, sit, make yourselves comfortable," Hiram said to the group with a shooing motion.

Hiram quickly took a seat in the low-slung leather chair. The shape and positioning of the chair now made sense to Darius. It fit Hiram's unique size and personality perfectly, stationed in a position where he could easily be the center of attention. Darius imagined hundreds of executive meetings had taken place in this room. Corporate policies were undoubtedly promulgated here, marketing strategies created, sales programs born, and the fates of innumerable employees and entire companies cast—all in this odd little setting.

Hiram leaned forward with a pleasant smile.

"Why don't you introduce me to these friends of yours, Simon."

Vicky sat closest to Hiram. She wore a Mona Lisa smile. Before Simon spoke, Hiram said:

"You look familiar. Oh, now I can place you. From the press conference...the lady with the probing questions from WQES. Right?"

"I'm actually not with WQES anymore." Vicky said.

"Doesn't matter. Once a Journalist, always a Journalist, I always say."

Hiram turned to Darius. "And you, whatever your name is, managed to disrupt my very important press conference with the inappropriate and asinine question you asked Simon."

Before Darius could utter a word in his own defense, Hiram turned to Simon. "I wasn't really prepared to meet with the media today."

"With respect sir, I think you'll find there are a number of things you weren't prepared for by the time we're done here."

"Hmmmm...That sounds ominous." Hiram turned back to Darius, still wearing a pleasant smile. "Are you here to ask more inane questions for your obscure newspaper?"

"My name is Darius McPherson and the truth is I don't work for a newspaper."

"Summing it all up, then, I'm in a meeting with two out of work reporters and a scientist with grave doubts about the product he spent the last ten years and a billion dollars of my company's money developing. Does that sound about right?"

"I asked Simon to call the meeting," Darius said.

"If you don't mind me asking, just how long have you known Simon?"

Crossing his ankles, Hiram sat back in his chair. He formed a steeple with his fingers with elbows resting on the arms of the chair, waiting for an answer.

"I've known Simon for less than two days," Darius replied.

"It may sound improbable but he's no stranger," Simon offered. "Darius is a very unusual young man."

"I'm sure it's possible to grow very close to someone in less than two days." Darius noticed Hiram push one of the buttons on the chair's console.

"I'm not out of my mind, Hiram."

"I'm sure you're not, Simon. But I have to say you do look a bit rough around the edges."

"We've been through a lot these past two days," Simon said defensively.

Darius noted Simon's agitation. He placed a calming hand on his arm. "Mr. Fyrum, what if I could show you beyond a shadow of a doubt that Plezenthol will result in unimaginable human suffering if it goes on the market?" he said.

"Do you have a PowerPoint slide show to illustrate this?" Hiram asked with a straight face.

"In fact, I have something very similar," Darius said.

"We'll need to use the computer in your study," Simon added.

"Fascinating," Hiram observed, maintaining his relaxed pose.

"Darius isn't a crackpot. He's shown us things, unbelievable things." Simon's voice rose. "Just give him a chance."

Hiram's eyes widened. He turned to Vicky and Javon. "You've seen these things too?"

"I've seen and heard things that will take me a lifetime to forget, if I'm lucky enough to live a normal lifetime," Vicky said.

"These folks ain't trippin'" Javon chimed in. "What we saw may sound weird, but it's for real."

"Interesting." Hiram turned back to Darius. "Some of the statements you've made indicate that you can see into the future. Are you a prophet?"

"No," Darius replied. "Let's go into the study. "I'll make my presentation. Then you can draw your own conclusions."

Hiram squirmed in his chair. He checked his diamond studded watch.

"I'll bite, but let's make this quick."

· · ·

The last images flickered and then disappeared from Hiram's desktop monitor. His eyes were still ablaze with the pictures Darius had channeled through the screen.

"This has to be some elaborate hoax," Hiram said with a beseeching look in Simon's direction.

"No one sneaked in here to put those horrible scenes on your hard drive," Simon assured him. "Why would anyone go to the trouble and expense of producing a streaming video of the last days of the human race? Every employee with access to the executive suite goes through a screening all the way down to their toenails. There's no way someone with that warped of a sense of humor could get through the psychological tests, not to mention your impenetrable security."

Hiram turned to Darius. He sat perfectly still, as he had during the entire presentation. He sat up in his chair and took a few moments to gaze out past his terrace to the azure waters of Biscayne Bay.

"I don't know what's going on here, but I suspect it's some kind of corporate sabotage. I'm not going to scuttle a billion-dollar project based on some bogus computer slide-show."

A soft knock at the door surprised all of them except Hiram, it seemed to Darius.

"Come in," Hiram called out.

A dark-haired man who looked in tip-top condition underneath his crisply pressed navy-blue suit entered the study followed by two security guards.

"What took you so long," Hiram said.

• • •

The man known as Kyle Huntilla no longer existed. He had simply vanished like dirty water under a mop cleaning up a floor. Here one minute. Gone the next. The man's body remained, in tombstone fashion, to mark the passing. Poor Kyle. He had worked like a slave to latch onto his little niche in the human business world and had not survived to enjoy the fruits of his labors.

Huntilla's personality had been slowly disintegrating, thanks to the increased frequency of his alter-ego shuttling back and forth from the underworld. If allowed to live, Kyle would have soon become a blubbering idiot. He had reached the end of his usefulness as a sort of bookmark for Glythren while he was away on important business.

No one would find Kyle's body once Glythren left it for the last time. The first item on the agenda, however, was the matter of establishing the new pecking order. The angel sitting across from Hiram Fyrum complicated matters, but not by very much.

"Show these people out of the building," Hiram said. "Take Simon's security pass and his Mamongen ID from him. Simon Worthington III is not to be allowed on these premises, or at any Mamongen event, ever again. Am I clear, Kyle?"

Glythren had observed Hiram closely through Kyle's eyes on many occasions. Fyrum was not a man who scared easily. He was not a man you could bribe with worldly success either. He had achieved it all on his own, which is why Glythren had never attempted to enlist the CEO in the Exile plan.

The angel must have shown Hiram something, Glythren concluded, and the CEO wasn't buying it. Good. He watched the neophyte raise both arms in a pathetic attempt to fire a volley of light energy aimed at him. There would be no battle in Hiram's study. Glythren would make sure of it. The Warrior Lord pointed his index finger. An instant later, a dark energy containment field settled over the angel and the three humans sitting across from Hiram. With his other hand, Glythren pulled a dispatcher weapon from the holster hidden under his suit jacket.

Hiram stared at the triangles on the end of Glythren's hybrid energy pistol. "My God, Kyle, what are you doing?"

"I'm not Kyle," the Warrior Lord said. "I'm your new boss."

"My new boss?"

Hiram was no longer "Fyrum the Fearless." Glythren sensed he was scared out of his wits. Fear rolled off him like fog from a warm sulfur spring in the dead of winter.

"I hate repeating myself. Yes. I'm your new boss. Let me ask you a simple question: do you want to live?"

Glythren heard Hiram gulp, his eyes still contemplating the weapon he held inches away from the little man's reddening face.

"I'm not used to being threatened," Hiram said.

"You have five seconds to answer my question."

"Yes. I definitely want to live."

"Good." Glythren motioned to the security guards. "Take these four downstairs while I orient Mr. Fyrum to the way things will be done at Mamongen Pharmaceuticals from now on."

Chapter Thirty-Three

DESCENT

"YOU SURE HANDLED that like a pro," Javon said above the pneumatic hiss of the falling elevator.

Darius wondered where the elevator and the two security guards book ending the four of them were going. He looked over to Javon whose expression was as dark as the ash blue dark energy bubble holding them captive.

"I wasn't fast enough to outgun a Warrior Lord in disguise."

"Well, you shoulda' been."

"Easier said than done."

Another surprise that had caught Darius off guard was the dark energy containment field surrounding them. It crackled and sparked when it rubbed against the walls, or an object, or one of them.

"Look at those symbols." Simon pointed to a small red square centered above the brushed bronze elevator doors. "It looks like the Exiles have re-programmed the LED readout in their language."

Darius watched the symbols change rapidly. He had the sense they were hurtling downward at a frightening pace.

A few seconds later, the symbols stopped their frantic whirling. Darius felt the elevator slowing to a crawl. Then, it came to a dead stop. The bronze doors slid open.

If this was hell, Darius thought, it sure looked a lot like a big, neatly arranged basement. Maybe new arrivals only saw what they wanted to see in hell, just like in heaven. Except, he was sure, the illusion wouldn't last long. Where were they?

Two electric boilers dominated the room like nuclear submarines docked in parallel berths. Wire mesh storage bins full of tools and maintenance equipment lined three walls.

One of their Exile-in-disguise captors used a hand-held device that looked like a cue ball cut in half to move the containment field out of the elevator. The mobile containment bubble forced Darius and the others to move along with it. Touching the force field with a body part felt like a sting from a cattle prod.

"Can't you blast us out of this thing?" Javon asked angrily.

"I'm afraid we would all be consumed in the fireworks if I did," Darius answered.

They trudged on helplessly, doing their best to avoid contact with the containment field.

Bright fluorescent lighting bathed the room. The floor smelled of fresh paint. There were no signs of dirt or dust anywhere. Everything in the room appeared to be in its proper place and safely stowed away. Even the air had a fresh, lemon scent.

They approached a bathroom facility on the other side of the room. Darius read the message on the triangular sign positioned in front of the bathroom:

"THIS FACILITY IS CLOSED FOR FIRE CODE UPGRADES. ALL MAINTENENANCE WORKERS MUST USE THE FACILITIES IN THE LOBBY UNTIL FURTHER NOTICE. FAILURE TO COMPLY WILL RESULT IN JOB TERMINATION."

The sign seemed to confirm where they were. Maybe it wasn't an illusion after all. Maybe the elevator had deposited them in the basement of the Mamongen Building instead of the lower depths of hell. Why were they here? It definitely wasn't for fun. Darius didn't like the ominous tone of the message on the sign. Something friendly like, "PARDON OUR DUST WHILE WE UPGRADE THIS FACILITY TO SERVE YOU BETTER," would have made him feel a heck of a lot more comfortable.

Despite the sign's warning, they entered the bathroom, pushed along by the containment bubble and the guards. What Darius saw next was startling.

The interior of the bathroom looked like it had suffered a direct hit by a smart bomb. The place was all rubble. It looked more like the surface of the moon than the inside of a bathroom under repair.

"Looks like the construction workers took their jobs too seriously," Vicky said in a hoarse voice. These were the first words she had spoken since the meeting in Hiram's penthouse.

"We gonna' be in as many pieces as this damn bathroom unless we do something," Javon said.

Yes, but what? Darius had not anticipated the complication of the containment field. He clung to the slim hope that it protected them from energy weapon attacks while holding them captive simultaneously.

The force field changed directions causing Simon's shoulder to rub up against it. He grimaced and rubbed the spot of contact. Now they were moving in the direction of a jagged hole in the bathroom wall. Someone or something had stripped away the sheetrock like a layer of flesh, revealing a ragged gash in the underlying cinderblocks.

To Darius, the opening looked like the feeding apparatus of a giant, deep-sea anemone; a hungry mouth ringed with a circle of needle-thin teeth.

Chapter Thirty-Four

STRONGHOLD

DOWN THEY WENT, slipping and sliding on a carpet of sandy soil. It was too dark to see much of anything in the narrow passageway. Darius strained to see what lay ahead, hoping his eyes would adjust to the light. He saw only pitch-black darkness ahead.

The dark energy containment field had collapsed to half its diameter in the tight space. Whenever Darius or one of the others brushed up against the barrier, it stung them severely like a nest of angry wasps. The guards kept pushing the force field along from behind without the slightest regard for their cries of anguish.

Darius wondered if this was the end of the line. Would they be stung to death by the terrible dark energy bubble as it collapsed into itself? What would happen to him after that? Would the Hyperspace Conveyor Tube scoop him up? Would he have to face Aaron and the Directors as a failure and a disgrace?

Darius heard sounds ahead of them—a jumble of voices—Exile voices. It felt like drops of sweat ran from every pore of his skin.

With a hefty shove from behind, their tormentors pushed them out of the passageway into an enormous chamber. When his eyes finally adjusted to the dull, blue-gray light, Darius was able to make out a towering edifice in the center of what now looked to be a cavern. The tower stood in stark relief against the spotlights that lit it up.

It was hard to tell on first impression if the cavern was a product of nature or the work of Exile hands. The structure sticking up from the middle of the rocky floor appeared decidedly unnatural. It looked like an Art Deco version of the Eifel Tower shooting up into the shadows overhead. A giant replica of the tuning fork weapon the Exiles carried in their holsters sat atop the tower. The surface of the weapon reflected the violet shafts of light beaming from circular lights studding the four legs of the tower from top to bottom.

As they neared the center of the room, more details of the huge tuning fork emerged in the odd lighting. Whoever made the weapon had cast it from a different material than the strange pistols Darius had encountered in the Amcor lab. The twin barrels glittered as if they were made of emerald cut diamonds, but no diamond of Earthly origin could ever be that large.

Like the Eifel Tower, there were arches between the four supporting legs near the bottom. It was anchored by a circular base with tubes sticking out all around at regular intervals. It reminded Darius of a spiked dog collar. On closer examination, Darius recognized the tubes matched the bullet-shaped canister he had observed on the crest of the collection machine in the projection room of the Conrad Hotel. Behind the tower, rows of these canisters were stacked in squat groupings like World War II bombs waiting to be loaded into the bays of B-52 Bombers.

Within the four legs of the tower, long translucent tubes spiraled upwards from the base. The tubes plugged into the platform supporting the mega-sized tuning fork.

Near the top, a small team of Exile workers leaped about the legs of the tower clinging to chains with two of their powerful arms while carrying construction beams in the other two. Another team of workers used welding torches to secure the beams into place to reinforce the underside of the platform.

There were Exile sentries stationed throughout the cavern with their horrid eyes peeled for the slightest irregularity in the workflow on and around the tower. One of them drew its weapon the moment

Darius and the others appeared in the purplish light of the cavern. Then four more sentries drew their weapons.

The creatures took off on their stout haunches and tails, leaping towards Darius and his captive friends. Instinctively, the prisoners moved closer together inside the dark energy containment bubble.

"Looks like we ain't invited to this party," Javon said.

The ferocious creatures were almost upon them.

Darius waited for a miraculous action plan perfectly suited to the occasion to suddenly pop into his head. He had coaxed and prodded these people, his friends, into this awful mess. And now, when they needed him the most, Darius had no idea what to do. Maybe the underground cavern interfered with intuitive flashes sent from heaven, he told himself. Panic set in. All Darius could think to do was to take a deep breath to calm down.

A shrill scream echoed from the far side of the cavern. The oncoming Exile death squad skidded to a halt a few yards away. Darius exhaled. One by one, the Exiles turned their oversized triangular skulls toward the source of the noise. A giant Exile creature, taller by at least a foot than the others, came leaping at them from the ranks of guards and workers scattered all over the cavern floor. The creature's skin color was a distinctive pale yellow. A pulsating purple aura surrounded the giant.

The monster leaped over Exile bodies that bent like sea grass to clear a path. Soon, the terrifying creature reached them, panting heavily. The other Exiles standing around the containment bubble withdrew in a widening circle.

Darius turned in time to see one of the guards touch the cue ball device in his hand. The dark energy containment field changed into a free-floating cage around them. The guards who had accompanied the group on the way down walked away into the gloom, presumably to morph back into their familiar, hideous bodies.

Darius and his friends stood alone in the center of a ring of fierce creatures. The tallest, most frightening example of Exile manhood, hulked in front of them. The monster screamed again, most likely to assert its position at the top of the Exile hierarchy. And, to scare the crap out of them. From the expressions of his friends, he saw that it had worked.

Chapter Thirty-Five

ULTIMATUM

DARIUS BEGAN SUMMONING light energy in the hope that he might get the chance to use it.

Simon held Vicky tightly around her shoulders. Their clothes were torn and muddied from the awful journey to this woeful destination.

"I can't look at this," Javon announced, turning away from the sight of the creature Darius believed more and more was the physical manifestation of the cloud entity that had visited him in his room during the night.

The monster touched a glass ball hanging from an onyx chain around its neck. Darius watched two opposing triangles inside the glass sphere emit an azure-colored halo of light. Soon, a velvet shroud of the unnatural light surrounded the creature. The light pulsed, obscuring the Exile's purple aura.

The four of them observed the grisly process of a four-armed bird lizard caving into itself and reforming into a fit, dark haired man standing six feet tall and nattily dressed in a pinstriped, navy business suit.

"I think it will be easier if you see me like this," the man said in an educated, authoritative, human voice. "I am Glythren. I alone hold the key to your future."

The man standing in front of them resembled Kyle Huntilla,

Mamongen's Chief of Security, who they had met in Hiram's study. The duplicate Kyle regarded them studiously.

"There are large plans afoot. Each of you can play a role in those plans, or I can dispose of you right now."

Glythren sure didn't waste time getting to the point. Darius had a few split seconds to think of an approach that might work against a being with an undeveloped sense of humor and zero reluctance to murder them in cold blood.

The Kyle duplicate turned to the circle of Exiles looking on. "I will turn you over to my soldiers for recreation if my offer doesn't interest you."

There was not a lot of wiggle room in Glythren's statement. Darius couldn't think of a scrap of leverage to bargain with, so he decided to be quiet and listen.

The Kyle impersonation turned to Vicky with a charming smile.

"To you I offer the position of Mamongen Director of Communications. The company can use a bright new face to put a fresh spin on corporate communications. It's a perfect opportunity for an ambitious person to put her talents to good use."

Darius thought it likely that Glythren was projecting a tempting image into Vicky's mind to sweeten the offer. It might be a TV studio or a stage where Vicky was the center of attention with a staff of underlings to assist her.

Vicky turned to Darius with pleading eyes. Darius projected this thought to her: *don't say anything.*

"Give it some thought," the man who really wasn't Kyle Huntilla said. He pirouetted gracefully to address Javon.

"My Captains tell me you are quite a resourceful young man. Someone like you could be a useful asset, perhaps as my personal chauffeur, a shining example of Human and Exile cooperation."

Javon's dull expression brightened. Darius imaged the teenager was in the grasp of a vision of beautiful women wearing nothing but spiked heels sprawled with Javon on a sofa that stretched to the horizon.

Javon stood enthralled. Darius feared his young colleague was seriously considering the tempting offer. Darius watched with a growing sense of dread as the Warrior Lord in disguise turned its attention to Simon.

"To you, Doctor Worthington, I offer the opportunity to untangle the unsolved mysteries of science with your human intelligence enhanced by microscopic computers swimming in your cerebral fluid. We can help you to solve pressing problems like the energy crisis, world hunger, global warming, and the shortage of clean drinking water. Human beings, by themselves, have proven themselves incapable of this task. The pitiful condition of your world with its petty wars and irreconcilable divisions is a daily testimonial to this failure. I offer you the power to correct this abysmal situation."

Darius thought Glythren was full of himself to think someone as smart as Simon would swallow a proposal so obviously loaded with booby traps. He supposed a being whose mind had fermented in destructive thoughts for thousands of years might have a slip in judgment every so often. Such an error might provide the sliver of opportunity Darius needed.

The grinning Chief of Security now turned to Darius, spreading his hands in an open inviting gesture.

"And you, Darius. What is it you crave most in the World? To be reunited with your lost love?"

The words coupled with the images they inspired cut a painful swath through his heart.

"I don't hold onto false hopes," Darius said woodenly.

Glythren's fake human face drained of all expression. "I'm impressed. Have you applied that principle to the likelihood of your own continued existence?"

The man in the navy blue pinstripe suit pointed a finger at Darius.

Darius blinked. The energy field surrounding them offered as little room for evasive maneuvers as Glythren's ice-cold opening comments to the group.

Then, the containment bubble opened, as if torn apart by a hungry kid ripping open a freshly popped batch of popcorn.

The thing powering Kyle Huntilla's body pulled a black tuning fork out from under his suit jacket.

Before Darius had a chance to budge, a stream of projectiles exploded from the double triangles at the end of the pistol. There was a flash, and then an intense burning sensation that felt like someone had dumped him into an iron-smelting furnace.

Then there was nothingness.

Chapter Thirty-Six

THE VOID

DARIUS FLOATED AIMLESSLY in a pitch-black void. His mind was a tangle of thoughts bouncing off one another like excited electrons. *Why did I have to open my big mouth? Now, my friends are alone with no one to guide them. They'll acquiesce to Glythren's demands. What else can they do without me around?*

"Hey, anybody home?" Darius shouted into the void.

This place was more than just lonely. He had nothing to keep him company except his thoughts. It would not be long before his mind split into dozens of personalities arguing endlessly with one another. He imagined himself degenerating into a shrieking lunatic listening to a radio inside his head tuned to a hundred stations at once.

"HELP," Darius screamed.

Don't panic...not yet. Darius closed his eyes and called out silently from the depths of his being. *Whoever you are, please come to my rescue. My friends need me. I don't want the world to end because I couldn't shut up.*

Silence. Emptiness. Blackness. Hopelessness. *I will not lose hope,* Darius vowed to himself. *Maybe time doesn't exist here. If I can just find a way out, I might get back in time to complete the mission.*

Darius kept repeating this mantra to himself while hoping desperately it was true.

Something *SWOOSHED* by him. Darius opened his eyes and was amazed to see the golden triangle floating around his neck glowing. Two of the three circles inside the triangle projected shafts of light into the darkness.

A voice called to him from out the void.

"Oh good. I can see you now. Wait. I'm coming."

"Who are you?" Darius called out.

"Ankroot Harbot, Senior Operative First Class."

"I can't see you."

"Hang on. Be with ya' in a sec."

He saw a faint blur highlighted by the two beacons streaming from the necklace. The blur *WHOOSHED* by again.

"Dang," Darius heard the blur cry out as it rocketed away.

The blur made a sharp U-turn. It came hurtling back at him. Darius tried to swim out of the way. The movement caused him to tumble head over heels. He tried flapping his arms, which only caused him to spin faster.

The blur caught up with him. One strong hand grabbed him by the arm. He felt another catch him by the waist. They tumbled together for a minute. The rotations slowed, then ceased. Darius caught his breath. His dizziness began to subside.

"It took me awhile to figure out how to navigate in this muck. Guess you haven't gotten the hang of it yet. You're the first Senior Operative I've found since we all got blasted out here. Or in here."

The blur turned out to be an old man with the build of an Olympic swimmer. He shook his hairless head. "I still haven't figured how to get outta' here."

"Don't ask me," Darius said. "I just arrived."

"Just arrived? Wait a minute. You're not an S.O."

"I'm Junior Operative Darius McPherson. He made a stab at shaking hands. The old man grabbed him quickly.

"Don't try any quick movements. Takes a while to get the hang of motoring around in this soup."

The old man's face was smooth. His cheeks looked a bit sunken, like someone who hadn't eaten in a while. He had bushy white eyebrows, the only hair on his face. His eyes brightened by the second in the widening glow emanating from the triangle. Darius judged the circle of light surrounding them had grown to a diameter of at least eight feet.

"How'd you get here?" Ankroot Harbot asked.

"Glythren the Warrior Lord fired a weird looking hand gun at me. The next thing I knew, I'm floating around in this…whatever it is."

The old man seemed to be weighing his answer. Darius filled the silence with a question of his own. "How did you wind up here?"

"My brothers and I were supposed to bring back information about some newfangled weapons the Exiles claimed to have invented. Turns out the weapons were more dangerous than advertised. They blasted me here just like you." Ankroot frowned. "And the truce Glythren offered was just a cover to ambush us. That bugger really bamboozled yours truly and someone else who should have known better."

"I think you mean the Archangel Aaron."

"You're mighty well informed for a Junior Operative."

"Aaron sent me to Earth to deal with the Plezenthol situation. Now, I understand why he sent a Junior Operative. He had no Senior Operatives to send. Aaron had to throw the training manual out the window when he briefed me for the mission. There wasn't time for a proper indoctrination."

Ankroot listened, shaking his head in a subtle way to avoid shooting off into the void, Darius guessed.

"Do you have any idea what this place is?"

"If we had to put a name to it, I'd call it 'uncreated space.' I believe this is the place the universe came out of before the Big Bang."

"The ultimate nowheresville," Darius offered.

"Right," Harbot said. "Your story adds credence to my theory. Somehow, those Exile energy weapons blasted us back to the place where things come from before they are created, before they're even an idea.

Ankroot Harbot rotated in place next to Darius.

"Don't mind sayin' I'm as glad to see you as you are to see me. I have to admit even a Senior Operative can run out of hope in a place like this. I was beginning ta' think there wasn't enough luminescence to find another angel 'till I saw the light shining from that necklace of yours. The Exiles musta' scattered me and the others too far apart to hear each other calling out to one another. Now that we've found each other, I think we got a shot at ditching this place."

"How?

"I couldn't blast myself out of this muck alone, but I'm thinkin' maybe if we combine our light energy, we can build up enough thrust to break out of here."

The old man stopped spinning. He took Darius by the shoulders. "You're gonna' have to listen ta' every word I say and follow my directions to the letter. You got that?"

Darius nodded eagerly. Then he said: "What about the other Senior Operatives?"

"Well try to find them later. First things first. This won't be easy. I can't have you questioning what I tell ya.' Understand?"

"Just tell me what to do," Darius said. Then a terrible thought popped into his head.

"What if we wind up in a worse place than this? I mean...are you positive we can get back to the right place?"

"I'm not sure at all," Anky replied.

Chapter Thirty-Seven

THE PRINCIPLES

"**ALL I CAN** do is use the three principles and hope for the best," Anky said. "The principles have always worked for me."

"I have to get back to my friends in the cavern. It's somewhere underneath the Mamongen Building."

"Calm down, son."

"I'm sorry Mr. Harbot, but…how can I expect you to know where the cavern is and more importantly, how to steer us back there?"

For starters, you can call me Anky. And don't give up before we begin to get cranked up."

"Cranked up?"

"You'll see. Like I said, you gotta' start by believing I know what I'm doin'. It just so happens I was in a cavern before I wound up here. The Exiles took us down in an elevator. They had to make several trips to get all of us down there."

"We have to be talking about the same place. They took us down in an elevator too."

Maybe old Anky has figured a way out. Who am I to question a Senior Operative? The least I can do is believe.

"My friends are in danger. We have to hurry."

"Whoa down, son. The golden triangle on your necklace tells me you haven't learned the third principle yet.

"I've gotten this far using Belief and Hope," Darius confirmed.

"The more you use the principles, the deeper your understanding of them grows," Anky said. "The more you understand the principles, the more you can do with them. Ya' follow?"

Darius was growing impatient. He was worried about Javon, Vicky and Simon, not to mention the rest of humanity.

"It makes sense," Darius replied with an effort to steady his voice as well as himself.

Anky took a deep breath and let it out slowly. "Let's talk about the third principle. If ya' ask me, this one's the most powerful of the three.

Darius listened intently, taking in each word as if it was a breath of life-giving oxygen.

"There's a power inside you, Darius. This power can do anything. You have to learn how to connect with it and trust it. You might want to think of it as your inner hero."

"Are you talking about faith?"

"It's more than faith. It knowing and trusting based on the knowing."

"I'm having a hard time trusting anything right now," Darius said.

"It's easy not to trust when things don't go your way."

"I was a good person. I was good to everyone. And I lost everyone and everything I ever loved. I didn't deserve to wind up in this God-forsaken place."

"Unfortunately, bad things happen to good people, Darius. It wasn't your fault. It wasn't the Chief's fault. A person can be in the wrong place at the wrong time, or have unlucky genes, or turn left when they should have turned right. I'm afraid to say not everything happens for a reason. Bad things can happen randomly. There's nothing we can do about it except to go on. We have to find the next step, the one that will bring us closer to the dream in our heart.

"I don't have any more dreams."

"I know you've been hurt, son. But here's the thing you need to trust in the most. At the very center of the life force, there's a treasure trove of pure joy. It's our job to find it. But it ain't easy and there's no guarantee every human being ever will. It's just a possibility. We have to begin by trusting the treasure is there waiting to be discovered. We have to develop our inner resources to break through to the ultimate inner resource."

Darius took a minute to consider these words carefully. The idea of experiencing more joy as his consciousness expanded sounded appealing. If he and Anky managed to find their way out of here, Darius would get the chance to dig for some of that treasure. Once he found it, he imagined, he could spread it around in many ways.

The "if" in finding their way out represented a yawning chasm they had to cross somehow.

Grab hold of my hands," Anky instructed.

The old man's hands were smooth as silk with strong, straight fingers. These were not the crooked, bony hands of an old man. Light energy passing through those hands in the performance of good works must have kept them so young, Darius figured.

"Summon light energy," Anky commanded.

Darius closed his eyes and concentrated on an imaginary point in the center of his solar plexus. Warmth radiated to every part of his body. Feelings of peace and joy blossomed in his heart. The light energy felt like water feeding a thirsty root system.

"We're gonna' have to use all three principles to work up enough thrust to get the heck outta' here. Open yer' eyes now."

Darius was surprised to see columns of light streaming from the three circles inside the golden triangle to the outer edges of the circle of brightness separating them from the black void.

"Bring your light energy to the point of release," Anky said. His neck arched. They broke eye contact. Darius sensed an incredible power rising from within. Soon his neck arched too, an involuntary reflex.

Darius strained to remain in control of the energy surging inside of him. His mind suddenly flashed on an image of his three friends kneeling at the feet of a monstrous figure in the sallow light of the cavern. Despair nibbled away at his resolve. He tried to refocus but the grim picture remained firmly rooted in his mind's eye.

"Believe in yourself and in me," Darius heard Anky say. "Remember that anything is possible with Hope. Trust in your inner power. Trust the treasure waiting to be discovered. Stay in control until I tell you to let go."

But Darius was drifting away like a rudderless ship in a choppy ocean. His mind would not obey his will. He saw himself back in the Hyperspace Conveyor Tube tumbling head over heels towards a dim light in the distance. The light source turned into a pair of headlights rushing at him and then there was a blinding flash.

Darius tumbled onto a scuffed linoleum floor. He opened his eyes and blinked. High intensity lighting washed the room of shadows. He knew this place—the teak wood classroom where he used to study comparative religions in college. It was a small room with about thirty chairs, all of them now empty. From the hallway, he heard singing. The lyrics sounded familiar—an old Irish ballade Darius had learned to sing to Rebecca on her twenty-first birthday. The sweet voices made him weep.

> *"I will build my love a tower*
> *Near yon' pure crystal fountain*
> *And on it I will build*
> *All the flowers of the mountain*
> *Will ye go, Lassie go?"*

Rebecca Donahue stepped through the classroom doorway. She wore a red cardigan sweater with white shorts and sandals. Her black, curly hair toppled over her shoulders and sparkled, along with her deep blue eyes in the pale light of the room. She walked up to him in the simple, graceful way Darius remembered. She was tall and slim, only an inch shorter than his five foot ten inches.

Rebecca took his thick hands in hers.

"Don't cry, my love," she said.

He couldn't remember the last time he had cried. Now he couldn't stop. He tried to speak. Nothing but awkward sounds came out.

"Don't mourn the past," she said. "Be grateful for what we shared. Nothing can destroy our love. Remember that forever."

She smiled in a way that had always made his heart cartwheel.

"I don't think I can live without you," Darius said.

She smiled again. "You're stronger than you know."

He had so many things to say, but her last words sounded like a goodbye. He did not want to lose her again. Their hands slipped apart. The floor moved under his feet. The room flew away. An irresistible force pushed him down a narrowing tunnel. Before he reached the end, the tunnel turned into the Hyperspace Conveyor Tube. He floated in the HCT for what seemed like only seconds before it spit him out—back inside the circle of light piercing the dark void.

"Stay with me," Anky said.

With every thread of his being, Darius willed himself to believe that he was capable of escaping the void with Anky's help. He refused to relinquish hope. And he trusted the power within him.

"Release the energy," Anky shouted. It felt like the pent-up energy of a hundred hydroelectric dams rushed out of his fingertips.

The circle of light surrounding them exploded outward in every direction—as far as Darius could see.

Chapter Thirty-Eight

THE TRANS-DIMENSIONAL TUNNELER

"I'**LL HAVE YOUR** decisions now," the man in the navy suit said. "Tell me quickly if you want to live." He pointed to Simon. "You first."

Simon turned away, unable to meet the penetrating stare of the creature behind the mask of Kyle Huntilla. Simon's averted eyes rested on the structure shooting up into the shadows in the center of the cavern. Bullet shaped canisters protruded from the circular base of the tower. He made an instant connection. The canisters likely contained the light energy stolen from the people at the" New You" seminar.

Simon noticed a pink halo of light glimmer to life at the top of the tower. The light outlined what looked to Simon like a giant version of the hand-held weapon The Warrior Lord had used to dispatch Darius. The thing glittered like a gem in the eerie light. It seemed to be floating by itself in the upper reaches of the cavern. Then Simon caught sight of an Exile standing behind the double barrels of the weapon.

The gun barrels arched upwards towards the cavern ceiling.

A second later, the rows of purple lights lining the four corners of the tower blinked off.

Simon felt Vicky's arms around him. Her eyes searched his for inspiration; some inkling of a plan to free them from this nightmare.

He held her tightly. He had no escape plan. Neither did she. They were hopelessly outnumbered. He watched the color of the halo surrounding the giant tuning fork cycle higher in frequency, from pink to red, to orange, to indigo, and finally violet.

He heard a high-pitched beeping noise followed by what sounded like a great bevy of birds taking flight. The cavern walls shook, and then, a loud explosion accompanied by a swirling cloud of purple light.

Simon watched the purple cloud slowly disperse. It revealed an astonishing sight.

The hellish machine had torn a perfect circle out of the cavern ceiling with the precision of a glasscutter. A full palette of colors shimmered from inside the hole. It reminded Simon of the colors reflected in a prism.

Enthusiastic shrieks rose from the ranks of Exiles clustered in groups on the cavern floor. The Warrior Lord in disguise thrust one arm in the air, then turned back to face Simon.

"I'm waiting impatiently for your answer."

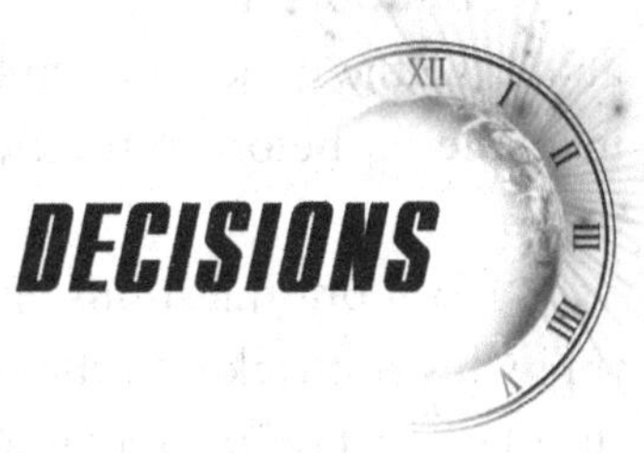

DECISIONS

IT SURPRISED SIMON how easy it was going to be to announce his decision. He didn't know what the firing of the weapon had proved. Maybe it was a doomsday weapon. Whatever it was, he knew it wasn't good news. He didn't care anymore. Everything was uncertain now, except his choice.

"I've already caused enough suffering," Simon said. "Helping you and your cause is out of the question."

The man glared at Vicky. "And you?"

"No," she said.

The man turned to Javon. The teenager shook his head back and forth. "I'm with the Doc and the lady," he said.

"Then I have another use for all of you," the man said. "We'll need to test the Trans-Dimensional Tunneler before we send our troops through. You three will be guinea pigs."

"Test this," Javon said with a middle finger salute.

"Don't you dare irritate me," the Warrior Lord said with the most terrifying look Simon had ever seen.

"What exactly does the machine do?" Simon inquired, unable to quell his scientific curiosity, even in the shadow of death.

"This machine will open a portal to distant planets and millions of worlds in other dimensions. With this invention, we can travel to the shores of heaven itself. This planet will serve as a launching pad for our unlimited conquest."

"How does it work," Simon asked. Maybe if he knew something about the theoretical principles, he could figure out a way to blow the machine up before it took him to some forlorn asteroid or lifeless moon.

"No more questions. I have much to do." The Kyle duplicate threw his suit jacket to the floor and tore open his shirt. He touched the glass ball on the chain hanging from his neck. The marble-sized ball looked like the one Simon had seen the tech at Amcor wear. The man who was not really Kyle Huntilla began to change shape. The creature sprouted an extra pair of arms and grew two feet taller. The human head disappeared into a rapidly transforming torso. A ghastly reptilian head emerged.

"I am Glythren."

The creature spoke in a hissing, whispery voice that was hard for Simon to understand. The beast roared in agony as its legs thickened to the size of tree trunks and a broad, flat tail unfurled from behind.

Shards of clothing littered the floor at the creature's Ostrich-like feet.

Glythren pointed to the dark energy containment bubble he had resealed after dispatching Darius to his unthinkable fate. The top of the bubble ripped open and the edges pealed back. Three Exile guards emerged out of the gloom. Glythren barked an order to them in a guttural language Simon did not recognize. The guards seized Simon, Vicky and Javon, pulling them towards the tower.

Chapter Forty

CLOSE UP

THE LIGHTS ON the four legs of the tower switched on. They emitted a ghostly, violet light.

Light energy from the canisters swam up the tubing like semen in search of an ovum.

"It looks like the damned machine runs on light energy sucked from the hearts and minds of people," Simon whispered to Vicky and Javon.

He followed the path of the energy up the tower as they walked towards it. At closer range, Simon could see that the tubes fed into a large funnel immediately below the platform.

As they drew closer, Simon noticed a ladder on the far side of the tower stretching all the way up to the platform on top—and something else. A substance resembling crude oil flowed upwards inside the tubes.

"What's that black stuff?" Javon said.

"I assume it's another form of energy, possibly derived from dark matter," Simon answered. "Light energy is pushing up this side of the tower, and the other energy is moving upwards on the other side. It appears the machine runs on a combination of light and dark energy.

"But Darius said dark and light energy can't meet without causing some sort of detonation," Vicky said.

"Apparently, these creatures have figured out how to combine the two forces," Simon replied. "They've managed to create an entirely new form of energy. From the looks of the hole in the ceiling, the new energy is extremely powerful."

They reached the base of the tower. What looked like swamp gas from afar now looked to Simon like thin, violet gauze draped over the structure. He guessed it was a protective energy shield.

One of the Exile guards touched a ruby red circle at the very bottom of the corner beam. The lights on the tower blinked out again. The violet energy field disappeared.

"Climb," one of the guards hissed.

Simon looked up. It was a steep haul up the ladder to the top.

Chapter Forty-One

NETHERWORLD

THE BRIGHT EXPLOSION of light gave way to a pale blue color. Darius thought they were tumbling down through the sky, until the atmosphere around them changed to cool orange and again to lime green. The colors kept changing with no apparent rhyme or reason.

There was no day or night, hot or cold, transparent or opaque. There was no wind in front of them or behind. It was impossible to tell if they were moving forwards or backwards. This was a netherworld, a place between here and there. He had only the slightest inkling of their direction. He sensed that they were falling.

Darius held a vision of the underground cavern in his mind and heart. He told himself to keep believing, hoping, and trusting they would wind up in the right place. He gripped Anky's hand tightly.

An object appeared in the distance below them. It grew larger, now recognizable as a small circle of blue-gray light. It appeared as a hole in a pinkish-blue sky. The stationary hole in the sky enabled Darius to judge they were falling rapidly like a boulder falling from the sky into a lake. The circle kept growing larger as they drew closer. Soon, it would swallow them up like two guppies swimming into the mouth of a giant sea bass.

"Grab my other hand," Anky called out to Darius. "Hold on tight."

Darius immediately grabbed his companion's free hand. The last thing he wanted was to fall through the gaping hole alone.

"Are you sure this is the right way?" Darius shouted.

"Nope," Anky replied.

They shot through the circle in the middle of nowhere.

The atmosphere inside the circle grew thicker and hotter as they plummeted. Darius found it harder to breathe. Tiny globules of colored lights swirled around him. Looking down, he saw nothing beneath his feet besides the balls of colored light that appeared to be shooting towards him as they fell.

His arms and legs began to sting. He closed his eyes to protect them from whatever was happening. The atmosphere around him suddenly felt like sand in a windstorm grating against his skin.

"Be ready to open your light shield," he heard Anky call out.

"When are we going to land?" Darius said through gritted teeth.

"No idea," Anky answered. Just be ready with your shield when I say so."

Darius summoned light energy. It was the only thing he could do, besides believing, hoping, and trusting that Anky, his newfound friend, had the instincts of a test pilot who lived to enjoy his retirement years.

With his eyes closed, Darius did not see the circular opening appear ahead of them from out of nowhere. They flashed through it an instant later.

"Now," Anky yelled.

Darius deployed his light shield three seconds before he crashed into a very solid object.

LONELY AT THE TOP

DARIUS HEARD A loud *clunk* behind him. He crawled under the huge tuning fork and found Anky sprawled on the other side of the platform where they had crash-landed.

Darius crawled to the edge and looked down. Simon, Vicky and Javon looked up at him from the cavern floor. They were surrounded by two Exile guards. Darius held his breath. It was a long way down, at least a thousand feet. Groups of Exile soldiers scattered about the cavern drawing their weapons.

A creature noticeably taller than the others ran through the throng of soldiers screaming something that sounded like *VARR LUMM*, whatever that meant.

Anky crawled next to Darius. He peered down at the commotion on the cavern floor. "Looks like we got a Warrior Lord comin' to pay us a visit." The old man sighed. "Oh boy."

Darius watched the Warrior Lord push the two guards aside before taking a giant leap towards the tower.

VARR LUMM the fearsome beast shrieked again.

"I think he's tellin' the others not to shoot. Must be he doesn't want to damage this tower we're settin' on. Can't be any other reason. Those boys have no use for us, that's for sure."

Darius and Anky listened to the creature's claws hitting the ladder. They sounded like four pistons in a motor operating in perfect unison. The *chug-a-chunk* sounds grew louder.

"All my brothers and sisters are floatin' around in the black void thanks to this fella comin' after us."

"What's our next move?" Darius was almost as afraid of the answer as he was of the monster coming for them.

"Sit here and wait for our chance," Anky drawled laconically.

"I'm not going to sit here without putting up a fight." Darius pushed up from the cold steel platform. Anky grabbed him by the arm.

"Whoa down, son. Putting up a fight now is futile. Their guns can pierce our light shields."

"How do you know?"

"How do you think me and all the other Senior Operatives wound up in the soup? We're not a bunch of idiots, fer Pete's sake. They took us by surprise. The Exiles have developed a bunch of powerful weapons by combining dark and light energy. We call it hybrid energy."

"One of your fellow Directors told me that dark and light energy explodes when combined."

"Glythren's son discovered a molecule that makes it possible."

"So now our light shields are useless against their weapons?"

"That's about the size of it."

His courage swooned. "So, now we face an army of Exiles without any protection?"

Anky turned to him with a reproachful expression. "We've still got the three principles."

"Oh, great."

A vicious scream rose from the darkness below. The sound was much louder than before. The monster was closer now. Any second, Darius knew, it would emerge out of the gloom, a killing machine with eyes as deep and black as the hopeless place from which they had just escaped.

Chapter Forty-Three

"WE GOTTA' MAKE A MOVE"

A SEA OF Exile eyes watched spellbound from the cavern floor as their leader ascended the ladder on the tower. They were like a crowd of Roman spectators at the Coliseum anticipating the bloody climax of a gladiator contest without the sound effects, Simon thought. Javon stood next to him.

"We gotta' make a move," he whispered.

Simon could not agree more. He jerked his head towards a stack of light canisters nearby. They moved slowly away, deftly ducking inside the nearest v-shaped stack. Not one of the Exile soldiers seemed to notice or care. Their attention was riveted on the impending slaughter of two hapless angels trapped on top of the tower.

Simon examined the stack of light canisters directly in front of him. A curved handle about four inches long protruded from the middle of each canister. The handles interlocked. They formed a spine from the bottom to the top of each row. He figured the handles were there to hold the stacks together. Another function might be to make it easier to handle the smooth metal cylinders when carried individually.

A wonderful idea came to him. There had to be a release device to allow the energy to flow from the tube. Could the handle on the canister also serve as a trigger? Simon carefully slid the canister on top of the pile away from the others. Javon copied his every move.

"Careful," he whispered to the teenager.

"Careful's my middle name," Javon assured him.

"Point it straight up while I try to figure out how it works."

Javon frowned.

"We don't want to shoot ourselves in the foot with one of these things. You know what I mean?"

"A'ight. Whatever."

Simon tried pushing the handle on the canister. It would not move in any direction. He ran a finger along the handle where it joined the cold metal of the cylinder. There was a crack between the two pieces. The handle was a moving part, no doubt about it. How did the thing work? He kept pushing and pulling with no success.

He heard footsteps. Javon peered over the top of the rock. "They're comin' at us," he reported.

Simon peeked around the side of the stack. He quickly pulled back. A group of six Exiles were bounding towards them.

Javon banged the canister he was holding against his knee. A light energy beam blew a hole in the cavern floor, just missing Vicky's left foot.

Simon grabbed the canister out of Javon's hands. The handle had turned into something else. "You've activated the release mechanism."

"You mean the trigger?"

Simon nodded. He handed the canister back to Javon. "Wait until I get my canister ready. Then we'll surprise them."

Javon grinned.

Simon pushed down on the handle of his canister with both thumbs. It still would not move. He reminded himself the Exiles looked to be ten times stronger than a Russian Olympic weight lifter. Activating the trigger mechanism would be a much harder feat for a human being to accomplish. He pressed down harder, until both thumbs hurt.

"Hurry up," Javon said, poking him in the shoulder.

The handle finally moved. Simon watched it recede into the canister. A triangular mechanism surfaced in place of the handle.

He lost no time aiming the canister at the advancing monsters. The creatures made frightening sounds, now only about twenty feet away.

Simon put his index finger inside the triangle and pulled.

Nothing happened.

The creatures were almost on top of them.

Simon pulled harder. The canister spat a light energy beam that missed the advancing creatures by a wide margin despite the close range.

"You have to pull the trigger hard," he said to Javon.

Javon aimed and fired. The light beam missed the intended targets, but not by much.

Simon fired again. The light beam crashed into the Exile in the middle of the group, exploding it into chunks and little pieces.

Javon fired again, slicing the head off of another monster.

The surviving Exiles broke off their attack and scurried away into the gloom.

. . .

The Warrior Lord emerged from the darkness, pummeling the ladder with all four hands like a crazed prizefighter. Every instinct inside Darius told him to rain down light energy bolts before the creature could reach the platform. Anky had specifically told him not to fire, for some unfathomable reason.

He was numb with fear.

Then Anky swung into action. He crawled over the ledge and scuttled down the ladder—right into Glythren's arms.

The angel and the Warrior Lord tumbled down into the darkness.

"Anky!" Darius screamed. The old man had sacrificed himself to give Darius a slim chance to complete the mission.

No goodbyes. No inspirational speech. No more Anky.

Darius had never felt more alone in his life, before or after his death.

With intense concentration, he imagined the Archangel talking to him as Paul Newman, as he had in the dream. Darius heard Aaron's voice inside his head.

The golden triangle. Use its power to protect you.

"How?" Darius said aloud

Now he heard Anky's voice in his head.

Use the principles. Ya' think I was flappin' my gums to hear myself talk?

Darius closed his eyes and concentrated hard on the three principles. Belief was the first. He saw an image of Javon driving like a mad man, saving him from Exile attacks.

He thought of Hope. He never would have made it out of the black Void and back to the cavern without Hope to expand the circle of light.

He thought of Trust. He had trusted Anky to know how to blast them out of the netherworld. Even before that, he had trusted Aaron's judgment despite his initial certainty that he was the wrong man for the job.

And yes, he had trusted three total strangers to help him get this far. It was nothing short of a miracle that all four of them were still alive. If a hero lived somewhere inside him, it was time for that guy to show up.

Then he remembered something his father had told him on the eve of a big High School track meet: *You never know what you can do until you do it.* Simple yet profound advice.

The next day, Darius won two of the three events he competed in, a personal best.

Everyone had a hero deep down inside, Darius now understood. He had to find *his hero* and connect with him more fully than he had ever done before.

He pulled himself up from a prone position. Standing tall at the top of the tower, he heard rustling sounds from below.

The tower lights blinked on again. An army of Exiles looked up at him from the cavern floor. They raised their weapons.

Some of them carried the Exile version of a pistol. Others carried something that looked like a crossbow, while others carried an elongated version of the pistol.

All of the weapons came equipped with opposing triangles at the business end.

All of those scary things pointed straight at him.

Chapter Forty-Four

PRINCIPLE POWERED

THREE SHAFTS OF light streamed outward from the triangle Darius wore on the gold chain around his neck. Each of the broad shafts of light originated from one of the tiny circles wedged into the corners of the triangle. He kept repeating the three principles mentally.

In response, the light surrounding him grew brighter. A circle of light formed from one of the shafts of light. A second circle formed inside of the first circle from another shaft of light. Then a third circle formed inside of the second one. They formed a shield of three concentric circles—triple protection.

Darius sensed the three-ply shield grow stronger with each passing second. Light energy coursed through his body in preparation for the coming battle.

The Exile Soldiers on the cavern floor fired their weapons on a signal from Glythren. Hybrid energy projectiles flew from row after row of Exile weaponry. The projectiles swarmed upwards like a squadron of tiny cruise missiles.

Darius trusted his shield would keep him whole. He held his arms out with fingers spread wide. Light energy bolts sprang from each finger. He realized immediately his ability to channel light energy had increased profoundly since the last time he had done it in the Amcor lab.

The first wave of hybrid energy projectiles crashed into his shield with ferocious speed. Each one exploded in a puff of blue-gray smoke. Darius found it difficult to aim through the tiny explosions outside the shield. He kept firing, however, concentrating on one section of the Exile army at a time.

At first, his constant barrage seemed to have no effect. Darius wondered if he had enough firepower to wipe out the fierce Exile mob before they wiped *him* out. He forced that thought out of his mind. *Believe in yourself,* Darius repeated to himself. *Believe in the people around you.* That one was not going to be easy. Javon, Simon, and Vicky were nowhere in sight. Were they still alive?

After several minutes passed, the mini-explosions on his outer shield diminished. Visibility through the shields increased. The gaping holes in the Exile ranks surprised Darius quite pleasantly. He had managed to wipe out more than half of the creatures in a span of only about five minutes. Exile body parts littered the cavern floor, some of them twitching in the after-glow of sudden death.

He felt a sudden weariness and stopped firing to recharge his energy. Where was Glythren? Where was Anky? If Anky survived the fall from the tower, it was likely Glythren had ripped the old man apart with his bare claws after puncturing his light shield. The probable loss of his ally stung Darius deeply.

A flurry of light energy bolts coming from a stack of canisters near the tower cut his grieving short. Darius could hardly believe his eyes. Simon, Vicky, and Javon were down there, barely holding off a small detail of angry Exile soldiers. He aimed and released a fusillade of light energy bolts.

The Exiles surrounding his friends splattered like bugs on a windshield traveling at high speed.

Javon waved his canister at Darius. There was no time to acknowledge the gesture. Darius resumed his attack on the Exile army with one merciless barrage of light energy after another. He picked them off in clumps of six, eight—a dozen at a time. The chamber stank of burnt tar, the odor of Exile blood. The blood coagulated in ragged splotches and clumps all over the rocky cavern floor.

Darius ran to the ladder, eager to rejoin his friends. Together they would mop up the few straggling remainders of what had been an invincible army when the tormenting guards had first shoved them into the cavern. He put a foot on the top rung of the ladder. The purple energy shield surrounding it prevented him from stepping down.

Then, he heard a single, ear-piercing scream echoing from the bowels of the cavern. The force field and the scream made his friends seem as far away as Alpha Centauri.

Chapter Forty-Five

WISHING WON'T MAKE IT SO

THE LIGHTS ON the tower blinked off again, plunging the cavern floor into darkness. Something scuttled up the ladder at a furious pace. Darius clung to the hope that Anky had somehow survived the fall and murdered Glythren in a Senior Operative surprise maneuver reminiscent of the newest edition of James Bond. The creature ascending the ladder might be an Exile Captain, or better yet, an ordinary grunt. The rattling sounds—heavy claws pounding the ladder in unison, came ever closer.

The shiny platform under his feet offered little support. Darius wished he could magically change his penny loafers into high-top sneakers, or even better, combat boots. The loafers would be about as useful on the slippery platform as a bouquet of roses would be in fighting the pissed off monster zooming up the tower ladder.

Darius slid behind the back end of the tuning fork. Each facet of the emerald cut surface looked to measure about a foot long and six inches wide. From up close, the giant-sized surfaces gave the weapon a surreal appearance.

He found a keyboard sunk into the butt end of the awesome gun. Geometric symbols glittered inside each key on the board. The keys themselves looked to Darius exactly like glittering square-cut rubies. Randomly pushing keys might easily result in the destruction of the cavern. He only had his depleted light energy resources to fight the thing hurtling up the ladder.

Whatever was coming sounded close to the platform. Darius summoned light energy. His body's response was less than enthusiastic.

Seconds later, a massive Exile scrambled over the top of the ladder. The monster appeared to be at least seven feet tall with the nimble movements of a cat. The creature's distinctive purple aura pulsed. This was no "ordinary" Exile, if one could use that word in connection with any of these hideous beings.

"I've had quite enough of you, little angel," Glythren said in a hoarse voice.

Darius leaned out from behind the rear of the double-barreled weapon. He raised his arms. His mind told his body to release a ten-fingered salvo of light energy. His body refused to cooperate. He was dry as a bone.

Glythren hopped on the top barrel of the gun. The monster stalked down the barrel in a low crawl towards the back end.

Darius pushed the gun hard to the right. Glythren wrapped all four powerful arms around the barrels.

The big gun and the Warrior Lord hung over the edge of the platform. Glythren's tail rose straight into the air. It moved back and forth like a metronome.

"Your death will be quick and painless if you give up now," the monster hissed, baring a mouthful of needle sharp teeth.

Darius tried again to fire off a volley of light energy. Nothing doing. He shrank back behind the end of the big gun with only his three-ply shield to protect him.

With a shrill cry that pierced the core of Darius' dwindling courage, Glythren leapt forward, landing adroitly on the platform a mere foot away. The Warrior Lord tried to lay hands on his prey, but the outer light shield repelled the attempt like an impenetrable weather balloon.

Glythren tried to tear the outer shield with the bony points at the end of his long nails. The surface gave slightly but held firm, prompting a roar of frustration.

Glythren's aura intensified. The monster lit up like a purple candle, casting a blanket of midnight blue color across the ceiling of the cavern.

If only he could summon energy from within as easily as Glythren did.

The Warrior Lord rubbed his aura against the outer light shield in the same way a large grizzly bear would rub its back against a thick tree trunk to scratch an itch. Pieces of the outer shield frayed and fell away.

By concentrating on the three principles, Darius closed some of the tears in the shield.

Glythren continued to rub against the shield, ripping open more holes, and then poking his arm through to tear open a gaping hole in the outer wall.

That was all Darius needed to see. He launched himself off the platform into the darkness.

Chapter Forty-Six

A SHORT REUNION

DOWN HE TUMBLED, hoping the protective shields would cushion the impact of his fall. He closed his eyes. *Believe. Hope. Trust.* The principles and his faith in them were all he had now.

Darius heard a loud *crunch.* The good news was he did not feel any pain. Opening his eyes, he immediately realized that the two inner shields had cushioned his fall. The outer shield, or what was left of it, had disintegrated. The crash had completed Glythren's handiwork.

From out of the shadows, Simon, Javon and Vicky rushed towards him cradling their light canisters like babies. Those babies had saved their lives.

The sight of his friends brought a smile to his parched lips, but there was no time to celebrate a happy reunion.

Darius searched the tower and the dark corners of the cavern for signs of Glythren. There was no movement anywhere.

He peered in every direction, searching for the opening where they had entered the cavern. He found no hint of the way out. Too bad the Exiles didn't believe in posting exit signs. A big one with the words THIS WAY OUT OF THIS HELL HOLE blinking in pink neon would have come in handy right about now.

He hoped that his light energy carpet-bombing had not buried the exit under a pile of dirt and broken rocks.

A loud BOOM filled the cavern, followed by a blinding flash of blue-gray light. Something similar to a gale force wind swept Darius off his feet and pin-balled him into the walls and then the ceiling of the cavern.

He caught a glimpse of Glythren behind the big gun before his harrowing journey ended in a rocky corner of the Exile stronghold.

A few seconds later, Darius came to a miraculous conclusion. He had managed to survive a blast from the Trans-Dimensional Tunneler without losing his senses or body parts based on a quick inventory of the aforementioned items.

The blast, however, had disintegrated his two remaining protective shields. Apparently, the shields had saved him from harm.

Before he had a chance to thank his lucky stars, something jumped from the tower. A blur hit the ground. A terrifying scream filled the cavern.

Glythren attacked, uttering another horrible war cry. Darius' teeth chattered with exhaustion and fear.

The monster picked up energy weapons from the corpses on the cavern floor before coming after Darius and his astonished friends. Now, Glythren carried four tuning fork pistols, one in each claw. The beast opened fire on them. Four streams of hybrid energy projectiles swam through the cavern's half-light. Darius and the others scattered.

The projectiles blew a hole in the wall behind them large enough to drive a Caterpillar earthmover through. Inside the hole, Darius saw an opening.

It had to be the exit tunnel.

Darius felt his strength returning. He called on his light energy reserves. By now, his inner batteries had had enough time to recharge themselves. He fired ten light energy bolts at the approaching beast.

Glythren parried the attack with his forearms. Apparently, the Warrior Lord had much more resistance to light energy than the Exile soldiers. It would take more than one volley of light energy to bring Glythren down. Probably many more, Darius figured.

A light mist from the raging battle hung in the cavern. The

residue from the apocalyptic energy explosions that had rocked the cavern earlier parted around Glythren's powerful body. The creature sailed through the mist like a giant battle cruiser with all of its long-range artillery guns trained on Darius.

Glythren fired again. Darius hit the dirt. In a few more seconds, the Warrior Lord's guns would recharge and Darius would be toast.

The tower loomed behind the approaching monster. He noticed the shields were down. In his rage, Glythren must have left the big gun in firing mode when he jumped from the platform. The gun consumed all of the tower's energy in order to fire, so the shields had fallen. The tower was momentarily defenseless.

Darius wasted no time. He aimed and fired at the huge energy weapon on top of the ten-story structure.

Light energy bolts slammed into the tower's steel girders. The tubing just below the platform glowed bright red. Darius had missed his target. He fired again and hit the same spot.

Another miss—or so he thought.

A deafening explosion shook the cavern.

"SHLAGGAHHH," Glythren roared.

The light energy blasts had fractured the beams supporting the platform. The cracks were visible to the naked eye.

The steel girders groaned.

The platform tilted downward at a precarious angle.

Simon, Vicky and Javon started raking the tower from top to bottom with light energy blasts from their canisters.

Glythren screamed again, like a mother who had just seen her baby run over by a drunken driver.

The steel girders buckled. The sprawling tower wobbled like a clown on stilts fighting to stay upright. The structure lost the battle and crashed against the cavern wall, breaking into two sections before it collapsed.

One section smashed against the ground only a few feet away from Darius, spewing debris in every direction. A flying piece of tubing just missed crushing his head.

The other section crashed down directly on top of Glythren, raising a tall shroud of dust.

The sight of the Warrior Lord disappearing under an avalanche of steel and tubing prompted a triumphant shout from Darius and his comrades. With Glythren neutralized and his army of Exile soldiers destroyed, Darius felt a surge of confidence. But, he still had work to do in the murky cavern before he could think of leaving.

The dust made it hard to breathe. Darius struggled to his feet. His gray suit pants were torn and tattered. He bled from scrapes on his hands and knees. His spectacles were filthy. He took a moment to clean them with a piece of his ragged shirt.

Fitting the glasses back on, Darius staggered over to his three friends. He pointed to the entrance to the tunnel. "Get out of here. I still have work to do."

He broke down into a coughing fit—not exactly the best move to inspire confidence.

"What the hell are you talking about," Javon yelled.

"I have to destroy that thing to make sure the Exiles can't use it again."

Darius indicated the glittering weapon that had survived intact in the fall. It lay amid the settling dust, like a jewel stranded in the debris of a sunken ship.

"C'mon with us." Javon said. "This place could cave in any second."

Darius had to smile. "Don't give me a hard time."

"Your mind is blown, man."

Darius turned to Simon and Vicky. "Please take Javon with you. Drag him if necessary."

"Are you sure?" Vicky asked.

"Yes. I'll find you topside when I'm through here."

"What if you don't make it," Simon said.

"You'll figure out what to do."

The dust made Darius cough again. "Go on. Go. There's no time to argue."

DUEL IN THE SHADOWS

DARIUS STOOD ATOP the Trans-Dimensional Tunneler wondering how to destroy the thing without including himself in the process.

He was not surprised the giant tuning fork had survived the fall from the top of the tower. The diamond cut transducers behind the barrels had to be made of an incredibly durable material to convert the massive energy flow from the tubes into projectiles. It followed, then, that all the parts of the gun were made of highly durable materials. The stress on the machine's inner systems would be enormous when the mysterious hybrid energy surged through it. This line of reasoning pointed to a single, unhappy conclusion: The machine, in all probability, would still work when re-connected to an energy source.

Darius could not risk leaving it behind in one piece.

A rustling sound interrupted his troubled thoughts.

Nearby, a fallen steel beam shifted in a pile of twisted tubing.

Darius jumped off the giant gun and ducked. Adrenaline rushed through his bruised and battered body.

Two arms rose out of the rubble like twin periscopes.

"HREESSHAASHARGH."

The cry sounded like the pitiful yelp of a wounded animal.

The crown of an Exile head broke the surface of the debris. The head had to belong to Glythren, not some lowly Exile soldier. No other living being could have survived entombment under tons of falling steel, ragged chunks of oversized semiconductors, and long strands of heavy gauge tubing.

A dark shape rose from the pile of rubble.

Darius backed away from the doomsday machine. He fired a volley of light energy bolts at the twin barrels of the machine. The volley danced harmlessly off the gun, illuminating the cavern for an instant like a lightning strike. In that brief moment, Darius glimpsed a monstrous figure extract itself from the wreckage.

The fall of the tower had reduced two of Glythren's arms to bloody stumps. The Warrior Lord unleashed a furious scream.

Although every muscle fiber in his body told him to run, Darius stopped moving. Ignoring the approaching monstrosity, he stared at the machine's emerald cut diamond surfaces. Light energy had no effect on them. What should he try next?

Darius glanced at the opening in the wall. The only exit from the cavern beckoned. The temptation to run was almost irresistible now. Time was short. Glythren advanced. The Warrior Lord had apparently lost his weapons in the fall. That would give Darius a little more time.

Not enough time, regrettably, to ring up Aaron for a chat about how, exactly, a weary angel went about blowing up a doomsday weapon that was more powerful than anything he knew of beside a hydrogen bomb.

Glythren bore down on him from out of the shadows.

Darius continued to stare at the Trans-Dimensional Tunneler as if the weapon might tell him how to kill it by speaking through its gun barrels. Then he noticed an odd-shaped handle sticking out of the dust near the machine. He raced over to the spot, bent down, and dug furiously. In a matter of seconds, he unearthed a hybrid energy pistol.

Holding the weapon at arm's length, he fired a stream of projectiles at Glythren. The Warrior Lord still retained enough reflexes to dodge out of the way. Darius had about thirty seconds before Glythren arrived in all of his pissed-off glory.

No divine guidance came from on high. It was possible that Aaron, the Board of Directors, and even the Chief Himself, had no clue as to what to do next. He was flying solo now.

There was only one card left to play. Maybe the Tunneler was vulnerable to hybrid energy projectiles. If a blast from the pistol turned him into vapor along with the machine, so be it.

Darius fired the pistol repeatedly at the Tunneler. The surfaces of the gun barrels came alive with a rainbow of bright colors—pink, yellow, orange, red and violet. He didn't know what to make of it. At least he was still breathing—and the hybrid energy blasts had had *some* effect on the giant gun.

He needed more time to assess the situation. A hiding place somewhere in the shadows would do the trick, preferably somewhere near the exit.

While Glythren stood motionless, gaping at the colorful light show, Darius crept low along the ground towards the opening in the wall. His scraped knees and tired muscles ached. Dehydration weakened him. He needed to drink about a gallon of Gatorade to feel human again. He could use a two-week spa vacation to rest up for whatever was coming next.

Enough wishful thinking. He forced himself to re-focus on the mission. Taking refuge behind a pile of rocks, Darius observed the diamond surfaces of the Tunneler glow brighter. The rainbows reflecting off the barrels grew taller and wider. The hybrid energy projectiles had started some sort of chain reaction.

Glythren made one great leap with the help of his prehensile tail, and landed on the back end of the giant gun. He attacked the computer keys in the inlaid console Darius had seen earlier.

Chapter Forty-Eight

DEATH IN THE SHADOWS

DARIUS WATCHED GLYTHREN work the keys furiously. He figured the Warrior Lord was trying to shut down whatever was happening to his precious weapon of mass conquest. Apparently, there was enough stored energy left in the machine to operate it.

More rainbows sprang from the gun barrels. An instant later, Darius watched the rainbows change shape. They became pinwheels with thin spokes.

The pinwheels rotated in the air directly above the machine. The sight was fascinating and terrifying at the same time.

Glythren began to pound the console with his massive fists. The keyboard shattered. Unleashing a deafening roar, the Warrior Lord leapt off the gun barrels. He swept the cavern with the three antennae-like appendages above his forehead. Turning towards Darius' position, Glythren scampered through the rubble.

One of the pinwheels broke apart. Then another. And another. The spokes shot outward like multi-colored javelins hurled at the cavern walls.

Darius heard Glythren coming—only yards away from his position. He retreated to the mouth of the cavern opening, pushing up the tunnel a few yards out of sight.

Glythren stopped in front of the rocks guarding the entrance.

The monster looked about for signs of its prey. Glythren's pulsing aura provided enough light to discern the slightest movement from among the rocks. If the creature found him now, he would never be able to outrun Glythren in the narrow exit tunnel.

Glythren turned towards the entrance. The monster took a few steps closer for a better look inside the tunnel.

Darius panicked. He turned and ran up the tunnel, slipping in his fright, dislodging a few rocks. The stones clattered against the rocky floor.

Glythren roared. "There you are troublesome angel."

He stuck his horrible head into the tunnel entrance. The large black eyes with purple dots in the center found him.

Darius raised the hybrid energy pistol and fired. Nothing happened. Not even a *click* from the trigger. The pistol had run out of hybrid energy.

A second later, a light spear from one of the decaying pinwheels punched through Glythren's belly.

The Warrior Lord screamed and fell back.

Darius heard a loud *thunk* outside the tunnel.

Darius moved cautiously to the mouth of the tunnel.

Glythren lay on the cavern floor, writhing.

Somehow, the monster struggled to its feet.

Darius knew he should run, but he had to make sure the Tunneler was destroyed.

Behind Glythren's wounded body, shafts of multi-colored light slammed against the cavern walls, rocking the chamber with one seismic explosion after another.

Black blood gushed from Glythren's abdomen, but the monster seemed determined to take Darius along for a grisly ride to eternal damnation.

Darius reflexively fired light energy bolts from his fingers that carved a deeper gash in Glythren's stomach. His light energy attacks had previously bounced harmlessly off of the creature's purple aura. Apparently, the pinwheel spoke had weakened Glythren's armor. Darius noted Glythren's purple aura had dimmed.

Although he felt at the end of his resources, Darius summoned the will to fire another fusillade of light energy at Glythren. The blasts tore squarely into Glythren's chest, dislodging chunks of flesh.

Glythren screamed so loudly Darius thought the cavern walls and his eardrums would burst.

The Warrior Lord's purple aura faded out.

With his last ounce of strength, Darius summoned the remaining light energy in his body.

When the light energy blasts left his fingers, Darius felt like he had spent his last dollar of life energy. What kept him upright and breathing?

He struggled to hold his balance as the last burst of light energy tore through Glythren's body. Whatever remained of Glythren the Warrior Lord collapsed into a steaming mound of monster parts on the cavern floor.

With Glythren's demise, Darius felt a rush of hope, but it only lasted for an instant.

One glance at the Trans-Dimensional Tunneler spawned a new sense of dread. Without any controlling device hooked up to shut down the chain reaction he had started, the machine looked to be reaching some kind of critical mass. Two more giant pinwheels blew apart.

He spent precious seconds waiting for light energy to begin welling up inside his exhausted human body.

Another energy rainbow blew apart in the center of the cavern.

He wondered if the explosion would be powerful enough to collapse the tunnel with him inside it when the chain reaction reached critical mass. He had to trust that he had done his job. He had to leave the cavern.

Darius turned and began the arduous climb up the rocky steps inside the passageway. He pushed through the narrow tunnel as fast as his bloodied hands and knees would carry him.

Chapter Forty-Nine

DARIUS CRAWLED UPWARDS through the tunnel in total darkness. It was like slipping through the throat of a beast with teeth embedded all around him. He bumped and cut himself on the sharp rocks. Every few feet of progress cost him pain and blood.

His mind played tricks on him. He imagined the spokes of light shooting off from the giant pinwheels and bouncing off the cavern walls. In the center of the cavern, the spokes congealed into a huge ball of multi-colored light. The ball began to pulse, slowly at first, and then rapidly, like the heart of a champion sprinter running the hundred-yard dash. There was a brilliant flash of light before the fireball engulfed him.

He kept digging. He kept believing. He kept hoping. He kept trusting. Every cell in his body screamed for rest, but there was no rest for the weary. He would have plenty of time for rest if he survived this ordeal.

These thoughts spun around in his head like the giant pinwheels until he glimpsed the jagged opening leading into the basement. He dug feverishly toward the faint light ahead.

Crawling out of the passageway, he toppled onto the restroom floor. The sirens of sleep called to him seductively.

Get on your feet Junior Operative, Darius screamed at himself.

He struggled to a sitting position. His legs cramped from dehydration. Massaging his calf muscles, he forced himself to stand. He looked down at his suit pants, torn and tattered, covered in splotches of sweat and blood. Closing his mind to the collective moan from the nerves in his maxed-out body, he hobbled out of the ruined restroom.

The freight elevator on the opposite wall of the basement was a welcome sight.

Darius stared at the Exile symbols next to the elevator door. They yielded no clue as to which button to push for the lobby. He pushed the third button on the bottom in the column nearest to him. In a worse- case scenario, he'd wind up on one of the lower floors of the building, assuming it didn't blow up first. Visions of a fiery explosion spreading from the cavern to the boiler room swirled in his imagination. He imagined the elevator cab shake violently before plunging back down a flame-drenched elevator shaft.

He held his head with both hands to stop these nightmares from looping in his brain.

The elevator stopped.

Darius held his breath.

The elevator door opened. A deserted lobby never looked more inviting.

Darius limped out into the empty lobby. The elevator doors closed behind him. Jerking his head left and right, he detected no signs of Exile or human life anywhere.

A waterfall on the Atrium wall flowed peacefully. A big square clock on the opposite wall read eight-thirty. Night brushed up against the blue-tinted glass doors of the main entrance. A few hundred yards of granite flooring separated Darius from the steps down to the front doors.

With the last scraps of energy in his battered body, Darius half-ran for the doors. A second later, an earthquake shook the lobby.

Spindly halogen light fixtures plummeted from the two-story ceiling like spears thrown by angry gods. It seemed like the turmoil woke the last two Exiles in the building. He figured the rest of them had abandoned ship. The Exiles jumped to the floor from a staircase leading up to the lobby's second tier.

Shop windows shattered. Shards of glass spewed over the balcony and smashed against the main floor in a deadly wave. Darius lost his footing. He lay face down on the writhing floor.

He wobbled to his feet. The Exiles whirled around and pulled weapons. Darius fell again. Hybrid energy projectiles *whizzed* overhead.

Darius looked up in time to see a halogen light fixture smash into the Exiles, splintering them into pieces. He pushed off the crumbling floor, lurching his way toward the exit doors. *Almost there now.*

The pool at the base of the waterfall cracked open sending a torrent of water across the ruptured flooring. Darius barely maintained his balance while sloshing through water up to his ankles. He crawled the last ten yards on hands and knees down the steps to the exit doors.

Grabbing a door handle, he swung out onto the front steps and staggered away into the black night.

It seemed like days since his last breath of fresh air. He had not had an extra second to gulp down a mouthful of water.

He might be thirsty as hell, but he felt twice as glad to be alive. He kept moving away from the building despite the fatigue and pain in every part of his body. Then, he felt his strength returning as more light energy percolated up from the depths of his being.

He walked for what seemed like a mile before taking a second to look back over his shoulder. In the distance, the Mamongen Building listed at a precarious angle on its foundation, as if it were deciding to collapse or remain standing.

Cars stopped. Horns blared. Pedestrians ran by screaming, almost knocking him over. Darius stopped walking. He turned and took a few steps back towards the building. Any second, he expected to see the Mamongen building collapse in a shower of gnashing steel and glass.

Incredibly, the building refused to die, like its ninety-year-old owner, Joseph Mamon. It leaned drunkenly to one side lit by a half-moon and a sparkling canopy of stars.

Chapter Fifty

THE GARDEN

DARIUS PACED CALMLY away from the Mamongen Building, away from the hysteria gathering around him, including the waves of emergency vehicles, police cars, news vans, sirens, flashing lights, shouts, screams, and police officers barking orders at confused citizens.

A police cruiser pulled up. The driver's window rolled down.

"Are you coming from the office tower?" the officer called to him from inside.

"Yes," Darius answered. He recognized the police officer.

Madison Tremane's blue eyes narrowed. "You look familiar. What's your name?"

"Darius McPherson." After surviving Exile captivity and saving the world, Darius wondered if he was about to be rewarded with an arrest for the stolen Bentley.

"I checked you out," Madison said. "You have a record."

"You must be mistaken. My only involvement with the department was as a youth counselor in Detroit."

"Yup, that's exactly what the computer records show." Madison stared at him intently. "It also says Darius McPherson died from multiple gunshot wounds. Your face matches the picture in the file. You're not supposed to be walking around."

Darius decided the best way to handle Madison's discovery was to tell the truth. He was tired of lying anyway, and this police officer was no one to trifle with.

Darius smiled. "You might say I'm walking proof of an afterlife, Officer Tremane. The last few days have taught me that many strange and wonderful things can happen if you believe, hope and trust. My life here ended too soon, but I guess you could say, I'm making the most out of my situation."

Tremane continued staring at him. "Something tells me you had something to do with whatever the hell happened down the street." He jerked his head in the direction of the Mamongen Building.

"I came here to help. I'm pretty sure I succeeded in accomplishing what I came here to do. I assure you it did not include damaging the Mamongen Building."

Tremane began to shake his head before Darius had finished speaking. "There's only two things I'm real sure of right now. You're not a bad guy, and this is one crazy-ass night."

The police radio squawked.

"Copy. On my way." Tremane turned back to Darius with his eyes squeezed in a look of semi-disbelief. "Whoever you are, do me a favor and go back to wherever the hell you came from. I don't feel like writing up a report about a dead guy walking away from a building that forgot how to stand up straight."

He put the car in gear and roared away with the cruiser's blue and red lights swirling.

Darius waved after the departing patrol car, hoping Madison Tremane would catch the gesture in his rear-view mirror. Then he walked away using his mental radar to locate his friends.

He caught a stray snippet of Javon wondering *where in the hell is old Darius at?* Darius smiled to himself. *I'm still on top of your hopeless case*, he thought, and projected the sentiment to his friend.

A freshening breeze from Biscayne Bay kissed his cheek. The smooth waters blazed with reflected starlight. Darius felt the warm glow of light energy flowing back into his body. His spirits soared much like the herons flying heavenward in his dream about Aaron at the top of the Mamongen Building. He felt the same sense of fitting perfectly inside his skin as he had in the dream, before glimpsing the ominous sight of the sun slipping into a black hole in the sky.

He followed Javon's thought trail to an all-night Taco Bell two blocks away. Javon had apparently convinced Vicky and Simon of the urgent need to chow down after the calorie-draining ordeal of saving the human race.

An urgent message flashed into his mind. It came directly from Aaron.

. . .

Darius brought his friends to a small park within walking distance of the restaurant. They sat on a bench beneath the sculpture of a tall, thin, winged angel. Either Aaron had more of a sense of humor than Darius gave him credit for, or the sculpture was a coincidence.

They had this small piece of real estate all to themselves. The commotion from the Mamongen Building twenty blocks away was subsiding. Darius faced the group, propped up against the base of the sculpture, his scraped knees poking through torn trousers, white shirt ripped in several places. He had not bothered to tuck the bottoms of the shirt back into his pants. He looked a mess.

"Looks like we gonna' have to do some more clothes shopping," Javon remarked. "This time for you."

"I don't think so," Darius said in a quiet voice.

"You can't go 'round like a homeless dude who just walked out of a hospital without the doc's permission."

Darius regarded the three of them in silence for a moment.

"The three of you will have to take it from here," he said evenly.

"What's that supposed to mean?" Javon exclaimed.

They stared back at him with curious expressions.

Darius turned to Vicky. "You've got the story I promised. Simon will help you with the background information."

"What about my exclusive interview with an angel?"

"I'm counting on you never to say a word about me or the Exiles to anyone."

"Why?" Vicky wanted to know.

"Because the world isn't ready to know that monsters and angels actually exist. It will interfere with the natural evolution of human consciousness as I've just been informed by my boss. I'm asking each one of you for your solemn vow not to tell anyone about me or the things I've shown you."

"You have my word," Simon said.

"Who's your boss?" Vicky asked.

Darius knew she couldn't help being a reporter. He smiled back. "None of your business."

"The only pictures I have are the ones I took of the gizmo we found in the projection room. I guess I'll have to make sure they get lost," Vicky said reluctantly.

"What I gotta' do besides keep my mouth shut," Javon asked.

"Straighten your life out. It's what you really want to do."

"How you figure that?"

Darius stood and faced Javon. "There's a good person inside you who wants to come out in the worst way."

Javon's eyes grew red. He buried his face in his hands. Darius tapped him on the shoulder. Javon sat up. Darius embraced him. "Your life is going to get a lot better. You're going to make it happen."

Javon stiffened. "We'll see."

"I'm still gonna' be on your case, even if you can't see me. Remember that."

Darius took the triangle necklace and placed it around Javon's neck. "This is yours now. Don't even think about pawning it. Wear it all the time. It'll come in handy when you need it most."

Javon fingered the golden triangle with an inquisitive expression.

"When the chips are down, believe in yourself, hope for the best outcome, and trust that it will happen," Darius said to Javon. "Each circle in the triangle represents one of those principles. They helped to save us from a horrible fate. They'll help to save you from a horrible one too. They'll help you to make your life the one you want."

Javon stared back at him wide-eyed. Darius saw the three circles in the triangle glow for an instant.

"As you would say, it's for real." With those parting words, Darius moved on to Vicky and Simon. They were holding hands. "I can't thank you both enough for what you did."

"We didn't do much except follow you around," Simon said.

"Don't be so humble. You believed me. You trusted me. You didn't give up hope. That is a world of doing. If it wasn't for your courage and your strength, we couldn't have pulled this off."

Darius placed a hand on each of their shoulders.

"I love you both."

Darius turned back to Javon. "And you too."

"Whatever," Javon said, while wiping his eyes before they had a chance to tear up.

"You have a great mind, Simon. Use it wisely for the highest and best good. Choose the people you work with carefully."

"I will, Darius."

"Be your own boss, Vicky. You are a brilliant Journalist. Keep believing in your instincts."

"I'll miss you," she said.

Darius took Vicky's hand and held it for a moment. Then he took Simon's hand as well.

"What are you waiting for, an engraved invitation?" he called to Javon. Darius remembered Aaron saying the same thing to him after the general meeting in heaven. It had only been a few days ago, but it seemed like a century.

Javon squeezed over on the bench and put his hand in the circle of hands.

"Our connection is strong. Each one of you will be in my heart everywhere I go. Keep me in yours. Remember one another. Remember what we have accomplished together. Let it be a source of strength for the rest of your lives. We never have to be apart.

It occurred to Darius this idea also applied to Rebecca and to his family. It felt like the stone weight against his heart had shattered into dust. The empty place it left behind welled up with relief and then a sense of peace.

A circle of light opened behind Darius. He waved a final goodbye to his three friends. "Remember, we never have to be apart."

Darius turned and walked slowly into the glow emanating from the Hyperspace Conveyor Tube.

It was time to go home.

JAVON

THE DAY WAS too beautiful to waste looking for a job. Javon had half a mind to turn around and head out to the beach for a swim. Instead, he forced himself up the stone steps of the vocational training center in his new suit. It felt like he was sweating through his store-bought Haines underwear. Wearing a suit in the heat of the summer had cooled his resolve to embark on a new career path. The last words Darius had spoken to him were the only things propelling his feet in the direction of a new job: "Your life is going to get better. You're going to make it happen."

He had waited impatiently for an hour inside the center before the receptionist called his name. Javon usually made things happen quickly when he decided to do something. Waiting on other people was definitely not his style. As it turned out, he was glad he had waited. Sitting a few feet across from him was the most beautiful young woman he had ever laid eyes on.

She had a mouthful of perfect white teeth that she kept flashing unselfconsciously with one radiant smile after another. Her chocolate brown skin was smooth and clear. The woman looked about his age. She had a cute, upturned nose, high cheekbones, and a pair of brown, caring eyes he had trouble looking into for fear of drowning. While taking his hand in a firm handshake, she had introduced herself as

Daisy Witherspoon. Some kind of electrical current had passed through his body when she touched him. The feeling traveled from a point between his eyes straight down into his solar plexus.

The beginning of the interview brought Javon out of his trance. "You have no prior employment history and the job skills you list are..."

Daisy leaned closer to the application on her desk to read Javon's cryptic handwriting.

"...Driver Expert and, let's see, Buying and Selling."

"I've always been self-employed," Javon said proudly.

"What do you buy and sell?" Daisy asked with yet another disarming smile.

"Oh, you know, this and that, general stuff, whatever I can find that people want. I got a natural instinct for sales and marketing."

"You mean selling drugs, don't you?"

"Did I say drugs?"

"Do I look stupid," Daisy said.

"You look damn nice."

Ignoring his compliment, Daisy picked up another piece of paper from her desk and examined it. "Well, congratulations, Mr. Quincey. I see that your I.Q. and abstract comprehension scores are off the charts."

"Is that a good thing?"

"A very good thing. Especially if you take advantage of a new career development program we're offering sponsored by our corporate partners." Javon fingered the golden necklace hanging from the collar of his light blue business shirt.

"You think I look like the corporate type?" He put his hand on the desk. Javon made it look like a power move. It was actually an attempt to keep his body from shaking.

"You look like the kind of man who could do anything he put his mind to," Daisy said, staring straight at him with those caring eyes of hers.

HIRAM AND JOSEPH

HIRAM FYRUM STARED at the Mamongen Pharmaceuticals Building through the one-way front windshield of Joseph Mamon's bullet proof Rolls Royce. Silhouetted against the rising morning sun, the once majestic skyscraper now resembled a modern version of the leaning tower of Pizza.

Police cars surrounded the ruptured base of the building. Portable barricades and a line of police officers prevented pedestrians and traffic from coming within a thousand yards of the slanting edifice.

Hiram had been up all night, mostly trying to figure out what he was going to say to Joseph Mamon, the ninety-year-old Chairman and Founder of Mamongen Pharmaceuticals. The building's precarious condition suggested that something had gone horribly wrong with Glythren's plans. He figured the creature that had made his life a living nightmare was on his way back to hell or whatever awful place he came from. Served the pompous son-of-a bitch right.

Hiram knew somewhere deep in his gut that the soft-spoken angel who had visited him in his study was responsible for the carnage on display outside of the confines of Joseph's fortress of a car. Monsters and angels—he had seen them alive and in living color. He would never tell anyone, not even his therapist about such things. He didn't want his miserable brood of worthless adult children to use it as an excuse to have him judged incompetent. And, he didn't want any future employer to bring it up in an interview. No, Hiram planned to blame the building catastrophe on the engineers. They would claim innocence, of course, but he had Joseph Mamon's ear, not the stupid engineers.

Hiram's stubby legs ached from climbing down seventy-five floors of stairs from his twenty thousand square foot Penthouse to an emergency exit on the ground floor. He had spent most of this painful odyssey screaming into his smart phone at various members of the Mamongen building staff. The rest of the time, he had spent catching his breath. It was fair to say Hiram was not in the best of mental shape for this crucial meeting with his boss. Despite his depleted condition, he was as determined as ever to do what he always did in a crisis—rise victoriously to the occasion.

Hiram pulled himself and his thoughts together to begin his pitch to the old man. It had been a long time since he felt grateful to report to the Chairman. It certainly beat the hell out of being under the thumb of an actual, hideous monster. Joseph was certainly chock full of monstrous qualities, but at least he couldn't crush Hiram into little pieces or zap him into thin air if the spirit moved him.

"I'm beginning to see an opportunity here, Joseph. What if we left the building tilted like it is, reinforced with polished steel supports, of course. We remodel all the interiors to fit the new structure. Stay with me now. The building becomes the company's new logo. The tag line reads: 'Mamongen Pharmaceuticals—Taking an Innovative Direction into the Future.' The building becomes a statement, like a modern art sculpture. Think of it, Joseph. It's what we're all about."

Hiram sat back confidently in the rear compartment of the Rolls Royce. His mind automatically began to compute the logistics of the plan he had just proposed. The more he thought about it, the more he liked it.

Hiram turned to Joseph, eagerly awaiting his reply. His confidence took flight. He bubbled with energy, despite a sleepless night and no morning coffee.

Joseph Mamon stared morosely out at the spectacle that now loomed in a sadly comic fashion amidst the other sterling examples of *Corporate Wellness* standing straight and tall beside it. He coughed into his oxygen mask.

"I'm looking at what's left of my life's work," the old man said.

"You're looking at a new beginning, that's what you're looking at," Hiram crowed.

The old man turned to him. "I'm looking at the biggest *schmuck* in the entire world."

"I'm not offended, Joseph. This is an emotional time. I know you don't mean that."

"I'm the guy who hired you, which means only one thing. I'm getting too old for this."

The old man broke into a coughing fit. Hiram patted him on the back. The coughing finally stopped.

"I'm going to dismantle the company and sell it off in little pieces. And, I'm going to scuttle your pet project—the Plezenthol program. There's entirely too much liability with the questionable test results."

"Let's not make any rash decisions. Let's give the situation a little breathing room. Let's also keep in mind that your passion built this company and *our* passion can keep it going."

The old man looked at him with big, rheumy eyes. "Get out of my car." He blinked several times. "I never want to see you again."

"You're firing me?"

"Only because there are laws against killing you."

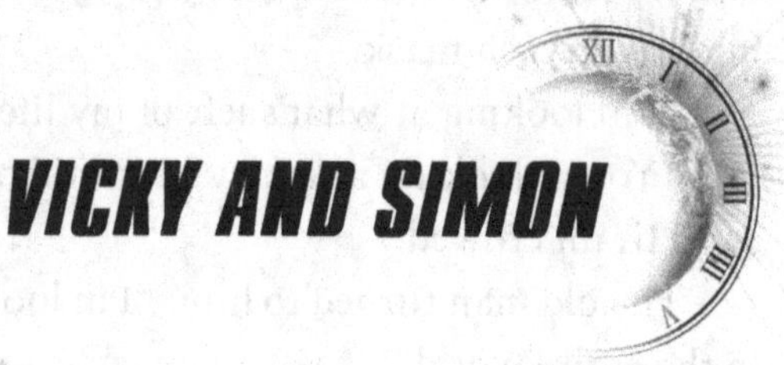

VICKY AND SIMON

"**GOOD EVENING. I'M** Vicky Matthews, your new host of Financial Matters. Roberta Fernbreath-Larson, who anchored the show for the past ten years, has taken early retirement to write her memoirs. We wish her all the best. In tonight's lead story, City Officials are still trying to determine what caused the Mamongen Pharmaceuticals building to nearly collapse last week."

The TV monitor switched to show a picture of the Mamongen building propped up by a giant, wedge-shaped scaffolding.

"Although the building was stabilized by the heroic efforts of emergency crews working around the clock to erect a support structure, the same cannot be said of the company's stock price. Mamongen shares dropped sharply on news of the company's sudden withdrawal of its blockbuster drug, Plezenthol. In a terse statement, Mamongen's Director of Communications, Patricia Fitzwalter, said, 'the phase three trials of the drug were unreliable.' This surprising revelation and the abrupt firing of the company's CEO have contributed to an eighty percent loss in Mamongen's market value."

The monitor switched again to a wide-angle view of Vicky seated behind her anchor desk with the WQES NEWS logo in the background. Vicky smiled at the handsome man in the camel blazer sitting next to her. The camera shot tightened, allowing Vicky to take Simon's hand without the TV audience seeing it.

"My guest tonight is Doctor Simon Worthington who resigned this past week as Mamongen's Chief Chemist. Thank you for agreeing to meet with us, Doctor Worthington."

"My pleasure."

"What do you think caused the Mamongen building to shift on its foundation?"

"I've been running some computer models and it looks to me like there was a geographic anomaly under the building that was so far down it did not show up on any of the engineering studies. It could have been something like an underground cavern that collapsed due to water erosion. There is absolutely no evidence of a structural failure in the building itself. There is also no evidence this was in any way related to terrorist activity."

"Interesting, theory, Doctor. Can you tell us what caused you to question the Plezenthol test results?"

Vicky squeezed Simon's hand. She was going to make damn sure the authorities and anyone else who cared to listen understood that Simon was the hero who initiated a review of the test data. There was one more thing she intended to ensure. Whatever this wonderful man's future turned out to be, she was going to be a part of it.

DARIUS AND AARON

PEACE WAS AN amazing experience. Darius always thought he had led a peaceful existence, until recently of course. But what he was feeling now, sitting in Aaron's office, was beyond words. It was utter contentment. It was joy. It was harmony. It was a deep appreciation for everyone and everything including his friend, boss and mentor, Aaron the Archangel.

He wondered how long the feeling would last.

"Don't do that," Aaron said.

"Don't do what?"

"Wonder how long the feeling will last. The minute you do that, the experience fades. The more you let go, the more you trust, the more you will feel it."

Darius nodded. "This is the first time I've had a chance to relax since coming back."

"So many nervous souls to reassure after you returned. They all wanted to hear the story in your own words. I'm glad all the commotion is finally subsiding. Did you enjoy all that attention?"

"I didn't feel comfortable answering all those questions, but it beats the heck out of running for your life."

"It's nice to see you've begun to develop a sense of humor. I thought you were entirely too serious when we first met."

"When I first woke up here, I was too shocked to have a sense of humor. Now, I feel more alive than ever. I'm continually amazed by the little details of life around me. It was beginning to happen on Earth, before events started moving so fast that it was hard to appreciate anything.

"You'll continue to feel more alive as your consciousness expands." Aaron paused. "Are you sure you don't want me to remove some filters?"

"I'd still like to see things the way I'm used to for the time being. Do you mind?"

"Not at all. Forgive me for being pushy. I'm just anxious to see you move along on your learning curve."

"I'll let you know when I'm ready."

Darius sat on a light blue leather sofa that fit his posture like the size forty suits he used to wear. It was a relief to feel comfortable again, and free of the physical pain he had experienced in his body on Earth. All unpleasant physical sensations had vanished after he had entered the Hyperspace Conveyor Tube on the trip home. His exhaustion had spared him from the scary journey back to heaven. He had apparently conked out soon after entering the Tube.

"You promised to tell me what happened to Anky," Darius said.

As if Darius had summoned him with his question, Anky shuffled through the door. "Am I interrupting?"

"Not at all," Aaron said.

"You made it back!" Darius exclaimed.

"Course I did. Ya' think I was gonna' spend the rest of eternity in a stinky underground cave? We got work to do."

Anky took a seat on the sofa. Darius smiled at the friend he thought he had lost.

Aaron turned to Darius. "We outfitted the Senior Operatives with a special homing device before they left for Earth. We took an imprint of each operative's energy vibration. Everyone has a unique frequency, just like a fingerprint. The HCT has a built-in scanner that we can set to any angel's frequency. Once the HCT locates a missing operative, it appears at exactly the right time for extraction.

Darius's experience in the garden confirmed Aaron's explanation.

"I wish it was that easy to find the other Senior Operatives stuck in the Void," Anky said with a mournful expression.

"Are they lost forever?" Darius asked. He looked to Anky, then to Aaron for some sign of hope.

"We don't know," Anky said. The Void has no physical coordinates. We can't send a Tube to a place that is basically 'nowhere.'"

"We'll keep trying to find them," Aaron said. "There has to be a way."

Aaron assumed a serious expression reminiscent of Morgan Freeman playing Detective Alex Cross in the movie "Along Came a Spider."

"Enough questions for now. Let me get down to the point of this meeting. Listen closely. This new hybrid energy the Exiles have developed is a real problem. Their energy weapons sent the Senior Operatives to the Void. We have no idea what the Exiles will do next with their new technology. The horde you wiped out in the cavern is only a fraction of their population. They've been breeding for thousands of years. We have to be ready for new threats. We need trained people to fill in for the missing Senior Operatives right away."

Aaron disappeared and reappeared next to Darius and Anky on the sofa. "I'm putting you and Anky in charge of a new 'Quick Learning Program.' It was the Chief's idea, actually."

Darius glanced at Anky. Anky winked back at him. He took a deep breath as Aaron continued to outline the assignment. Darius had learned at least one lesson since becoming an angel. There was never a dull moment in heaven.

ABOUT THE AUTHOR

After a career in marketing and business communications, David Gittlin began writing short stories and screenplays. He eventually graduated to writing novels. In addition to *Three Days to Darkness*, his other two novels; *Scarlet Ambrosia* and *Micromium: Clean Energy from Mars*, are available at major online retailers worldwide.

For more information visit
www.DavidGittlin.com

Also by David Gittlin

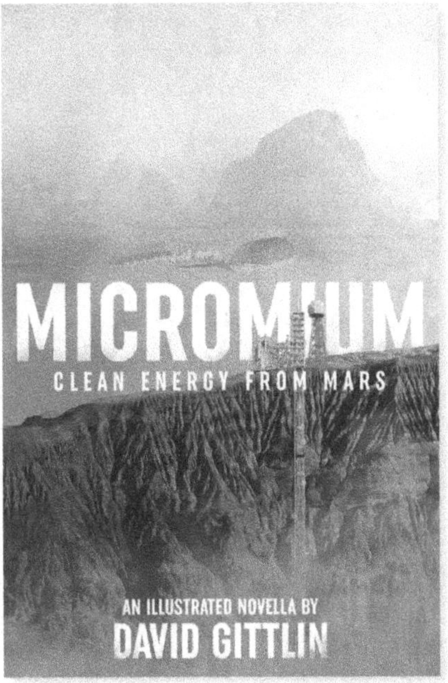

While investigating the deaths of two mining colonists on Mars, Logan Marchant and his crew uncover evidence of a conspiracy that threatens their lives and the survival of Mankind.

Available on Amazon and all major online retailers and Audible.com.

"The story that unfolds in this novella is very compelling and carries the reader along with a fast-paced tale that isn't difficult to follow. The characters are at their most interesting when they are working to solve the central problem of the book and working together as a team. When major twists are thrown their way, readers are eager to follow along with the team wherever they're headed. There is drama and excitement, and all of it serves the larger story."

—*Joshua Patton for IndieReader.com*

A one-night stand thrusts Devon Furst into the arms of a beautiful vampire lover, leaving him with a terrible choice: death or eternal life as a vampire.

Available in digital and paperback editions on Amazon and all major online retailers worldwide.

"With so many vampire novels on the market today, one could wonder at the need for yet another; but *Scarlet Ambrosia* is a vampire story of a different color, seasoned not so much by the drama of blood-letting as by the more universal themes of self-discovery, human nature, and redemption. Ultimately this is what makes or breaks any genre; especially one such as the urban fantasy or vampire story, which too often tends to eschew self-examination in favor of high drama. And this is just one of the reasons why *Scarlet Ambrosia* stands out from the urban fantasy genre crowd."
—*Diane Donovan Midwest Book Review*